FOREVER
Music

Play, music you love!

HOPE TOLER DOUGHERTY

MANTLE ROCK
PUBLISHING LLC
MantleRockPublishingLLC.com

Published by Mantle Rock Publishing LLC
2879 Palma Road
Benton, KY 42025
http://mantlerockpublishingllc.com

Printed in the United States of America

ISBN 9978-1-951246-38-9

Cover by Diane Turpin at dianeturpindesigns.com

To Anna, Hattie, Lane, and Quinn Dougherty.

You rock my world in more ways than you can imagine. You make me proud. You make me laugh. You make me strive to be the mother who deserves you. You keep me honest and on my toes. You will always be the best stories of my life.

LOVELOVELOVELOVE
M

CHAPTER 1

*A*nticipation for the evening revved Josie Daniels' heart rate as much as discovering original sales tags on a thrift store find. She surveyed the ballroom glittering with Lights and flowers and people in sparkly dresses and suits. Three musicians played James Taylor's "Carolina in My Mind" on a piano, guitar, and cello. Nice. In a couple of hours, the wait would be over, and she'd have a promise, if not a check, for thousands of dollars in her hand.

How many thousand remained a mystery.

Instead of a little black dress, she wore a little navy dress with a boat neck and a scoop back. Her ears featured dangly diamond earrings borrowed from her mom's jewelry box, a twenty-fifth wedding anniversary gift from her dad.

A tennis bracelet, graduate school graduation present from her grandmother, encircled her wrist. The ends of her hair curled exactly the way it did on a good hair day thanks to a quick shower after teaching her last class, so she left it down, framing her face.

Yep. She felt confident. She could hold her own in this room full of downtown Charlotte lawyers and bankers and businesspeople. So, what if she found her dress on the clearance rack? The rack resided in a trendy boutique in South Park. She looked good. She felt good. Tonight would be fun especially with her oldest brother Ben escorting her as her plus one. His six feet assured she could stand to her full height without slouching in the sweet heels she'd coveted all summer. Last week's coupon sale came at the perfect time.

"Ready to go in and slay the beast?" Ben jiggled her elbow.

She huffed. "I annihilated the beast when I wrote my killer grant proposal. I'm here to collect my hard-earned cash for the library." Writing the proposal had taken three months. The breakup with B.J. had almost derailed it, but in the end, it helped her focus on the library's needs and not her own misery. She shook her head. Absolutely no thoughts about B.J.

They stepped over the threshold and into the crowd. "Thanks for bringing me."

"Are you kidding? Who'd pass up a free meal?"

"Hey. What about the company? What am I? Chopped liver?"

"You know I love you. You look beautiful, by the way. Inside and out." He glanced behind her. "But aren't you cold?" He brushed his fingers across her shoulders. "The back of your dress..."

"Is fine. There's nothing inappropriate about this dress, *Dad.* I didn't even have to buy a special bra."

"Ahhh. I'm not listening." He plugged his ears. "You want a drink? Ginger ale with a cherry?"

"Yes, please."

"Those things are gonna kill you, you know."

"I only eat them every now and then. How about two if you can swing it?"

The last comment bounced off his back as he sliced his way through bumping shoulders. Josie scanned the room. The anchor for the eleven o'clock news chatted with someone who looked vaguely familiar. A professional athlete? Possibly, but his name escaped her. A few feet to the anchor's left, a small group of people nodded along with the mayor who punctuated a story with both hands. The A and B list of Who's Who in Charlotte comprised most of the attendees, and among them somewhere in this room were four others like herself, not movers or shakers, just volunteers hoping for the big payoff.

A violet skirt caught her attention. An intricate braid swirled around the hem in an interesting pattern. It definitely didn't look like a clearance item. Detail work. Beautiful color. Swingy fabric. A special piece indeed.

Someone jostled against her shoulder, and she shuffled sideways to regain her balance. The violet skirt dropped from her sight, allowing a new vision to take its place. Blue eyes. Blueberry eyes coming straight for her.

Her insides seized. Prickles danced up the back of her neck. She hadn't seen Lloyd C. Windham IV since August at the airport's car park. Five weeks. So why the crazy reaction to him? Maybe the surprise of his appearance? Maybe the embarrassment of almost crashing to the floor in front of him? Or maybe the frown wrinkling his forehead foretold a blip on an otherwise special night.

"What are you doing here?"

"Ahm. Well, nice to see you again too."

A glass with bubbly liquid materialized at her chest. Her ginger ale with two cherries speared on a plastic sword. God bless her brother. "Here you go." His arm slid around her waist. God bless him again. "She's here as one of the five recipients of the grants."

Before she could comment on the frown standoff between the two men, a hand with electric blue nails snaked around Lloyd C. Windham IV's arm. The owner of the hand, a brunette with a perfectly tousled up 'do, met Josie's gaze, then swept a quick glance all the way to Josie's toes and back to her eyes. She tipped her head to her companion. "I think it's almost time to take our seats, Ches."

Drat.

That quick glance sucked every ounce of confidence the new dress and shoes had provided. And her nails. She'd forgotten to have them done. She grabbed the drink with both hands, threading her fingers around the glass to hide the tips. Too late, Ms. Blue Polish had already seen her naked nails.

And wait. Did she call him Chess? Chess. Lloyd C. Windham. C for Chess?

A waiter carrying a tray of empty dishes confirmed the beginning of the dinner. "Please find your tables. Salads will be coming out soon."

"Good idea. This way." Ben nodded to the couple and guided her to their table near the front. "Who was that anyway?"

"Never seen her before, but he used to park his brand-new Lexus Sport Coupe at the Park 'n Go."

Ben snorted. "Right. Your summer job driving travelers to the airport. Glad you're back to teaching a full load and don't have to supplement your salary."

"It was a fun job. Mostly." The working crew was a great group of people. The Lexus driver? She'd pegged him as a jerk the first time she met him. In his defense, he was bent out of shape because of a broken pair of high dollar sunglasses. When she'd apologized, not as the culprit but as a human being familiar with lost or broken items, he'd chastised her not to apologize "for something you didn't do."

She'd riled him by refusing his tip and offering one of her own...to do something fun before the day was over. Not really her business, but the sadness that flickered in his blue eyes demanded some sort of action on her part.

Ben held a chair for her. "They weren't exactly a welcoming committee."

"Did you see the way she gave me the once over?" Josie

glanced over her shoulder. "What was that about? I felt like I had on cutoff shorts and a tank top." She laid her purse in her lap, spread a napkin on top.

"She was sizing up her competition."

"Don't be ridiculous."

"I'm not. I told you, you look beautiful tonight. She wanted to see what made him find you in this crowd." He unrolled his utensils. "She doesn't have much confidence."

"You missed the boat on this one, big brother. She's dating the hotshot something who drives a Lexus. Let's forget about them." Great advice for herself especially with scenes from her summertime experiences with Mr. Windham IV vying for attention in her mind. "Oh, look. The dessert's already on the table."

A chocolate mousse cheesecake beckoned her with chocolate shavings and berry puree drizzled in artful swirls. The night shifted toward an impressive upswing.

BEN PUSHED his empty dessert dish to the side and glanced at the program.

"Do you think it'd be tacky to take the rest of this home if it fits in my purse?" Josie contemplated the remaining portion of her cheesecake. Her stomach rebelled at the thought of one more bite, but she hated the idea of leaving it.

"You'll have to get some paper napkins at least. It's almost time for the announcement. Nervous?"

"No, of course not." She dragged her fork through the berry puree. "Okay. Maybe a little. Fine." She pulled in a quick breath, blew it out. "I can hardly breathe."

"You're here. You're getting something, right?"

"Right. Five people representing five nonprofits receive grants tonight, plus the free chocolate mousse cheesecake." She jiggled the plate with the half-eaten treat. "The top winner earns fifty thousand big ones straight out. Three organizations earn ten thousand each. The first runner up wins thirty thousand dollars with a chance for twenty thousand more if the organization raises ten grand in the next twelve months."

"Never heard of strings like that."

"Me either." Butterflies waged war all over her insides. She forced herself to breathe in through her nose, out through her mouth. "Ben, we've got to win the top prize."

"Of course, you want to win."

"Not just 'want to,' have to. We need to win so we don't lose a position."

"Somebody could be let go?"

"They slashed programs and events. They've trimmed to the bone. The next move is eliminating a position. Once you start eliminating positions, it's a downward spiral to closed doors altogether."

"It's that serious?"

"Yes, indeed."

"Well, it's a good thing the library has you in its corner." He chucked her chin with his knuckles. "My stubborn sister's a bull-dog." He glanced at the head table. "Hey, look. Someone's behind the podium. Here we go."

God, thank you for the ten thousand dollars minimum we're getting tonight. But it'd be really, really, really fantastic if the library got the top prize. Please help me not to trip when I'm called to the podium for the check. Please help me be gracious, and just one more little but kinda big thing, let me not blink when the pictures are taken.

"Congratulations, sis!" Ben hugged her and kissed her on her cheek. "Good job. Thirty K. That's a nice boost for the library."

Familiar notes of "Unforgettable" from the piano trio ushered party goers out of the ballroom.

"Yeah." Delicious tingles ping-ponged the length of her spine, boosting the grin on her face."And now I need to think up some tremendous fundraisers so we can get the whole pot." The thought of raising money couldn't quell the dance party inside her tonight.

Thank you, God, for the grant and for keeping me upright to and from the official handshake. She collected her mom's beaded purse, careful not to squash the bulging center. She already looked forward to snack time tomorrow afternoon. She wiggled it for Ben to see and grinned. "Yummy."

"Congratulations, Joselyn."

She whirled to the voice she recognized from the summer. Heat flamed in her face. Lloyd C. Windham IV. She tucked the purse in the crook of her arm. "It's Josie. Thank you."

"Josie." He nodded. "The announcer...I didn't realize." He cleared his throat. "I didn't know your name."

A smile tipped the corner of her mouth. "You never asked." Not once in all the trips from the car park to the drop-off at the airport. He wasn't even paying attention when she glanced his way from the stage during the check presentations. His girlfriend had been whispering in his ear.

He lifted his chin. "You changed jobs."

"What?" The hopscotching conversation, his unexpected second appearance, the exhilaration of the win—all of it tilted her world.

"You're not at the airport anymore."

"Right. It was just for the summer."

He glanced toward the double doors, a familiar tic appearing in his cheek. "You wrote a very good proposal. I helped review all of them for the firm."

Warm, melty sensations curled throughout her body from the unexpected compliment. "Thank you."

He nodded again. "Well deserved." And with that, he left for the waiting brunette, scrolling her phone with a blue-tipped ring finger.

So. Mr. Windham IV was a hotshot lawyer who worked for the firm in charge of doling out the grants. Interesting. Not that it mattered. The firm had no control over fund-raising ideas or anything now that the grants were given. Good. No more Park 'n Go. No more fancy dinners. No more Mr. Windham IV. She resisted a Sunday-evening-downer kind of mood, sought the more appropriate Saturday-night-party-time vibe that should accompany a thirty-thousand-dollar win.

"Josie, I'll go get our horse and buggy, so we can leave." Ben waited with his arms crossed, a goofy smile on his face.

"What?"

Ben chuckled. "Just checking to see if you're back from wherever you went with your Park 'n Go guy just now."

She punched his bicep. "I don't know what you're talking about. He's not my Park 'n Go guy."

"I asked you three times if you're ready to go, and you stood there looking after Mr. Personality. He's not much for small talk, is he?"

"No. I guess not." He never volunteered too much on the way to the airport, for sure.

"Come on. Let's get you and your cheesecake home. You remind me of grandma stealing sugar packets and creamers from restaurant tabletops."

"Thanks a lot. I'm not stealing my cheesecake. They'd throw it away. I'm helping. I'm not being wasteful."

"Grandma justified her tabletop hauls too." He guided her through the double doors.

She stepped into the foyer and scanned the area for the Park 'n Go guy.

Already gone.

CHOCOLATE POWDER DISINTEGRATED INTO MILK. Ches swirled a spoon until white turned brown. Father would have a field day if he ever found out his son's night-cap was chocolate milk instead of scotch and soda, Lloyd III's drink of choice. He carried the glass into his den and settled in front of his big-screen TV, cued up the next episode of *Home Improvement* and thumbed the edge of the folder.

Retrieving the folder hadn't been a problem. Although almost eleven o'clock when he arrived at the building, three new hires had still been working. Extracting himself from Mallory had been a difficult task.

Mallory. The first month they'd seen each other had been fun. Flattered that the great-granddaughter of the firm's founder had flirted with him at a company dinner, he'd asked her out on a date. She accepted and wham. They were a thing.

His parents patted him on the back and reveled in their idea of his future. His mother made a game of choosing the wedding venue. His father liked to estimate how many months the relationship would shave off Ches's pursuit of becoming a partner.

Ches squeezed the bridge of his nose, the dull throb in his brain taunting him that the aspirin he'd choked down dry after dropping off Mallory lost its power with every passing minute. He checked his watch. He'd take some acetaminophen later, or was it time for ibuprofen? One or the other. Maybe he could sleep away the pain in his head.

He sighed, slipping fingertips across his sensitive forehead. What had he been thinking about? His parents' games. Right. He played along with those games for a while, but sometime during the summer, Mallory's presence began to chafe. He sipped the chocolate milk and stared at the TV. Tim Taylor demonstrated proper use of a power drill.

A power drill. Reminiscent of Mallory's perpetual chatter.

Tonight's topic? The annual family barbecue at her grandparents' estate. He heard the details most of the night. He'd come edge-of-the-cliff close to shushing her to hear the chairman of the board's comments about Joselyn.

Josie. He'd refused to let himself ask her name during the summer. Knowing her name would have bumped her one step closer to reality. Even after choosing her to drive him to the drop-off every time he flew, he didn't allow himself personal details or chitchat. No. He'd kept her in his mind as Park 'n Go Girl only.

She looked different tonight. No more parking attendant uniform. No more ponytail strangling her dark blond hair. Tonight, she'd left it free with soft curls tumbling over her shoulders, but her smile and her eyes were the same. Green rimmed with a circle of gold around the irises.

Yeah, she looked different, but the ping in his gut confirmed the woman he spied in the navy dress before dinner was the Park 'n Go girl. The same awareness pinged every time he drove into the parking lot last summer. The same ping warned him she wasn't part of the plan.

He opened the folder. *Grant Proposal for Thomas Byrd Regional Library by Joselyn Daniels.* He began rereading, this time with an image of the author in the back of his mind.

CHAPTER 2

*J*osie hoisted her book bag higher on her shoulder and pushed through the library's front door. One of the high school volunteers chatted with a man in cargo shorts who leaned across the circulation desk. The reference librarian caught her eye, greeting her with applause and a cheer. "Thank you, Josie, for winning the grant for us!" Startled patrons glanced from books and computers.

Volunteers joined in. Josie laughed and held her index finger to her mouth. "Okay. Okay. Tone it down. We've still got a lot of work to do." More like a ton of work to earn ten-thousand dollars by next fall. Most extra programs had been shelved when the county reduced the library's portion of the budget last spring. The next money-saving move would be to cut an employee. Josie was determined not to let that happen.

The man at the desk straightened. "Fancy meeting you here."

Her stomach dropped. B.J. Did the surprise of seeing him here cause her body's reaction, or was it a lingering attraction to him?

Do not be interested in him. Do not be interested. Do. Not.

"Saw your picture in the paper. You look good today too."

He smiled and, yep, the dimple in his left cheek flashed.

Thank goodness she'd come straight from work and hadn't stopped to change into weekend duds, vintage shorts, and a t-shirt. *God, I need some help here. I know B.J. isn't the one for me, but that dimple...*

She regrouped. "You look comfortable."

His gaze swept his shorts and untucked madras plaid button-down. "Yeah. I'm on my way to Wrightsville Beach, so I'm dressed for the ride. I stopped here first to get some preliminary notes."

Beach weekend? Wonder who—stop. Not her business anymore. "Notes for what?" She emptied her books into the return bin and folded the canvas bag in front of her.

"He's writing a feature article on the library and the grant." The teenager directed a dreamy smile toward B.J.

"You, big-time crime reporter, are writing a feature? On a library? Has a major crime wave hit these hallowed halls? Somebody checking out too many books? Or embezzling the overdue fines? Or, I know. Taking too many free Charlotte Knights baseball tickets?"

He guided her away from the desk to an empty table near a bank of computers. "Funny as ever, Josie. Maybe this isn't my usual gig, but it's kind of a big story. Lots of interesting questions to answer. This library's been on the chopping block for two years. Now it receives a shot in the arm, so to speak, at the eleventh hour. Just wondering why and highlighting that sometimes the little guy wins."

"I can help you with the *why* part. The money's from a private grant, not the county. And I wrote a very good proposal. Heard it from the horse's mouth." It felt good to be confident in front of B.J.

"What horse would that be?"

"Lloyd C. Windham IV."

"Ches? How do you know him? You're not dating him."

She frowned at him. "I didn't say I was. But is that idea really as incredulous as the look on your face suggests?" He didn't want her and couldn't imagine anyone else dating her either? This conversation would warrant a double scoop ice cream cone for dinner. And peanut M&M's for dessert.

"Hey, sorry. It wasn't a dig against you. It's just...Lloyd Chester Windham IV is all about making partner as fast as possible. He doesn't allow anything or anyone in his way. Mallory Padgett is the fast pass to his holy grail. He's not about to give that up."

"Thanks for the heads-up. Here's one for you. I'm not interested in Mr. Windham." Not exactly. "He just complimented my proposal. That's it."

B.J. rubbed the side of his nose. "Well, that's news right there. Ches Windham is never forthcoming about anything. I've interviewed him or tried to, a couple of times over the past few years. Like pulling teeth."

How many silent rides from the parking lot to the departure lane had she endured last summer with Ches? Not forthcoming sounded right.

"So, let's grab something to eat and start on those notes I need. How 'bout it?"

"You're on your way to the beach, and I have plans." No need to tell him her plans included ice cream and peanut M&M's.

He glanced at his watch. "You're right. I ought to hit the road, but there's another thing." He dropped his voice and leaned closer to her. "What's the deal with the strings attached to the grant? You've got to raise money on your own? Then you get matching funds or something like that? Sounds odd to me."

"Sounds like more work for me. The firm's giving the money. The owners can tie any strings they like to it."

"Maybe. And what about third, fourth, and fifth place? Scuttlebutt says those recipients were supposed to get more money."

"Top prize was always fifty thousand. The grant description offered fifteen thousand as a possible beginning point, never a promise. We found out more details when we received notice about winning. I knew entering the ballroom the library had at least ten thousand."

He nodded. "Gotcha. So, we need to talk some more. What about next week? Tuesday maybe?"

"I don't think so."

"Hey, ah." He shoved his hand in his pocket. "I'm sorry about what went down between us. And how it went down. I was a jerk. Just wanted you to know."

The breath caught in her throat. An apology from B.J.? Nice. "Oh, I knew. But I appreciate that you know it too. And," she dipped her head, "thank you for apologizing." A long time in coming, but it sounded sincere. "To use an old cliché, it was for the best."

He narrowed his eyes. "You think?"

"I know."

He bit the inside of his cheek. "Yeah, well. So how about Tuesday? The Pewter Rose? I've got questions for the article, and I need to get on it."

The Pewter Rose? As in their first date, Pewter Rose? "Sorry. No can do. Email me with your questions. I'll get back to you."

"But—"

"You won't miss your deadline. I wouldn't sabotage you."

"I know you're not that kind of person, Josie."

She grinned. "Although six months ago, I might have fantasized about doing it." Zinging him felt good. If she could tease him, withstand his invitation, then her heart must be healing. *Thank you, God.*

He blanched. "Josie, really. I'm sorry."

She nodded and stood. "Have fun at the beach, B.J. I'll look for your email." She headed for the door, enjoying being the one walking away from him this time.

THE LAST BITE of chocolate chip brownie ice cream, the first course of dinner, melted on Josie's tongue. Dessert, a ramekin of peanut M&M's, waited beside her laptop. She'd fed Winston Churchill, the family basset hound, thrown a load of laundry into the washing machine, and read her mail while she enjoyed her ice cream.

Now, the moment she'd been waiting for since the idea that hit her at the library had arrived. Social media stalking Mr. Lloyd C. Windham IV. Ches. She opened her laptop and waited for the screen saver to appear.

She gave herself a pep talk to calm her accelerated heart rate and scooped up a handful of M&M's. She was doing nothing more than what people do when they need an attorney, researching a law firm, trying to decide if the firm fit their legal needs.

What were her legal needs?

Nothing, thank goodness. But she was curious about one lawyer in particular. She typed in the firm's name. Bingo. Four areas of practice. Real estate, banking and finance, tax law, and corporate law. Interesting. No litigation, so did that mean Ches didn't appear in court? That fit what she understood about his personality. Reading briefs? Researching finer points of tax law? Real estate questions?

She scanned the first page, her eyes catching an information list. Firm Overview. Firm History. Pro Bono Work. She bit her bottom lip. Listed attorneys. Yes. She chose the tab and scrolled to the bottom of the alphabet. Windham. She clicked on his name, and his picture filled the top left-hand corner of her screen. Her fingers flew from the keyboard and curled into fists.

You're doing nothing wrong. He doesn't know you're about to read his profile. His information is available for anyone who's clicked this far into the website.

She grabbed four M&M's and tossed everyone into her mouth. She crunched and swallowed before placing her fingers back on the keys. She scrolled down his page. Undergraduate magna cum laude from Vanderbilt University. Law degree from the University of Virginia. Editor of UVA's law journal.

A writer. His compliment about her proposal was real then, not just words. A warm glow spiraled through her chest. Not that she cared what he thought of her. She didn't. But a sincere compliment is a sincere compliment.

She grabbed four more M&M's and stared at the profile picture, munching. The same haunting sadness she discovered during the summer hovered around his eyes in the professional portrait. What was the deal with this on-the-path-to-partner corporate attorney with the gorgeous girlfriend, not to mention the sweet ride? What was going on behind the sad eyes?

Being the sister of three brothers ramped up her nurturing gene. Even as the little sister, she mothered Ben, Heath, and Sam, plus all of their friends whenever they allowed it, usually when they were starving for home cooking. Those sad eyes reached out to her and tugged on her heart. What was the rest of the story, the story his firm profile didn't reveal?

Not that she was really interested. Just wondering.

The ramekin neared empty. She plucked out a red M&M and bit it in half. Bits of candy coating floated into her lap. She popped the remaining candy into her mouth. So much for trying to slow the dessert.

What about Mallory Padgett? Josie pulled up a social media site and typed in the name. Mallory's page, complete with minimal privacy settings, popped up. She met the brown-eyed gaze from the profile picture, residual embarrassment from the grant party creeping up her neck.

She broke the eye connection and perused the About section. Owner of Lasting Impressions Art Gallery on Providence Road. Attended Clemson University and Campbell University Law

School. She scrolled to the Album section. Sweet. Tons of pictures.

And, boom. There he was. Pictures of the smiling couple in a boat. At least Mallory smiled. Ches's attention centered somewhere to the left of the camera.

Pictures from, according to the captions, a polo match. *At the Caroleigh Polo Charity Classic with my man!!!!* Four exclamation points? Safe bet she really, really likes him.

More pictures of another dress-up party. Ches bending his ear toward Mallory. That short girl loves selfies and exclamation points.

Wait a minute. Why all the snarky comments? You don't even know this babe, and you're judging her? Step back and relax.

Josie turned her computer to sleep mode. Enough of that. She'd never been a snarky person and wouldn't start now. Ches's relationship status was none of her business. She'd discovered what she'd set out to discover, more about him and his work.

So why stalk Mallory? Simple curiosity. She wanted to know more about what made him tick through an important person in his life.

But why? Why keep digging when you already know the kind of person he is? Driven, serious, status hungry.

Pretty much the same as B.J. And you've been down that road before. Remember where that road led? Disappointment and heartache.

Quit the detour and get back to reality. No more stalking people online. No more thinking about Ches. Focus on teaching, planning fundraisers for the library, and taking care of the brothers.

Plenty of things to do.

Not thinking about Ches should be easy.

CHAPTER 3

*C*hes leaned against the wall beside the open door. What was he doing here, sweating through his undershirt outside a college classroom like an eighteen-year-old freshman instead of an adult man with a law degree? Would he really go through with his plan to talk with Josie? At work? What would Mallory say if she knew? What would his father say?

He was doing nothing wrong. He wanted to find out how the plans for using the grant money were going. Lame excuse but valid. If they talked about more than the grant over lunch, so what?

Movement in the classroom claimed his attention.

"Okay, people. Listen up. Put your desks back in order, please. You'll have two more weeks to finish this project. You're welcome for the in-class work period, by the way. Have a good weekend and, please, be careful, not stupid."

"Hey, Ms. Daniels, what about the JH squared house you mentioned?"

"Ooh, thank you, Ryan. Yes, if you're interested in volunteering for Joined Hands Joined Hearts, the address is listed on my web page. It starts bright and early somewhere in downtown Harrisburg tomorrow."

"We'll build a whole house tomorrow?"

"Not exactly. This site began in the summer and has several months to go."

"Any extra credit for showing up?" A smart-aleck chimed his two cents from the back.

"I'm promising nothing but a good feeling for helping people. We'll wait and see about anything more."

Quick come back. Good for you, Ms. Daniels.

"You're going, right?"

"Absolutely. See you in the morning."

Students streamed from the door, barely missed his Ferragamo wingtips, and jostled each other down the hall. He swung around the door frame. She leaned over the desk, intent on gathering a couple of books, keys, and papers.

He cleared his throat.

The welcoming smile crumbled on her face, replaced with an open mouth and a gasp.

"Sorry to scare you."

"No. You didn't. I wasn't expecting." She shook her head. "What are you…"

"I was hoping we could talk about your plans for the grant money."

Her brow knitted. "I thought you read the proposal. I included all the ideas there. I'm not sure…"

"Right. I did." She didn't make this easy for him. "I meant I'm following up. For details." Lame. Lame. Lame.

"Sure. Absolutely. Follow me. We can talk in my office."

Okay. Better.

A floral scent drifted along with her as she stepped by him for the door.

"I'm just a ways down the hall."

Before she could unlock the door, another woman hurried by them, craning her neck to give him the once over.

"Hey, Josie. I've got some pancake breakfast tickets. I'll stop in at the end of the day."

Josie, fiddling with the lock, huffed a breath. "Sure. I'll be here. For a few minutes."

An interesting smirk captured her mouth as she held open the door and offered him a seat. She slid a small glass canister of peanut M & M's to a corner and plopped down her books.

"Sorry. It's a mess during the day when I'm teaching." She shifted papers in piles, stuffed colored pens into a stone mug.

"No problem. I surprised you." He noted the two diplomas on her wall. "So. A pancake breakfast?" What? Asking about pancakes?

She narrowed her eyes, gave a quick shake of her head. "Yes, and I already bought tickets. My friend," she emphasized the word, "Lucy, is just being nosy." Back ramrod straight, she perched on a swivel chair, clutching her hands in front of her. "Okay. What questions do you have?"

In the minute and a half since he'd ambushed her, she'd recovered from the surprise. Back on her game. Good for you, Ms. Daniels.

She tilted her head. "Mr. Windham?"

"What? Call me Ches. Please."

"Ches." She reached behind her. Loose blond curls cascaded over her shoulder, obscuring the quick view he'd had of her neck.

Focus, man.

She flipped through files in her desk drawer. "Ahm. Here's the tentative schedule of planned events." She slipped out a sheet of paper and offered it to him. "A few are definite fundraisers. Some are just ideas. Others are free events geared toward community goodwill and garnering support."

His stomach gave a warning. He rose to cover the eminent

grumble. "Could we talk about this over lunch? I have another appointment later, and I'm starving."

She glanced at the sheet in her hand and back at him. "Sure, but I have a class at one. We'll have to be quick."

A PARKING SPOT opened for them right at the door of a nearby bistro. Known for its good food and quick service, the place was a favorite choice when Josie and colleagues needed a break from campus for a lunch in under an hour.

She unbuckled her seat belt, and Ches opened the console. He sifted through the contents twice and slammed it shut, rattling an aspirin bottle in the cupholder. Last summer a bottle had held. Acetaminophen.

He reached behind him for his suit jacket, patted all the pockets, and tossed it back on the seat. He pressed into his seat.

"Is something wrong?" Clearly, the tic in his jaw indicated a problem, but he closed his eyes instead of answering her. "Ches, tell me. What's up?"

He turned his head partway in her direction but kept his eyes on the touch screen between them. "I, ah...I don't have my wallet."

A relieved laugh escaped her mouth. "Is that it?" Of all the tragic things she could have guessed, leaving a wallet hadn't made her list.

He jerked narrowed eyes toward her. "It's not funny. I've never done this before."

Poor guy. Asking her out to lunch, then not being able to pay for it. Of course, he was upset. Discomfort hung on his shoulders like a letterman jacket. This new perspective made him more human, more approachable than the closed-off Park 'n Go guy of last summer. "I'm sure you haven't. I'm just glad it's not something serious. That muscle twitching in your cheek had me going."

"It is something serious. I asked you to lunch, so—"

"So, I'll pay for it. No big deal."

"It is a big deal." He looked away.

She touched his sleeve, and he stiffened. She retrieved her hand. "Seriously, Ches. Let it go. Things happen. No harm. No foul and all that. Hey. My lunch hour is dripping away here. We need to get inside."

"I'll reimburse you."

She opened the door. "Let. It. Go. One twenty-five-dollar lunch isn't going to break me. Come on."

They snagged one of the last two open tables. Except for pouring a water glass for Josie, their waitress had eyes only for Ches. No wonder. He looked like a walking advertisement for button-downs or ties. Expensive haircuts or toothpaste. Thank goodness she was immune. Been there. Already done that with B.J. No thank you for another helping of smooth-talking, good looking men.

"Will this be one check or two?" The waitress bit her pen and inclined her chin toward Ches. "And I'm Sandy, by the way."

"One, and it's to me, please." Josie waved her hand, making sure the server remembered her. She smiled at him. "Everything's good here. Local vegetables. Homemade bread." She turned to Sandy. "I'll have the chicken salad on sunflower bread, please." The besotted woman scribbled on her pad, still gazing at Ches.

"You're enjoying my predicament." Returning the menu, he ordered the steak sandwich on ciabatta.

"Only a little bit." She squeezed lemon into her water. "I figure I'm saving you from a headline like *Hot Shot Corporate Lawyer Washes Dishes for Lunch.*" She licked the tart juice from her fingers.

No response.

"Come on. I'm kidding. Relax. I won't make you wash dishes. And here's a news flash. If things don't work out with your girlfriend, I think Sandy would love a date. She might even pay for dinner." She unrolled her napkin, placed the utensils in correct positions in front of her.

He clenched his jaw. "You like to tease."

"With three older brothers, I had to learn to take it and dish it out too."

The waitress returned with a basket of skinny breadsticks and set it down square in front of Ches. The pungent aroma of garlic and herbs heightened her appetite.

"Ooh, these sticks are fantastic. Do you mind sharing?" Josie chuckled as he slid the basket toward the middle of the table.

"So, you have a big family."

"Yep. How 'bout you?" She crunched on the end of an herbed stick. Yummy. The breadsticks made the company of a prickly companion worth every moment.

"Just me." He selected one, broke it in half.

Interesting. An only child. "No siblings to fight over the remote, huh?" She twirled her stick in a circle outlining his face. "All the love and attention centered on you. Cushy gig."

"Not quite. So, you're working on a Joined Hands Joined Hearts house tomorrow?"

Whiplash much? Shut down the family talk with a new conversation right out of the left-field, why don't you? She wrinkled her brow. "Yeah, but how..."

"I heard you remind your class." He bit the stick.

"You were lurking at my classroom, eavesdropping?"

He swallowed. "Waiting. I was waiting for your class to end. So. Tomorrow's the build?"

"Yeah. I can't wait. Tomorrow night I plan to check Building a House off my bucket list."

"That's on your bucket list?"

"Among other things." She finished the stick and brushed the loose herbs from her fingertips.

"You know how to build a house?"

"No, but I can hit a nail with a hammer." She grinned at him. "That should be a good start, don't you think?"

"Hitting nails is involved along with a lot of other skills like electricity, plumbing, finishing work."

"You sound like you know something about the process." Ches with a nail in his mouth and a hammer in his hand? She couldn't picture it.

"I do." He leaned against the back of his chair.

She waited for him to elaborate. In vain. "Yeah, well." She moved her water glass from the pool of condensation underneath it. "I'm hoping we can get a lot done tomorrow. The last email mentioned a youth group had backed out. Sounds like we're down some volunteers, but I've wrangled at least two of my brothers into helping. For a home-cooked meal afterward, of course."

He sipped his water, set down the glass and made eye contact. "I could help."

She startled. "I wasn't fishing…"

"Didn't think you were. It's in Harrisburg, right?" He fiddled with the napkin-rolled utensils.

She nodded. "You can volunteer tomorrow? You don't have to read a brief or attend a polo match or—?" She bit her tongue. Foot in mouth. Foot in mouth.

He frowned. "What?"

"Nothing. You really want to help?"

"I do. Just tell me what time." He glanced at the front door. "I could pick you up and we could drive together."

"You don't have—"

"If it's downtown, parking might be scarce near the site." His face was closed, no indication of what was going on behind those vivid blue eyes. "Sharing a ride will be a good thing."

A good thing, huh? Picking her up at her house? Driving for

a half-hour to Harrisburg? What would they talk about? A whole day with Ches Windham? What if he got hurt? What if he messed up his clothes?

His clothes.

Did he own grubby clothes? Nope. No image with him dressed in worn-out blue jeans and faded t-shirts could replace the uptown picture in her brain. No social media photo showed him in anything less than GQ-worthy outfits.

But help was help. If he knew something about building... "If you're serious."

"I've helped on a build before, Josie."

Ches Windham as a volunteer. A new perspective, for sure. "Okay."

"I'll need your address. What time do we start?"

Despite his initial embarrassment about leaving his wallet, Ches rallied and proved to be an interesting lunch companion with helpful insights for her fund-raising ideas. Their waitress rarely let the water level in their glasses recede beyond a few sips, so Josie could ask for a quick check. As she counted out bills to leave as a tip, Ches commented, "You're a nice tipper."

She shrugged. "Tips are important to most people."

"Yet you didn't want me to tip you last summer."

Interesting. He remembered when she declined his tip too. He'd chucked the bills toward her with a warning to "be careful with the car." What a jerk that day. "It's different. You..." She made a face.

"What?"

"You irritated me." She concentrated on the change in the receipt tray. She touched all four pennies, turning over the ones showing the face.

"Why?"

She shook her head and focused on the coins.

"What are you doing?"

"I collect wheat pennies. They still turn up sometimes. I

always check." She pocketed the change.

"You never answered why I irritated you."

"Yeah. I know." She pushed back her chair. "Okay. I need to get back. My class starts in nine minutes."

"WHAT DO YOU MEAN, 'you might have a problem with tomorrow'? I promised you homemade spaghetti in return for a day of hammering nails or whatever else is necessary." Josie set two cartons of vanilla ice cream on the counter to soften.

"Calm down, Josie girl. We're coming." Heath advocated for peace, as usual. "We won't make it at first bell is all."

"All three of you'll be late?" She cradled the phone between her cheek and shoulder, ripping open the bag of Oreos. "How late?" She counted twenty cookies and plopped them into the food processor. Threw one into her mouth too.

Maybe their not coming was a good thing. What would they say when they saw Ches there? Ben knew him, the dressed-up lawyer at the grant party. They hadn't discussed Ches after the banquet, but she'd seen the questioning look in Ben's eyes. Would he turn suspicious and go all fatherly when he saw Ches at the worksite?

And did Ches know anything about wielding a hammer? All three of her brothers were handy with carpentry tools thanks to their dad. How would Ches's skills line up with theirs? He'd learn firsthand how much her brothers liked to tease if he didn't measure up.

"Okay. If you need to be somewhere else, I understand. You can help me with something else later." She tore into a sleeve of small Butter Finger candy bars.

He grunted. "Did you not hear me? We're coming. We'll stay all day until the last screw is in place and all the trash is picked up."

All three brothers would be there. Ches too. Maybe she could run interference for Ches if they rode him hard about a lack of skills, but she'd have to play it cool or she'd end up as the target of her brothers' teasing.

All that and learning how to build a house. Tricky day tomorrow.

"You're crinkling packages. Are you eating or cooking?"

"If you must know, I'm right in the middle of making dessert for tomorrow night."

"Excellent. Your homemade spaghetti sauce and dessert. A great end to a day, little sis. What is it, by the way?"

"Not telling. You'll find out soon enough. See you tomorrow."

"Hey. If you can catch a ride with somebody, we'll get you home."

Right.

The problem wasn't catching a ride. The problem might be catching the grief when the brothers saw the driver.

FOCUSING on the soft instrumental version of "Every Rose has its Thorn," Ches steeled himself against Mallory's sulk.

"But I thought we'd go shopping tomorrow." She skimmed her right hand down the hank of hair framing her face, then fluffed the ends several inches below her shoulders.

"I don't remember making plans." A dull ache signaled the return of his headache. The acetaminophen he'd swallowed at the end of the workday was wearing off. He'd take some ibuprofen before bed.

Her left hand mimicked the same smoothing-hair pattern on the other side of her face before she posed as if for a picture. "We didn't exactly but remember when I mentioned the sale at Brooks Brothers, you said you needed some new shirts."

"Yeah. I said that, but I didn't mean—"

"So, I thought we'd make a day of it. Shop till we drop at my mom and dad's place on the lake." She dipped her chin and trained a sultry gaze on him. "I sold two pieces this week and want to reward myself."

"Congratulations, but it can't happen tomorrow. Sorry."

"Why?" She clutched his wrist, her manicured nails painted a color matching the strawberries on their dessert and her lacquered lips. "How about postponing?"

Ches remembered another hand on his arm. Another voice, teasing instead of whining. He extracted his arm to signal the waiter for the check. "I'm volunteering, and tomorrow's the day."

Her mouth hardened for an instant. "You've already done your pro bono work for this month."

"This isn't for the firm."

"Oh." She raised an eyebrow. "And your father's okay with that?"

He narrowed his eyes. Was that a veiled threat? Mallory liked getting her way. Would she mention her disappointment to her grandfather? "There's no problem. No conflict." He stuffed cash into the receipt folder.

"Except conflicting with our plans."

"Your plans. I'm sure you'll find a new dress or necklace to make you happy. Or should I have said dresses and necklaces?" He stood and offered his hand.

She smiled. "You know me well, Ches."

"Sorry I've got to call it a day already. Early morning tomorrow."

His pulse tripped a tad at the thought. An early morning working on a community build. A hammer in his hand would feel good after such a long time.

Yeah. Anticipating construction work definitely caused that blip. It had nothing to do with spending a day with Josie.

CHAPTER 4

*T*he ringing doorbell fractured Josie's nerves. Oversleeping, thanks to her dead phone, had wrecked her schedule this morning. She'd taken twenty minutes too long to decide what to wear. In a final fit of I-don't-care, she snatched one of Ben's old baseball t-shirts out of the bottom of her drawer and shrugged it on.

What to wear to a work site? Who stresses about that? Someone crazy, that's who. If Ches comes to work in pressed khakis and a golf shirt, who cares?

Lord, I'm being ridiculous. Help me stop. Please.

She tugged at the hem of her shirt and opened the front door. Ches knelt beside Winston, lolling on his back, his limp tongue hanging out the side of his pointy mouth. He patted the dog's stomach. "That's it, buddy." Ches rose and dusted his hand on his jeans. Faded jeans with a ragged hole hinting at his knee. He smiled. "Good morning."

Josie sucked in a breath.

"What's the matter?"

"Nothing. I, ah. I've never seen you dressed like, like..." Like a blue-collar worker. Like someone with a day's growth of whiskers. A plaid flannel shirt on top of a navy t-shirt instead of a button-down under a suit coat.

"I came to work, right?"

"Right." Get a grip, girl. But those jeans and that shirt. And his hair wasn't gelled into place today. It looked more like he'd just woken up and ran his hands—

"Josie, I've changed clothes, not grown two more ears."

Her mouth dropped. "Wait. Is that a joke? Did Mr. Windham just crack a joke?"

"Mr. Windham IV. Don't forget the Fourth."

She held up both hands in mock surrender. "What's happening here? Two jokes in less than a minute. I can't take it."

"Are you letting me in or are we leaving right now?" He cocked his head and sniffed. "Smells like garlic, but I was hoping for coffee."

She backed up and swung the door wide. "Oh, coffee. Yes. And, no. I need a few more minutes."

"A few more minutes?"

"I'm making spaghetti sauce for dinner tonight."

"Gotcha. Special date?"

"Yeah. With three brothers who'll be starving after hammering nails all day. Help yourself to the coffee." She gestured to the side counter. "Everything you need's right there. Milk. Mugs. Sugar."

He poured himself a mug and sipped it black. "You're cooking for your brothers?"

"Yep." That's right. We're all big loser nerds. No dates on a Saturday night.

She tossed in several pinches of dried basil to the crushed tomatoes already waiting in the crockpot, added a good portion of oregano. "I promised them dinner in exchange for volunteer time today." She poured in Worcestershire sauce along with generous shakes of a local hot sauce.

Ches leaned against the counter, one ankle crossed over the other, and scanned the workspace. "Where's your recipe?"

"Mmm." She tapped her temple. "It's all up here." She added in a couple more drops of the hot sauce.

"Do you even know how much you've put in?" He bent to peer into the crockpot.

"I have a pretty good idea."

"But you don't know for sure."

"Listen. I cook for my brothers at least once a week. No complaints. Not real ones anyway. Just requests for more, even though they ream me about pretty much everything else. I learned to cook by watching my mom feed three ravenous boys plus various friends who had a knack for showing up right at dinner time. She cooked a lot and cooked it fast."

She lifted her shoulders. "Most recipes are forgiving. Cooking isn't rocket science." She stirred the pot, rinsed the spoon, then laid it on a spoon rest beside the crockpot. "This will simmer all day into a fantastic meal tonight." She clamped down the lid.

THIS KITCHEN RESEMBLED nothing like Ches's childhood one. No stainless-steel appliances. No granite countertops. No mom checking a recipe after adding each ingredient, demanding everything be perfect. Certainly, no mom throwing out the whole dish if the tiniest bit didn't make par, then calling a delivery service to bring a gourmet dinner. In recent years, his mother skipped the cooking step and moved straight to the delivery service.

Josie cleared the counter of the spices and refrigerated the sauces. She wiped the drips and herb sprinkles, rinsed the dishcloth, and surveyed her domain with arms akimbo. Satisfied with what she'd accomplished. Free and easy in the kitchen. Completely confident. Fearless.

She fished a couple of M&Ms from a bowl on the counter and popped them into her mouth.

"Chocolate in the morning?"

"Is there a bad time for chocolate?" She leaned against the counter and grabbed a few more. "My payment for a job well done." She sighed before popping those into her mouth. "Don't let me forget to take this with us." She slid an unopened bag of peanut M&M's to the middle of the counter.

"Are you addicted to those things?"

"These will give us a boost this afternoon. You'll thank me about three o'clock."

"Oh, so you share?"

"Sometimes. If people are nice to me."

He lifted one of the many pictures from a side table. Josie surrounded by three young men. All smiling. No. Laughing at the camera. Their hands-on her shoulders. One of them, yes. He'd seen him before. One of the men, the one in the middle, accompanied her to the grant dinner. So, her date, no, escort, had been her brother. He ignored the tiny surge of relief at the discovery.

"Okay. I think I'm good to go." She pointed a remote toward a receiver, quieting the Top 40 contemporary hits playing in the background. "You want a to-go cup for your coffee?"

He replaced the picture and drained the mug. "No, thanks. Great picture." He rinsed the mug and placed it in the top rack of the dishwasher.

She grimaced. "The photographer had us going so bad. Such a goofy guy. The real portrait's in the living room, but my mom loves this one best. She says he captured us with real smiles, not fake ones."

"Fake smiles?"

"You know." She angled her head and twitched her mouth.

"Could I see?"

"The other one? Fine. This way." She led him into the next

room off the hallway. "There you go. The entire Daniels clan. Smiling for the camera. Mom, of course, wanted a picture of just us. Ben dated someone for a while, and we thought it could end differently than it did. Therefore, the picture." She gestured her hand like a game show model.

Another room, more formal than the others, but still comfortable, still lived in. "Your parents look nice." He studied the portrait.

"They're great."

He nodded. "You like them enough to live with them."

"They're not here. They're on a mission for two years. They decided to serve as short-term missionaries in their retirement. They've been gone a few months. I'm keeping the house while they're away."

"Missionaries, huh." He moved to the piano and sank onto the bench. Sheet music and piano books flanked both sides of the bench and spilled out of a wicker basket. "Do you play?"

"Yeah. Not that great. My brothers got all the talent. How about you?"

"Took lessons for ten years." Hated every minute of it. He picked up a book. "*Star Wars*. You have a *Star Wars* music book?" He flipped through the pages, then sifted through the other books. *Billy Joel's Greatest Hits. Disney Classics. The Fifty Greatest Movie Theme Songs. Easy Jazz. Johnny Cash Favorites*. "You've got almost every kind of music here." He looked at her. "Johnny Cash?"

"Sam went through a phase. My mom tried to keep us interested and bought the music we liked, or she liked. What do you like to play?"

"What do I *like* to play?" He shook his head and pulled out a magenta-colored book. *60 Progressive Piano Pieces You Like to Play*. "This is what you'd find at my piano." He tossed it back onto the pile.

She shuddered. "I remember that book. What torture. My

teacher insisted I learn "Spinning Song" before moving on. It took me forever."

He swiveled on the bench and played the first section by heart. He grinned at her over his shoulder.

She thumped his back. "Show off. But that was great. Good job."

He rose from the bench. "Speaking of jobs."

"Uh oh." She glanced at her watch. "We'll never hear the end of it if my brothers get started before we arrive."

"They can't be that bad."

She glanced her emerald eyes toward him and groaned. "Famous last words."

CHAPTER 5

"So Sleeping Beauty has finally arrived." Sam's words curled around the nail in the corner of his mouth. He made a great show of pushing back his sleeve, pretending to check the time. "If I'd known you'd show up this late, I would've asked you to bring snacks for break time."

"Funny as a doorknob, Sam. Watch it or you'll be answering, 'Want fries with that?' for your dinner." Josie scanned the work-site. "Where's Jerry?"

"Over by his truck. Checking with group leaders, I think." He removed the nail from his mouth. "Who's your friend, Jo?"

Great. Exactly what she wanted to avoid. If she'd gotten to the site before her brothers, they wouldn't have seen her arrive with Ches. He would've been just another volunteer. She would've hopped a ride home with the brothers, and all would be normal. But, no. They arrived at 7:50 to every eye watching them ascend the brand-new walkway together.

"Sam, this is Ches. Ches, meet one of my annoying brothers, Sam."

"Ches. That's an interesting name. Kind of unusual." He rolled his shoulders into a stretch. "Sounds like a board game or like that pie you make, Joey." He threw a cheeky glance at his sister. "Is that what we're having for dessert tonight?"

"Sounds like you might not find out what's for dessert tonight, Sam. Honestly." Way to welcome the new guy. Why did she ever agree for him to come?

"Ches, huh? Sounds like you might have misplaced part of it or—"

"Like you misplaced part of that casing?"

Sam glanced at the frame around the door and back at Ches, a slow grin stretching across his face. He repositioned the errant board and nodded. "Good call. Nice to meet you, Ches."

Josie chuckled. Score one for the new guy. Maybe Ches could hold his own with the chiding. Time would tell if he knew how to wield a hammer or an electric screwdriver. "Don't mind this guy," she jerked her thumb toward her brother. "His manners are stuck somewhere in seventh grade. And I apologize to all seventh graders."

Sam repositioned his ball cap. "Careful, girl. I know secrets about you."

"Right back at you, Twinkle Toes."

"Hey, now." Sam leaned back, mock horror animating his face. "Don't play so rough."

"You started it." She shook her head. What was she doing? Picking back and forth with her annoying brother. And in front of Ches. If Sam was in seventh grade, that meant she was in sixth. "Let's go find Jerry and get our assignment."

They rounded a corner. "Twinkle Toes?"

"Old family story I'll keep to myself unless I need to use it for leverage."

"Are all your brothers like that?"

"You mean charming, warm, welcoming to strangers?"

"More like irritating, annoying, irksome like a mosquito?"

She grinned. "You're good. Looks like you can tease as well as—"

"Howdy, Joey girl." Heath appeared from a room to the left, tugged her ponytail, and faked a yawn. "Did you get enough beauty sleep?"

"Not you too."

"I promised Sam. Anyway, we got here ten minutes before you rolled up. And nobody'd started working at that point. No worries." He looked at Ches and held out a hand.

"This is Ches." She started the introductions. "Sam beat you to the name game."

"Good to know."

Ches clasped the extended hand. "I'm sure you'll think of something else."

Heath raised his eyebrows and smiled. "You may be right. Jerry said they'd need extra hands in the kitchen. The cabinets should be here any minute."

"Installing cabinets, huh?"

"Guess so. Unless you want to be in charge of sweeping sawdust. We need a sawdust sweeper."

"I can hang cabinets." Ches hooked a thumb in his belt loop. "You look like a good fit for a broom."

Josie started for the backyard. "Boys, let's get to work." Yep. Ches could take care of himself.

"I THOUGHT I was riding home with you bozos." Josie slapped her gloves against her thighs and glared at Sam. Ches had climbed to the roof to check something for Jerry. He'd also discarded his flannel shirt at some point during the day, revealing a navy t-shirt with UVA emblazoned in orange letters on the front and big, solid muscles. Nice biceps told the story of long workouts probably at some swanky gym or country club.

She chastised herself. That wasn't fair. He'd worked hard

today and knew what he was doing, too, usually one step ahead of what was needed. He'd done this before.

She lowered her voice. "In fact, Ben told me you'd give me a ride."

"Well, big brother was mistaken." Sam stretched his arms straight up and rolled his neck. "We're taking the two high schoolers who don't drive back to Charlotte. So the car is full up. What's wrong with riding back with your boyfriend?"

"One. He's not my boyfriend." She slugged his arm. "Two. I'm supposed to ride with you." Picking her up was one thing. Dropping her off? It could be a little awkward.

"Hey. Jerry said everybody's packing up." Ches, down from the ladder, draped his flannel shirt over his shoulder. "Ben said if we leave now, you could get a head start on having dinner ready. I think he's starving. Oh, and...ah. He invited me to dinner."

"See?" Sam gave her a side hug and jiggled her twice. "Problem solved, Jo. See you in a few." He stepped away, then turned back toward her. "Hey. Did you get another bottle of Ranch? I'll need it if we're having a salad."

"Grab a gallon of skim when you pick up the dressing, bro. See you at home."

CHES CLOSED HER DOOR, then stretched his arms over his head on the way to the driver's seat. A good day's work. The twinges from his muscles felt good. Like the summer spent with his uncle.

He pressed the start button for the engine, and his cell sounded. He hesitated. He didn't want to talk to anybody from Charlotte or anywhere else today. He wanted to keep talking to the Daniels family. The ringing insisted on his attention. The screen on the dashboard flashed his father's number. Father. He clamped his mouth just before a profane word slipped out in front of Josie.

Fastening her seat belt, she glanced at him. "You can take it. We have time."

He jerked a smile and pushed the hang-up icon. "My father. He'll leave a message." Or five. He pressed his palm against the burning in his gut and pulled away from the curb.

With simply his name on the screen, his father had soured the whole day. Ches wanted the free spirit of the day back, but his father had swooped in and crashed the scene. He complied with everything his father wanted. Couldn't he have just one day? Just one day to live outside the strangling confines of the firm?

Law school. The firm. Even Mallory. He was following the path his father set for him, and still, he wanted more. Every day. Working toward the plan. His father's plan.

He merged onto I-85, set the cruise control, and shifted to a more comfortable position. A movement beside him interrupted his musings. Josie. Focus on Josie.

"You need to pick up anything before dinner? We could stop somewhere."

"Sam's on it. Thanks anyway." She smoothed flyaway tendrils from her face, secured them behind her ear.

He tightened his grip on the steering wheel before his fingers could follow the same path behind her ear and settle on the creamy skin of her neck. Nope. Not where his thoughts should be landing. Focus on her brothers and the camaraderie they'd shared building a house today.

He cleared his throat. "Your brothers. They like to have a good time, huh? What're their stories?"

JOSIE MANAGED to talk the whole way back to Charlotte. Thirty minutes or so about her crazy brothers. She talked right through the second call from his dad. Did Ches listen, or did he simply need help ignoring the persistent phone?

She finished the last story about Heath as Ches brought his car to a halt in the driveway. Perfect timing.

The phone vibrated again. A tic appeared in his cheek.

Maybe the timing wasn't perfect.

She opened her door and nodded to the phone. "You can answer while I boil the pasta water."

"I don't need—"

She locked eyes with him. "This is the third call in thirty minutes. Maybe you should answer it. Come in when you're finished." She hopped out and headed for the house before he could reply or grunt or yell, it wasn't her business.

He wouldn't have yelled earlier today, but the phone calls had changed him. He'd returned to the guy in the power suit with the fully-loaded Lexus. Besides nodding and offering a monosyllable or two, he'd contributed nothing to the conversation on the drive home.

Could a call from his dad change his personality that much? Maybe someone was sick in his family, and he didn't want to hear bad news. No. Most people would jump on the phone, wanting information, not ignoring it.

She turned the burner under the pasta water on high and unwrapped the Italian bread. She peeked out the kitchen window. He hovered at the corner of the car, rigid as a soldier at attention. His mouth etched a straight line, no room for words. He listened instead.

He tapped his finger to the screen and shoved the phone into his pocket. She retreated from the window. *God, something is going on with Ches. I have no idea what the problem is, but You do. Help him, please.*

Flutters teased her stomach. Praying for Ches? Really?

Well, why not? She prayed for her brothers all the time.

The front door opened after a quick knock.

She stuck her head into the refrigerator, retrieving salad fixings. His footsteps thudded on the wood floor.

"Josie, sorry. I gotta go."

She set the vegetables on the countertop and faced him. Except for the clothes, the Ches she'd volunteered with all-day had vanished. His face lacked any trace of feeling except for his eyes, glittering with some strong emotion. His hands curled into fists. The transformation sent a shiver down her spine.

"Is it a family emergency?"

"No. No emergency."

She ran a finger along the countertop. "Did your parents ask you to dinner?"

He snorted. "No. No dinner." He raked his hand through his hair.

"Well, then. You have to eat." She shrugged. "It's practically ready. The guys'll be here any minute."

He turned for the door.

"Ches. Wait. You seem—"

He whipped toward her. "What?"

She sucked in a breath and stepped back. Ignore those hard eyes flashing daggers. They're directed at something else. Someone else. She swallowed. "Upset. Angry. I don't know, but you got some bad news from that phone call. Maybe take a few minutes, eat, then drive." She slid the M&M bowl toward him. "At least have a few of these. They'll make you feel better."

"You think the phone call was bad news?"

"I'm not a mind reader, but you're torn up. You got that muscle in your cheek happening again. Driving like this might not be a good idea. Think of it as protecting your sweet ride out there." She smiled, hoping the teasing would bring the carpenter Ches back.

"You like the car?"

"Well, duh. Who wouldn't like a Lexus Sport Coup that still

smells faintly new? So." She raised her eyebrows. "Will you stay?"

Working his jaw, he studied the picture on the side table. "Yes. Thank you."

"Great." She pressed on the oven light button. "Could you set the table, please." She checked the bread.

He dropped his jaw. "What?"

She laughed. "Do you mind? Setting the table?"

He shook his head. "No. No, but—"

"Good. Don't worry. I won't ask you to fold the napkins into fleurs de lis. The plates are right up there." She pointed to the cabinet near his head. "But wait. Wash your hands first. The powder room is down the hall to your left."

"You like giving orders." The tightness around his mouth softened.

She grinned. "I'm good at it too."

Nice. The muscle in his cheek had disappeared, replaced by a fledgling smile. Now if she could drive out the tension knotting his shoulders, the day would be a success on all counts. The brothers would help.

CHAPTER 6

A potted plant partially concealed a rip in the carpet near a portable shelf system. A fluorescent light flickered and buzzed near the stairs. Would a thirty-thousand-dollar grant be enough to fix all the problems in this library? Ches rubbed his chin and studied the last page of the proposal. Josie had listed several ideas for fundraisers. A 5K, some kind of antique event, a night of chocolate tasting. But could they garner the funds necessary to keep the library in the black?

He checked his watch. Ten minutes before she arrived. Ten minutes to jot down some notes, make good work of thirty minutes he'd allocated for the library. Then he could leave to be on time to pick up Mallory.

But he didn't want to think about fundraisers or Mallory either. He wanted to remember Saturday night's dinner, the bantering between siblings and directed toward him too. The delicious spaghetti sauce drenched over perfect noodles. The simple, but wonderful dessert, ice cream sandwiched between Oreo and Butter Finger crumbs. He hardly ever indulged in dessert, but Saturday night he'd dug into a second piece before the concoction melted in the serving dish.

The contented feelings from that one dinner sustained him through the second irate phone call from his father later Saturday night and the third one on Sunday afternoon. His work would not suffer by helping with the library or by working on a build or by being with Josie. If anything, all those activities would enhance—

"Hi. Did you have a good day?"

He jerked to attention. Josie. Her sudden appearance kicked his heart rate to a fast thump. "It was normal." Today her hair, styled away from her face, fell in soft curls caressing her shoulders. A few loose strands had escaped from whatever held the rest in place behind her head.

She sat across from him and opened a notebook. "Is that good or bad?"

"Good question."

She wrinkled her brow. "Okay. I don't even know what that means. Sounds very mysterious and like you don't want to talk about it." She tilted her head, raised her eyebrows. "Well, are you going to ask me?"

"What?"

She pursed her lips. "How my day was, of course."

"Oh. How was your day?"

"Pretty good. Especially in the last few minutes. I got every green light all the way through downtown. Can you believe it? Ten or eleven. I lost count. All green. I just kept going, and they just kept turning green." She snapped her fingers and flashed him a satisfied grin.

Who was this girl? She could cook a delicious meal while she helped build a house. She didn't mind hard work. A simple thing like a green light tipped her joy to bubbling. "You're easy to please."

"Not true." She shook her head. "But I appreciate the little gifts offered all day long." She rummaged in her bag, retrieved a purple ink pen. "Okay. Should we get started?"

He flipped the proposal back to the cover page and leaned back in his chair. "First, I'm wondering why this library is so important to you. Charlotte has, I don't know, maybe fifteen libraries."

"This neighborhood needs its library. Children can walk to it now. They can't walk or even ride their bikes to Scaleybark, the next nearest branch." She pressed her lips together. "I addressed all that in the grant." Heat blotches crept up her neck. "The grant you read."

"Don't worry. I can't revoke the grant. I just wondered why this library?" He glanced over the common area.

She swallowed. "I see what you see—torn carpet, blown light bulbs, worn furniture. The budget has been slashed by tens of thousands of dollars over the last few years. I just started volunteering after grad school. I like helping people. I'm young and able, so why not help a good cause?"

"Oh, like do what you can for your country?"

"You've completely ruined the Kennedy quotation, but yes, I guess it's sort of like that." She moistened her lips. "You sound like you regret that the library received the grant."

"Not at all. Just wanted to know why you're so passionate about this particular one."

She chewed on the inside of her cheek. "When my brothers left me to go to school, my mother used to bring me at least twice a week to this library." She tapped the table with her index finger. "Storytime. Puppet shows. Craft make-and-take sessions." Her gaze settled on the children's area. "I loved being here when I was a little girl.

"When I walk in now," she glanced back to him, "the same book smell greets me and makes me happy." The corners of her mouth twitched. She fashioned an L on her forehead with her thumb and forefinger. "I'm a geek. I know."

"Having a happy memory doesn't make you a geek."

"I want the same happiness for the children of this neighborhood. Plus, the next budget item to go will be a paid position. I don't want one of those ladies—she nodded to the circulation desk— to lose her job."

"Got it."

"So you've got the proposal out. Good. Do you want to discuss the fundraisers now?"

No, he didn't. He wanted to find out what else made Josie happy. He wanted to hear about the rest of her day which surprised him. Instead, he dragged his attention to the list before him.

"Tell me about this 5K."

THE YELLOW MARKER squeaked against the paper as Josie high-lighted the date to send out press releases announcing the race. "Didn't you hear me the first time? I'm not running in the 5K. I have to man the registration table."

Ches continued to be stubborn about her participation. "Wimpy excuse. One of the librarians can man the table. You should be one of the runners. Lead by example."

"I'm not a runner. In fact, I hate running, so I'll contribute my upbeat personality and administration skills to registration."

"How can you ask people to run if you're not willing to?"

She leaned against her elbows and pretended to share a secret. "I don't understand it, but they're actually people who love running." She straightened. "And anyway, I'm bringing three people to run in my place."

"Your brothers." He rubbed his fingers over his chin, just beginning to show a five o'clock shadow.

She wiggled her eyebrows. "Exactly."

One corner of his mouth tipped. Not a real smile, but a start. "They always do what you tell them to?"

She smirked. "Don't I wish? But they know how important

this is to me." She twirled her pen and grinned. "What about you? Will you run for a good cause?"

The other side of his mouth tipped. "I will if you will."

Her smile vanished. "No. Wait a—"

"I was hoping I'd catch you here." A cloud of spicy cologne wafted between them.

B.J.

She dropped her pen, crossed her arms in front of her. "I thought you were emailing me questions."

"Face to face is better." He laid a leather embossed folder on the edge of the table.

She gestured toward B.J. "Ches, this is—"

Chess's mouth flat-lined. "We know each other."

"What's up, Ches?"

"I was going to ask you the same. Crimewave hit the library?"

"You might be surprised." He glanced at Josie. "Hey, when you're finished here, how about we catch a bite and go over the questions together?"

She shook her head. "No. Sorry. Email them."

"Some of them require explanations."

"Email the explanations, B.J."

"A quick dinner won't—"

"I think she's saying 'no,' B.J." Ches straightened in his chair, curled his fingers around the edge of the table.

B.J. shifted his stance, widening the space between his feet. "Josie and I go way back. We're friends. She's helping with a story."

"No. We're not friends. We used to date. That's all."

"Sounds like she's not interested in dinner."

The testosterone level in the room had multiplied with each exchange. Josie searched for a way to diffuse the manly vibes. "Ches, don't you have an appointment?"

He flicked his eyes to his watch and grimaced. "Yeah. I do."

"B.J., I can give you about fifteen minutes before I have to leave. We can go over the questions here." She patted the table.

"I'm not sure…"

She leaned on her elbows and steepled her fingers. "Take it or leave it."

Ches looked at her and again at his watch. "Are you sure you'll be fine?"

She smiled, a warm feeling rising through her midsection. "Completely."

He gathered the proposal and rose. He inclined his head to B.J. "She doesn't want dinner." His mouth allowed a tiny smile to Josie. "We'll continue the 5K discussion another time."

Her pulse quickened. No, no, no, heart. Do not leap at the idea of seeing Ches again.

He turned back and waved before exiting the library.

"So you won't have dinner with me." B.J. clicked his pen in the silence as he studied her. "Are you waiting for Ches?"

"What?" Shock brought her attention back to the table.

"Because if you are, I can tell you right now. It's not going to happen." The clicking picked up speed. "He's on the fast track to partnering. With the firm and with Mallory Padgett."

Way to douse all my happy feelings, B.J. "Thanks for the warning, but I'm not your business anymore." She extracted the pen from his fingers and laid it to the side of his notebook. "What's your first question?"

He clasped his hands, rubbed his thumbs together. "You two looked real cozy, smiling and laughing. Flirting maybe. I don't want you to get hurt."

She laughed. "That's rich, B.J. So you're the only one for that job?"

His mouth tightened. "I said I was sorry."

"Yep. You did. And for the record, Ches and I were discussing the library, not flirting."

He regarded her for a couple of beats. "What if I said I think I made a mistake?"

"I'd agree. But your mistake worked for my best."

"Yeah. I agree. You look great."

"Stop. Flattery doesn't look good on you, and no need for the dating advice. I've already checked off dating-a-success-driven-Type-A from my life's goals. Not planning to do a double-take. With you or with Ches." She tapped his folder. "Get to those questions. You've already burned five minutes."

TWENTY MINUTES. Josie followed the minute hand circling the clock face on the kitchen wall. Twenty minutes since leaving B.J., and her nerves were almost back to normal. The frozen yogurt with mini chocolate chips and almonds helped soothe her insides but being away from him was the best medicine.

She dragged a broken piece of sugar cone through the yogurt, making sure to catch some chocolate chips and some kiwi bits. Several food groups mingled in her cup of deliciousness. Dairy, fruit, protein. Pretty healthy dinner. And no dishes.

Padding into the family room, she ignored the echoes of her brothers' whines for permission to eat on the couch and snuggled deep into her dad's recliner. Tonight she needed comfort, and the oversized, overstuffed chair and a bowl of frozen yogurt soothed her spirit.

What was the deal with B.J.? Coming around again. Messing with her mind. Why was he acting interested? Was the interest real or a ruse to...what? Why would he want to see her again? Six months ago, when B.J. shattered the dream she'd begun to weave around him, he made it pretty clear she wasn't his future.

If he wasn't interested in her, then...something about the library? The grant? The firm? He'd asked a lot of questions about the grant. How and when was the firm paying the money? Why this library? Had Ches always been slated to help with the fundraisers?

What did it matter if the big check used for the photo ops listed the full amount, but the library and all the other non-profits would receive incremental checks throughout the next six months? So what if he'd never heard grant money paid out like that before.

B.J. Always the pot-stirrer. This instance would prove to be no different. If he thought he smelled a rat, it was his own stinking Docksiders. Padgett, Gibbons, Tyler, and Rose was an old, respected, community-minded, solid business that could give out money any way it saw fit.

He wanted to dig up dirt on the firm. He wasn't interested in her. Good. She didn't want to get back together with B.J. He wasn't the person she'd imagined him to be in the early stages of their relationship. The hardnosed side of his personality blossomed through the time they spent together, culminating in an impersonal break-up scene.

No thanks, B.J. My head is on straight this time. I'm not fantasizing about a get-back-together scene with you. I'm not signing up for another round of heartache.

Still, his compliments and attention boosted her self-confidence. Even though she didn't want them to. Even though she could hear her mom admonish her with "Your worth comes from being a child of God, not the superficial trappings of this world. Not from a pretty dress or a new pair of shoes. Not from what others see on the outside, but how God sees you, His special treasure."

Yada yada yada.

True, Mom, but a compliment sure does feel nice. Especially one from an old boyfriend.

Besides the compliment, though, B.J. wasn't exactly nice today. He didn't use kid gloves in his warnings about Ches.

The *unnecessary* warnings about Ches.

She knew he had a girlfriend even if the girlfriend was all wrong for him. Yeah, Mallory looked beautiful and seemed smart with her own business, but Ches liked to volunteer with Joined Hands Joined Hearts and work with his hands. Did she even own a pair of old jeans? Wouldn't she be afraid she'd break a perfectly polished nail?

Wait. You're dishing out some serious catty attitude.

She stretched her legs over the arm of the chair and pushed Mallory out of her mind. Ches needed someone who appreciated his wood-working talents. Someone who appreciated his sense of humor. Someone who helped remove the tic in his cheek, the barometer for his stress level.

Just like she'd done at dinner the other night and the day she'd paid for his lunch. Yep, quelling his tic wasn't easy but she'd managed it a few times. So someone like herself would...

Someone like herself?

Me?

She bolted upright in the recliner. The tiny thought had sneaked up from the recesses of her mind, her crazy mind, and ambushed her.

No. No. No. Ches didn't need her. She wrangled the absurd thought to the back of her brain. Ches needed someone who could help him with his career but make him laugh at the same time, who could banish the sadness hovering at the corners of his eyes and make him smile. He didn't laugh enough. Or smile either.

Ches needed someone else, not her, and he certainly wasn't the one for her either. B.J.'s lesson had taught her plenty about dating the wrong person.

An image of B.J. and Ches squaring off over the library table floated into her mind. What was up with the tension between them?

Burrowing deeper into the cushions, she fancied she caught a whiff of her dad's aftershave. *Watch over my parents, please, God.*

Scraping the bottom of the cardboard bowl, she startled at her phone's signaling a text. Ugh. The cell rested on the kitchen counter. She didn't want to move, but her brothers would drive over here if she didn't reply.

Tossing the cardboard bowl into the trash, she retrieved the phone and checked the screen. Her insides seized.

Ches.

"Did you have dinner?"

"Yes."

"Did you enjoy it?"

Was that his way of asking about B.J.?

"Yes."

No reply. She gave more details.

"Stopped for froyo after the library."

"That was dinner?"

"Yes. Delicious and nutritious."

"Got to work on your definition of nutritious."

She grinned at the phone.

"Covered most of the food groups."

"Are you free Saturday at 8 am?"

Her stomach dipped again. Breakfast? Slow down, heart.

"Eight on Saturday morn? Sleep much?"

"Eastfield Park? Wear workout clothes and running shoes."

It didn't sound like breakfast.

"Not getting a good feeling here."

"For the library. Saturday?"

"I agree to meet. That's it."

"Goodnight, Josie."

"Night."

She dropped the phone onto her lap. What had she just agreed to? Meeting him. At eight o'clock in the morning. In workout clothes. Which could mean sweating and a red face and limp hair and not exactly a look she wanted to cultivate in front of Ches.

Not just in front of Ches. In front of any man.

But especially not Ches.

CHAPTER 7

"*B*ut as I told you the other day, I'm working the registration table, not running the 5K." Josie crossed her arms and waited for Ches to rise from his stretching exercise.

"Look at it this way. The librarians I've seen in your library aren't about to run three steps much less three miles." He flattened his hands to the asphalt and spoke to his shins. "You'd be letting them participate in the fundraiser by working registration in your place while you're running the race."

She smirked. "You'll be a good parent one day."

He popped up from his jackknife position. "You think so?"

"You're working the guilt trip like a pro."

Did he look disappointed? Not for long. The look retreated, and a teasing one took its place. He arched an eyebrow. "It's for a good cause, remember?"

"I. Despise. Running."

He crossed his ankles and touched his knuckles to the pavement. "Wow, Josie. Strong word. It's only three-point one miles. Even a slow pace will get you done in thirty minutes."

She huffed. "Thirty minutes of torture."

"Torture? How about dialing back the drama a notch. You

look like an athlete. I know you can do it. I'll help you train for it."

Like an athlete. Did he mean a big ol' sweaty, weightlifting kind of athlete or the more svelte, graceful type of gymnast athlete? Did she really want to know the answer? But did he say he'd help train?

"I played volleyball in high school to avoid running. I think all the press about a runner's high is just hype to sell more shoes."

He laughed and pushed his hands above his head. How could she get him to laugh again? Could she sacrifice sleeping-in time for training? Could she seriously allow him to see her huffing and puffing?

No, the real question was could she run for thirty minutes without dropping?

"Come on. You run in the race. I'll help you train, and—" a slow grin called up a dimple— "I'll bring ten more runners."

She narrowed her eyes. "You're holding four hundred dollars hostage against my running or not?"

"I prefer to think of it as getting people to contribute to a good cause."

"You're very good with words. No wonder you're a lawyer."

"Flattery will get you a longer workout. We'll start slow. We've got, what? Six weeks to train?"

"Yeah. First Saturday of November."

"Should be perfect running weather."

"There's no—"

"Uh-huh." He held up a hand. "No negativity. Let's go. I'll stay with you. We'll run for two minutes. Walk for one. Build up to running."

"Why are you doing this?"

"A good cause. Remember?" He gestured for her to begin.

Right. The library.

HEATH PLANTED a kiss on Josie's forehead. "Thanks for dinner, Joey. Delicious as always."

"Hey, what's your hurry, big guy?" Sam slid a plastic container of leftovers into a brown paper bag. "Gotta date?"

"Wouldn't you like to know? Have a good week everybody." Heath slipped out the front door.

Her phone vibrated on the counter. Sam beat her to it. "Ooh. I think Jo might have the date. Guess who's texting lil' sis, Ben."

"Give me that." She lunged for the phone, but Sam held it over her head, high out of reach. "Nosy Ned. My phone is none of your business." She grabbed his ear and tugged. Hard.

"Ow." Sam bent closer to her but cradled the phone away from Josie's hands. "I can't help if your phone shined his name, and I just happened to look at the screen."

"Whose name? And give her the phone." Ben grabbed his keys from the basket on the counter.

Josie stopped struggling, held out her palm, and glared at Sam. "I'm waiting." She tapped her toes for good measure.

Sam wiggled the phone in the air. "Ches Windham. That's who."

Ben glanced at Josie, eyebrows scrunched together. "Ches? Why's he texting you?"

"I haven't read the text, so I can't answer." She waved her hand at Sam. "Hello. The phone."

Ben jabbed a finger in Sam's side and grabbed the phone when he doubled over.

Sam twisted away from Ben. "No fair. Quit tickling me."

"Here." Ben handed the phone to Josie. "I thought Ches was seeing—"

She tucked it into her pocket. "He is."

"Then—"

"We're working on some fundraising ideas for the library."

Sam shifted his bag of leftovers to his left hand. "I thought—"

"We still have to raise extra money to get the matching funds."

Ben nodded. "Just be careful, okay?"

"Don't worry. No need for the warning." B.J. already beat you to it.

"Ches isn't exactly a rebound kind of person."

It was her turn to frown. "What does that mean?"

"Are you really over B.J.?"

"Are you kidding me? I've been over him." The last meeting at the library confirmed she was thoroughly over B.J. Nichols. *Thank You, God.*

"But you haven't started dating again."

"Not that this is any of your business, big brother, but I kinda got my hands full right now with my students, the library, not to mention keeping you yahoos fed." She poked his chest. "And when was the last date either of you had? I can't remember one, for sure."

"Hey, Jo. Ben's right. Ches is—"

"Dating advice from you?" She chucked Sam on his shoulder. How could she end this bizarre conversation and get them out of the house? "Now I've heard everything. Go home, you two. I have to get my beauty sleep."

Sam gave her a quick hug and left, but Ben lingered in the foyer. "Josie, Ches isn't a bad guy. He was cool building the house and at dinner—"

"That you invited him to, remember."

"Right. It's just... He's..."

Her stomach knotted. She lifted her chin. "Out of my league?"

Ben's mouth widened into an O. "You seriously didn't say that. I don't know anybody in your league, by the way. But from all I've heard, he's got a plan, and his plan—"

"Includes Mallory Padgett. I know, Ben Buddy. I'm good. Thank you for caring about me." She squeezed him tight. "Have a good week."

He searched her face for a couple more seconds before exiting the house.

She waved at the retreating headlights as Ben backed out the driveway.

Then she closed the door and read the text.

THE HOW-ARE-YOU text sent ten minutes ago. Ches checked the phone again just in case he'd missed a new notification. Nothing. Maybe her phone was dead. Maybe she was busy with students' papers. Maybe she was on a date.

He chunked his phone to the end of the couch and selected the next episode of *Home Improvement*. Maybe Tim Allen could help take his mind off Josie.

But what if she was on a date? Would it be with that B.J. pest? They used to date. Did they want to start up again? Maybe he does. He'd be stupid not to, but she's too smart. Isn't she?

What was the deal with B.J. anyway? Why did he appear in so many of the same places all of a sudden? At the library with Josie and then at lunch the other day with a client of one of the partners.

Researching a story on the library? Not likely.

The Tool Time girl on the screen had blond hair, but hers was lighter than Josie's. Josie's curled at the bottom, too, whether she left it long or put it up in a ponytail as she wore it yesterday.

He smiled to himself. Yesterday started promising with the run in the park. She had a nice stride for someone who professed to hate running. Straightforward. Smooth. Halfway through the run, she'd given up the walking minute and stuck to running. A slow pace, yes. But running, nevertheless.

Yeah. She was an athlete all right, a good sport too. She powered through the little rain shower at the end of the run and never mentioned it.

His phone vibrated. He grabbed it with one hand and muted the TV with the other.

Yes. Josie. His pulse rate ticked up a notch. Concentrating on her words, he didn't explore the reason for the upswing in heartbeats.

"I'm fine. You?"

"I'm good. Sore?"

"Not yet. Probably tomorrow, right?"

"Right."

What else could he type to keep the conversation going? *Are you seeing B.J. anytime soon?* Absolutely not. *Seeing anybody special?* Quit with her dating life. His thumbs hovered over the screen.

His phone buzzed again.

"Busy week?"

"The usual. You?"

"Couple of tests and a project due."

"You a mean teacher?"

"Brutal."

He chuckled. Could she really give a lazy student a teacher glare? He didn't want to find out. Her smile interested him more.

"Still up for another training session Saturday?"

"You. Are. Killing me."

"No. Training you."

"Same thing."

"I owe you lunch."

"No."

"And dinner."

"Don't think so."

"Yes. Jog at least twice this week."

"Who's mean now?"

"Saturday 8?"

"Tyrant."

"See you then?"

"Fine."

"Good night."

"Night."

He smiled and relaxed against the couch. Could he suggest grabbing something, breakfast or a smoothie, after the run? Not to start anything. No, definitely not. Despite how the local gossip columnist portrayed him in her column, he'd never cheated on a girlfriend and never planned to.

But, yeah, he'd like to spend a little more time with Josie. She made him laugh, helped him breathe.

The phone sang in his hand. Mallory's ring tone. She'd pirated his phone months ago and changed the ring without his permission to a Top 40 song she claimed to be theirs. He fought impatience as he answered the call.

"Hello, Mallory."

"Whatcha doing, sweetie?"

He smoothed the wrinkles on his forehead with his fingertips. "Just enjoying Sunday night. Getting ready for the week." He followed the muted actions on the TV screen.

"Wish I was with you?"

How to answer? *No* wouldn't cut it. "I'm sure you'd be bored."

A throaty giggle annoyed his ear. "I can make sure you aren't bored if I come over there."

"Well..." How to respond in a kind, but truthful answer? He wasn't in the mood for company or phone conversations either.

"Not still mad at me, are you?" The pout she'd perfected to get her way resounded through the speaker.

Yeah. I'm absolutely ticked. "Why would I be angry?"

"Ches, I thought your mom would like to know I was

thinking about her yesterday. I thought she'd like to hear from me."

"Yeah. You were thinking about her and invited her to go shopping even though she's in Virginia."

"In my defense, sweetie, I said I wished she could come with me."

Splitting hairs. "She appreciated the thought nonetheless. My father appreciated the call as well." He'd endured a fifteen-minute harangue from his father about not being available when "the Padgett girl wanted to have brunch."

"Could we change the subject? My grandfather's having a pig picking' at Lake Norman this coming Saturday. He's invited us and a few people from the firm, but mostly friends and family. Sound good?"

No. It sounds like work. "Depends on the time. I've got commitments till late afternoon."

"My grandfather mentioned hoping he could spend some time with you."

Right. Part of the vetting process. The barbecue would please his father and maybe keep him off his back for a week or two. He ground his molars. "What time's dinner? I could be free after five."

"Fabulous. Pick me up at six-thirty. I've got a new outfit perfect for the party."

He ended the conversation with a quick, "See you then."

Pressing the message icon, he began rereading the texts from Josie.

CHAPTER 8

*J*osie stirred the smoothie with the thick straw and sipped a long swallow of frozen mango puree, enjoying the cool feeling wash down her throat. The October sun shined warm rays on the park despite the red and yellow leaves signaling a new season. She swept escaping tendrils of hair away from her forehead. Three weeks of cooling down with smoothies and quick conversations after their runs had made her more comfortable with looking sweaty and tired around Ches. Plus, he was dating Mallory, so it shouldn't matter what she looked like.

Except that it did matter.

"Do you still hate running?" Unwinding on the memorial bench at the edge of the parking lot, Ches pulled a mouthful from his triple berry smoothie, his long legs stretched out in front of him. His black running shorts were hiked midway up his thighs. Toned, muscular, tanned thighs.

She forced her eyes to a mom pushing a running stroller and pumped her straw, the plastic squeaking against the lid. "Of course."

"I don't think so."

"Why? Because I don't groan when we start anymore? Because I'm hiding my bad attitude better?"

He raked off condensation from the side of the cup with his fingers. "No. But I appreciate the absence of groans. Thank you." He transferred his gaze from the cup to her. "I think you like running a little."

"Wrong."

"Come on. A little bit."

She shook her head. "Not even a tad."

"But you're really getting good. I'm thinking you have a shot at placing."

"Are you kidding? Don't start pushing the winner's podium. I'm running. That's it." She sipped the dregs of her smoothie, stopping before she slurped in front of him.

"But since we've started training, you've shaved several minutes off your time. We still have three weeks to go. You could be in the hunt. You're an athlete, Josie. You're a runner."

"No. I'm not a runner, but you're right. I'm an athlete. I like to swim, bike, do Zumba classes."

"Zumba? Wait. Let me picture that." A teasing smile played around his mouth. Just like Sam.

Not.

Why mention Zumba? She scraped her feet underneath the bench, sat straighter. "No. Don't. And anyway. How do you know about Zumba?"

His gaze bounced off his watch. "How are the other fundraisers shaping up?"

Okay. New topic. Was Mallory the connection to Zumba?

Probably.

It doesn't matter.

"Fine. I'm excited about the January crafts fair, but I need somebody to head it up, someone who knows a lot of crafters. Someone with organizational skills would be a plus too."

He clunked their empty plastic cups into a nearby receptacle. "I know someone." He wiped his hands on his shorts.

"Great." She smiled. "Who?" She pulled the covered elastic from her ponytail and shook out her hair. She smoothed all of it back into a tighter catch, twisting the elastic in place as she waited for his answer. Silence. She tossed her head, and her hair flipped over one shoulder. She glanced at him.

Shifting from the ponytail to her face, his eyes darkened from blueberry to a deep lapis. Stomach flutters rose and swirled warmth around her heart.

"Ches?"

He hooded his eyelids and took a breath. "My uncle."

"Sweet. What does he do?"

"He carves things." He raked his hand through his hair. "All kinds of things with wood. And he's talented. Used to be in some kind of a guild, I think."

"Sounds perfect." She reached for her phone in her arm pack. "Give me his contact information." Her fingers hovered over the phone. "Unless you want to ask him?"

He rubbed the back of his neck. Stalling? Was he regretting the suggestion already?

"We could ride out to his house together." He scanned the edge of the park. "You could see his work and talk about particulars then." He studied the seat between them.

Butterfly wings rippled through her midsection. Didn't see that invitation coming. More time with Ches. She bit the inside of her cheek to focus.

Calm down, heart rate. He's got a girlfriend. He's helping the library. "Sure. When?"

"How about Tuesday afternoon? I have appointments out of the office. I can pick you up at your house after your classes. He lives between Charlotte and Gastonia. Not far from here."

"I'll be ready."

"Sounds good." He checked his watch again. "I gotta go." He

caught her eyes. A tiny movement tipped the corners of his mouth. "You ran great today. See you Tuesday." He waved as he headed away.

She slid into her car, turned on the ignition, and pressed the A/C button. The morning had turned warmer than expected. She directed all the vents toward herself. Cool air whooshed over her flushed face.

Breathe in. Breathe out.

Oh, God. This, whatever this is, is beginning to feel like a crush. My heart has never gone giddy planning for the library before. I don't want to have a crush on Ches. He has a girlfriend. But I enjoy being with him. He's turning into a friend. Isn't that okay? Help me keep my head on straight. Help me fundraise for the library without getting burned, please.

The dashboard clock flashed 9:10. He always left before 9:15. Going to meet Mallory?

Didn't matter. None. Of. Her. Business.

"A PRETTY GOOD reproduction of mom's roast, Jo." Sam tossed his napkin beside his plate and rocked back in his chair. "Good job." Leave it to Sam to turn the touching end of Sunday dinner into a healthy dish of competition.

"Pretty good, huh? Is that why you stopped at three helpings instead of asking for another?" Josie threw her balled napkin and scored a hit in the middle of his forehead. "And four on the floor, remember?"

Sam plopped his chair upright again. "Hey, cut it out. You don't want to mess up this work of art," he framed his face with his hands, one thumb sporting band-aids. "Do you?"

"It's getting thick in here." Heath drained his water glass.

"Sam, you never told us what happened to your thumb." She peered into the crockpot.

Ben grabbed his plate and silverware. "Let's clear the table. Don't listen to Sam. The roast was fantastic, Josie."

"Thank you, dear brother. Actions speak louder than words." She poked the serving spoon in the ceramic crock. "And we have just about one serving left. Who wants to take it home?"

"I'll take it since Sam didn't think it was that great." Heath dragged the crock toward himself.

"I never said I didn't like it." Sam reached for the pot.

"What's with the band-aids, Sam? For the umpteenth time."

He twisted his wrist back and forth, gazing on the double band-aid covering most of his thumb. "A little carpentry accident. Bruises and a little swelling, no cuts. I just keep the band-aids on it to get sympathy from the ladies."

"For heaven's sake. Did you hurt it or is it just a ruse?"

"Oh, I hurt it all right. Ask your boyfriend. He heard me yell bloody murder when the hammer whacked it."

She frowned. "My boyfriend? What are you talking about?"

Ben stopped mid-stride between the table and sink. "You're dating again, Josie? And you didn't share the news?"

"No. I'm not dating. I told you. I'm out of the game for a while."

"Too bad. Mom joked about staying in the D.R. till we give her a reason to come home. Mom code for grandchildren, you know." Heath clasped his hands behind his head.

"Well, one of you can start dating."

"But you're the girl in the family." Sam winked at her.

"What does that mean?" She glared at her youngest brother."And what's up with the build?"

"Mr. Ches Windham. That's what. He's been helping finish the house." Sam snagged two chocolate chip cookies from the jar on the counter.

Josie stilled. "You and Ches have been working on the house. The house we helped on?"

"Yeah. They needed extra help with some finishing jobs and

called a few people. Yesterday was the last Saturday. He doesn't get there too early, but he usually stays until the end. He's a hard worker. Oh, and, ah, he says you're a good runner." He saluted her with a cookie then bit it in half.

Heath signaled to his brother. "Bring me a couple, will ya? And the milk too. I thought you hated running, Joey."

"I do."

"You're running, Josie?" Ben returned to the table and sat. He watched her with narrowed eyes. "What does Ches have to do with your running?"

"He's training her." Sam popped the rest of the cookie in his mouth not bothering to hide the smile creeping across his face.

All eyes focused on her. Ben spoke for the group. "So, you've been seeing him?"

"To train. If I run in the library's 5K, he'll bring ten extra people. That's four hundred dollars more for the library."

"Sounds a little like extortion."Heath poured milk into his empty glass and dunked a cookie up to his fingertips.

"Yeah. I kinda thought so, too, but it's for a good cause. You're all ready to run, right? You're training too?"

"Jo Jo, I can run three miles without training for two months." Sam flexed his arms. "Have you forgotten what a superb athlete I am?"

"Did I ever know it?"

He thumped the crown of her head as he passed her chair. "Let's get this show on the road. I need to get going."

Swallowing the last of his cookies, Heath carried the bread and a vegetable bowl to the island. "Me too."

The youngest two brothers picked at each other all the way down the driveway, and Josie waved when they entered separate cars. Ben waited for her full attention. "I'm surprised you're running. Surprised Ches is helping too."

"I'm surprised myself. It's not that bad, but I'm looking forward to checking 5K from my bucket list. Not that it was ever on it." She tossed leftover rolls into a plastic bag. "And I don't plan on running another one, either."

"What about Ches?"

"What about him?"

Ben sighed. "Josie—"

"Don't start. He's training me. That's it." *Please, God. Let this be the truth. No crush. No hope for anything more.*

"It's just, you didn't tell us. It seems like a secret."

"Well, I kinda wanted to surprise you on race day, but no problem. I saw your shock tonight."

Ben stood his ground, staring with darkening green eyes that usually matched her own.

"I am fine. It's prayed over. Don't worry, okay?" *Please don't launch into another lecture about why Ches isn't the guy for me. I've heard it before. I. Get. It.*

"That's what big brothers are for."

"No. Big brothers are for big hugs." She stepped into his arms and hugged him tightly.

"I love you, Joselyn Daniels. Thanks for dinner."

"I love you, Bennett Daniels. Thanks for worrying about me."

Sunday evening melancholy settled on her shoulders with Ben's exit. She closed and locked the door, turning off the porch light at the same time. The secret was out now. No problem except for the concerned looks from Ben. *Don't worry, Ben Buddy. I've got my eyes open. Ches is a fun friend.*

A fun friend who'd texted on Sunday night for the past three weeks. Would he continue tonight?

She grabbed her phone on the way to the family room couch, stretched out, and waited. The house, full of her brothers' teasing five minutes ago, now sounded silent as a tomb. She flipped on the TV, scanned the program guide. A girl choosing a wedding dress. No. People with tattoos gone wrong. Double no. People dating naked. No. No. No.

She checked the recorded programs. Three romantic comedies. Better, but no. She returned to regular TV and settled on a golf game.

Boring but the oohs and ahs from the crowd could fill in the silence while she—

The phone buzzed, bouncing her straight up into the air. The screen flickered a name.

Ches.

"How are you?"

"Fine. Good weekend?"

"Yes. You?"

"Yes."

Should she ask about working on the house? No. Wait for face to face time. Her phone buzzed again.

"Busy week?"

"Mid-terms."

"How many classes?"

"Five."

"Is that a lot?"

"Normal."

Normal? That's it? One-word answers wouldn't keep him texting. Think. Think.

"Tuesday still okay?"

"Yes. Looking forward to meeting your uncle."

"Him too. Pick you up about 4?"

"I'll be ready."

"See you then."

"Sounds good."

Sounds really good. What else could keep him on the phone? Nothing? Her skull held mush, no fascinating topics, no thought-provoking questions.

"Night, Josie."

"Good night, Ches."

The rush from the texting slowed and pressed on her chest.

Do not sink back into the dumps. Tuesday will be here before you know it. She caught her breath. Do not look forward to seeing Ches either. Look forward to meeting his uncle. That's it. Look forward to getting help for the library.

She pulled up the DVR'd movies again and chose the first one. Losing herself in the story was easy.

Too easy. The male lead character looked a lot like a lawyer with sad, blueberry eyes.

CHAPTER 9

*S*oft strains of jazz guitar streamed through the car's speakers, relaxing Ches's shoulders.

"That's nice." Josie's eyes focused on the dashboard screen.

"Yeah. I like Earl Klugh." He liked her smile too. The first ten minutes of the drive they'd had a minimal conversation. Also, nice. The music, Josie, being out of the city—a welcome respite in the middle of his meeting-packed day.

She fished through her purse and extracted a pen and pad.

"You're taking notes?"

"I really like this guy. I might want to download some of his music later. Didn't want to forget." She dropped the pen and pad back into her purse and relaxed into her seat.

"You know you could keep a list on your phone."

She shrugged. "I like paper. So," she flipped down the visor, "Sam, my brother, said you've been back to work on the house."

"Yeah." He glanced at her. "Why?"

"Just surprised. That's all. I didn't realize you were continuing."

"Surprised I'd volunteer more than once?" Why did that

thought disappoint him? Why did he care what she thought of him? "I helped out that whole Saturday, remember?"

"Yes, and you were good, but I figured you had a busy schedule." She shrugged. "No reflection on your compassion for humanity."

He loosened his grip on the steering wheel. "The project manager caught me before the end of the first build and asked about helping with some finishing projects." He skipped the next song with a not-my-favorite explanation and turned right onto a side road. "It's been good to get to know your brother. He's skilled and funny too."

He chuckled. "You enjoy your brothers. I envy you that."

"Oh, they're a riot—butting in on my business, trying to boss me around, criticizing the food I cook for them every week." She nodded. "Great guys."

"And you love them."

"Of course. They're family. I have to."

"No, you don't."

He felt her questioning gaze.

"That's kind of a loaded statement."

Yeah. Not going there today. He checked his mirrors and shifted in his seat instead of answering.

"I do love them. They get on my nerves slightly less each year." She sighed and pulled the seat belt away from her neck. "They're really good guys, and they love me back."

How many times had he asked for a little brother? Every year for birthdays and Christmas. He relented, finally, and asked for a little sister. Instead, his parents gave him bicycles and the latest computer games and then a brand-new car for his sixteenth birthday. No brother or sister, just a lot of expensive presents.

Ches chewed the inside of his cheek. Was this a good idea? She really didn't have to meet Jack to let him head up the crafts fair fundraiser. Why bring her out here? He wiped a palm on his thigh. The last time he'd visited his uncle was June a year ago.

He'd been grateful for the invite but acted cool most of the day, anticipating his father's reaction if he discovered the visit.

How would Jack receive him today? Warm and interested in their sporadic phone calls, Jack always invited him to visit. Anytime, he'd say, but Ches's schedule didn't allow many visits. His father's attitude toward his brother didn't allow them either.

"So, your uncle. He's talented in woodworking?"

"Very. He taught me everything I know about carpentry."

"Cool. Then you grew up out here?"

"No. I spent a summer with him." Why did he admit that? He ignored the second unspoken question hanging between them. "Here we are." He turned into his uncle's driveway, wondering why he thought this afternoon would be a good idea.

NOTE TO SELF. Don't talk about family with Ches. He'd shut down or changed the subject both times the conversation skittered close to the topic of family. Then why bring her to meet his uncle? Pondering the question, Josie unlatched her seatbelt. Ches rounded the hood of the car to help her out the door.

A man almost as tall as Ches descended the front steps. He greeted them with a warm, genuine smile and grabbed his nephew into a bear hug.

"It's been too long, buddy. Heidi was so disappointed to miss you, but she couldn't get out of her commitment. You've got to promise to come back or she's threatening not to cook dinner for a week." The man loosened his grip and stepped back, keeping his hands on Ches's shoulders. "Whadda ya say, man? Don't let my stomach down."

A fledgling smile hovered at the corners of Ches's mouth. His arms hung at his sides. "Your stomach is safe. Tell her I'll check my calendar and figure something out."

"No firm date, but I'll take it. You know your aunt, though.

Don't leave her waiting or she'll do something about it. In fact, she'd love for you to come with us to church on Sunday." He released Ches and gestured to Josie.

"Uncle Jack, this is Josie Daniels."

He completely disregarded that invitation. What's up with that, Ches?

"Josie Daniels, welcome to our house." He clasped her hand in a firm grip belying his silver hair and focused his attention solely on her. His eyes, exactly like his nephew's deep blue, reflected joy, however, not sadness. "We've never met a friend of Ches's before. So glad to have you."

"Nice to meet you, too, Mr. Windham. I'm looking forward to seeing your work. Ches has been singing your praises."

The older man glanced at his nephew, raised his eyebrows, but didn't comment. "Well, he's no slouch himself. Call me Jack, please."

"He says you taught him everything he knows. He showed serious skill at a community build a few weeks ago."

"Is that right?" A grin slid across his face. "Nice job, bud. Putting your skills to good use. I like that."

Ches shrugged and stuffed his hands in his pockets.

Jack turned toward a corner of the house. "My shop's around back. Ches mentioned something about a library fundraiser?" He led the way with Josie at his side. Ches followed behind them, silent.

She spent the next half hour explaining the library's needs, the idea of a crafts fair fundraiser, and marveling at the talent of Ches's uncle. Miniature carved wooden boots, bread bowls, and puzzle boxes filled the studio. A butcher block table near the door featured a nativity set. Ches fiddled with tools hanging on the far wall.

"A crafts fair is a great idea. I know plenty of people who'd want to participate since our crafts warehouse kept raising the rent and finally closed up shop."

"Ches suggested you might be willing to head up the fundraiser."

"Is that so?" He threw an amused glance at his nephew. "Free and easy with other people's time, huh?"

Ches laid down a rough, honey-colored rectangle. "I thought—"

"Oh, well, if you can't, maybe you could direct me to—"

Jack waved away their protestations. "Just teasing, Ches. I'd be glad to. Helping a library and my friends? A win-win, right?"

"If you're sure." She studied the carvings of Joseph and Mary. "This set is gorgeous. Some pieces look like a deep purple."

Jack picked up the baby. "It's made of Madagascar Rosewood or Bois du Rose. I bought this wood years ago, but you can't get it now. Legally anyway. I saw it for the first time on a mission trip to South Africa."

"My parents are missionaries in the Dominican Republic."

"Nice. Did you grow up there?"

Ches joined them at the butcher block and ran a finger along Joseph's back.

"No. They retired early and left for the mission field last spring. It's been their dream. The commitment's for two years. Then we'll see."

"How's it going for them?"

"Great, so far." Josie picked up a box fashioned with three different kinds of wood and examined it. "My mother's threatening to stay down there until my brothers and I give her reasons to come home."

"Reasons?"

She chuckled. "Grandchildren."

Jack grinned at Ches, stepping beside him. "Grandchildren, eh?"

Ches's hand dropped from the wooden pieces along with all emotion from his face.

Her stomach tightened. Why had she mentioned grandchildren? Clearly not thinking. "Ah, no, Mr. Windham." She focused on the uncle, didn't want to see the shuttered expression change to irritation or even amusement on the nephew's face. "I didn't mean...Ches and I..." What were they? Friends? Maybe. "We're not..." She shook her head. How to save herself from this mess?

Ches cleared his throat. "We better get going. I have to go back to the office tonight."

Great. She'd slammed the afternoon down with an embarrassing thud. "So nice meeting you. You're just as talented as Ches said. I look forward to working with you. I'll send you all the information I have so far." She peeked at the top of Ches' loosened tie, too chicken to meet his eyes. "I'll be in the car." She nodded to Jack. "Thank you for today." Now get out without creating another humiliating moment.

Before she could turn for the door, the older man reached for her in a loose hug. "Come back anytime. Don't wait for Ches or it could be years. My wife would love to meet you."

As much as she'd love to get to know Jack better, visit again, and meet a wife she imagined to be just as welcoming and interesting as her host, Josie didn't see a future visit happening. She made no promises, simply thanked him and exited the shop.

Grateful for the hug, she returned to the car with a warm feeling replacing the misstep she'd taken with the offhanded grandchildren comment.

Note to self. Joking about grandchildren with her brothers? Fine. Joking about them with Ches or any of his relatives? Not fine.

CHES KICKED himself for not defusing the situation, but what could he have said? Better just to leave it alone.

"Sorry about that. I didn't mean to embarrass her. I like her.

She's a good one." Jack scratched behind his ear, narrowed his eyes. "So you're not—"

"No." So much for leaving it alone.

"Does that mean you're still seeing that other one? The one from the firm?"

Ches's head whirled to his uncle. "Mallory?"

"Oh, yeah. That sounds right. Heidi keeps up with the About Town section of the Charlotte paper. Points out your picture when you make the column. She's a looker, all right."

Which one was he talking about? Both women were beautiful.

"Are you really serious about her?"

"Mallory?"

An eyebrow twitched. "Who'd you think I was talking about?"

"Mallory, of course." He lifted a shoulder. "I don't know. We've been seeing each other for a few months."

"I just wondered because I thought I saw you blush a little when I stuck my foot in my mouth while ago. You need to pray about it, son."

"Uncle Jack."

Jack splayed both hands in front of him. "That's it. No sermon. Just reminding you of who I am. Where I stand."

"Got it."

"But if it doesn't work out with Mallory…" He jerked his thumb toward the outside of the studio. "That one out there. She's solid. She's got depth."

"You got all that from a thirty-minute meeting?"

"In a word? Yes."

Ches turned for the door.

"Son, be careful with her. She said no while ago, but…" He shook his head. "Just watch yourself. Don't play with her. You know what I mean?"

"We're just friends, Uncle Jack."

"Does she know that?" Jack stopped him at the threshold.

"I'm helping her with the library fundraisers."

"Why?"

"If the library succeeds, the firm looks good."

"The firm needs PR?"

"No. It's one of those win-win scenarios you were talking about. Good for the library. Good for the firm."

"As long as it's good for Josie too. I like that girl."

"Don't worry. She's fine. Everything's fine."

Jack threw his arms around him. "I love you. The invitation to church is always open."

Ches accepted the hug and headed for the car. Head down, Josie was swiping her phone. Good. If she continued checking messages, they wouldn't have to talk on the way back.

She closed the screen, dropped the phone into her purse.

No such luck.

Instead of speaking, however, she stared out the window. Her fingers knotted together in a clump. She looked as uptight as he felt.

He backed the car down the driveway and onto the road. What to talk about? Should he forget getting dinner with her? Would dinner lead her on? But he needed to reciprocate for the spaghetti dinner and the free lunch. He also needed to eat before going back to the office. And...complete honesty? Spending more time with her just plain appealed to him. Was being with her such a bad thing?

Maybe. Mallory would probably object, and rightfully so. He'd been distracted lately and not as attentive as he'd been at the beginning of their relationship. Not exactly stellar characteristics for a boyfriend.

Still, a quick meal couldn't hurt.

Having dinner with Josie would be like a working date. No. Not like a date. A working dinner. To continue discussing—

"Ches."

He blinked and whipped his head to Josie. "I'm sorry. What?"

"I said, your uncle is very talented and nice. I like him. Thanks so much for connecting us. He'll be a real help for the crafts fair." She hugged her purse like a life preserver.

"No problem. He likes you too."

Her hands relaxed, released the purse, and stretched over her knees.

"I'd thought about getting dinner."His eyes found the dashboard clock.

"But you need to get back to the office."

"Well, yeah, but—" His phone rang. Father. Great. Not now. He sent the call to voice mail.

"You can take that. I won't listen."

He shook his head. "What do you like to eat?"

"Thanks for the offer but take me home. Then you can grab whatever you like."

"I owe you dinner. We're going. Where?" He winced at how harsh his voice sounded.

"No. Thank you. We planned to meet your uncle." She dipped her head. "We met him. We didn't plan dinner."

"Right, but I owe you—"

"No. You don't, so stop saying that. I don't think you're in the mood for dinner anyway." She crossed her arms on top of her purse.

"Why?"

"That tic flashing again in your cheek for one." She nodded toward his profile. "For another, you're strangling the steering wheel."

He released his grip on the wheel, tried to loosen his jaw.

"You weren't exactly overly friendly to your sweet uncle either. Maybe you're in a bad mood today. Maybe you should go home and start over tomorrow."

"Except I have to go to the office tonight, and I have to eat first." He enunciated each word with precision. "Where do you want to eat?"

"I want to eat at home. You can eat wherever you want."

"No. I owe you dinner."

"Stop. Saying. That. You do not owe me dinner. I cooked spaghetti for my brothers, and you happened to eat with us after volunteering all day. You didn't get anything special."

Her rising voice—was she yelling at him?—caught his attention. Her eyes were narrowed, and her mouth set a stubborn line. Was this her teacher's face? She sounded really ticked off. He raked his teeth over his bottom lip. How to fix the situation? He chanced another quick peek at her.

She blinked and softened her mouth. "But I guess you do owe me for the lunch you mooched off me."

He threw back his head and laughed. "Then let me pay up." He glanced her way. "What changed your mind?"

"You made me so mad with the owing-me-dinner thing. Ben invited you to eat because it was a nice thing to do. I wasn't trying to snag another dinner. When I yelled, you looked so shocked. I felt bad." She bit her bottom lip. "Sorry, I scared you with my mean eyes."

"I can take your mean eyes. What's for dinner?"

She considered him. "You like cheeseburgers?"

"Am I American?"

"Take the second ramp in a couple of miles. Best cheeseburgers in the southeast."

"Only the southeast?"

"Fine. The whole United States."

CHAPTER 10

*J*osie stretched the seat belt away from her stomach. Why did she eat the whole cheeseburger?

Because it was delicious. That's why.

And in front of Ches too. Thank goodness she'd declined the fries.

"I'm going to be useless at the office tonight. All I want to do is lie down. I need to run, but I don't want to throw up." He shifted in his seat.

"Do you agree, then, you just ate the best cheeseburger in the United States, maybe even North America?"

"And the sloppiest. I can't believe I didn't get a spot on my tie." He ran his hand down the silk fabric as if to assure himself. He'd kept the tie on for the afternoon excursion but loosened it at least.

"Flipping it over your shoulder may have helped."

"The way those chili, slaw, and burger juices flowed and slid and dripped, I could have spots on the back of my shirt."

"But it was good." She couldn't help the grin splitting her face. She'd changed his mood. Or maybe the burger had, but still.

"It was fantastic. I'll have to remember the exit for future reference. Any time I haven't eaten in three days."

"And you'd never heard about that place before? Plenty of people in Charlotte know about Harold's burgers. Even hotshot lawyers."

He didn't come back with a quick reply. He centered his attention on the road beyond the windshield. Did she say something wrong again? Maybe he was thinking about work. Maybe the conversation had come to a natural end.

Not that it mattered. She was almost home. Eight o'clock. She'd have time to grade some papers waiting in her satchel and maybe revamp a test scheduled for Friday.

Would he still want to run on Saturday? Probably not if he thought she pined for a way to give her mother grandchildren. The dinner was clearly a payback. He'd hammered that idea home, for sure. More than likely, he'd step back from the training. She didn't need it anyway, but his company was nice.

He rolled to a stop in her driveway, shifted to park, but didn't move to exit the car. He always opened the door for her, getting in and out. Not this time.

Okay. Message delivered.

She reached for the door. "Thank you for dinner and—"

"Wait." His hand on her arm stalled her. "What you said back there. Is that what you think of me? I'm a hotshot lawyer?"

"I, ah…" How to answer? Lightly? With humor? "Well, you know, you've got the car and the gorgeous suits."

"No." He tightened his grip on her wrist. "I asked a real question. Give me a real answer. Please."

She glanced at his hand encircling her arm. He freed her and turned off the engine.

Furrows stacked on her brow. "That's hard to answer. I've never seen you working in law." She fiddled with the purse strap. "You seem smart and driven."

He nodded. "All right. What was your first impression of me?"

She shrank back, shaking her head. "Oh, Ches."

Scrubbing his hand over his face, he sighed. "That bad, huh?"

He was serious. He wanted to know. Something was going on. She didn't know what, but she'd help him if she could. She surrendered to the entreaty in his eyes. "Fine. Last summer, when you slid into the Park 'n Go in this fantastic, shiny car, I thought you were arrogant, aloof.

"In other words…" She waved her hand in a circle in front of her face. "All about me." She shrugged. "You were busy. Too busy to be bothered with unimportant stuff."

She tipped her head. "As many times as we drove to the drop off together, you never even asked my name. Which was fine since I never expected to see you again, but it was kind of odd. Most repeat customers asked my name and used it."

His shoulders sagged. "You can be direct all right."

"But—" she reached for his arm this time, "since I've gotten to know you, I've seen you be compassionate, interested, help-ful, even funny. You hold your own with my goofball brothers. You're a hard worker too. It's like." She blew out a breath. "Like you're two different people. One in a power suit and tie. Another one in faded jeans and a flannel shirt. You can change like flip-ping burgers on a grill. Especially if your dad calls."

His head shot up eyes narrowed.

She held up her hand. "Don't worry. I'm not going to try and psychobabble that problem, but clearly, something's going on with you two. So...I guess I don't think of you as a hotshot lawyer anymore. Maybe. No, you are, but you're more than a lawyer."

He captured her gaze with dark eyes filled with a vulnera-bility she'd never seen in him before. "Thank you." He lowered his eyes to her lips.

Zings sparked through her body, stole the breath from her lungs. His mouth parted. Did he feel the same crazy electricity fizzing between them? Or was she imagining it?

He smoothed wispy tendrils behind her ear and captured a lock of her hair with his fingertips, the ends curling around his knuckles. Clinging to him the way she wanted to.

Ches met her eyes. Fingers still entwined with the lock of hair, he tugged her toward him.

Headlights shattered the early evening darkness, flashing through the back window. They both jumped as if they'd been, what? Kissing after curfew?

Would he really have kissed her? She sucked in a trembling breath. No. No, he wouldn't have because he's dating Mallory. He didn't feel anything between them because he's dating Mallory. She imagined all of it because she wanted him to kiss her.

She wanted him to kiss her.

She planted her back against the seat and craned toward the headlights. Ben's car. Her stomach somersaulted. What would he think of her being with Ches? Heat burned in her cheeks.

"That's Ben. I don't know why he's here at eight-thirty." She faced Ches again. "I've got to go." She brushed his arm, fisting her fingers to keep from hanging on. "You're a good guy, Ches. Thank you for introducing me to your uncle and for dinner."

She hopped out of the car, grateful for the cool air on her face, and waved at Ben, backing out to let Ches leave.

Calm down, girl. You've got sixty seconds to get to normal before you have to face big brother.

Normal.

Would she ever feel normal again?

Not likely.

BEN JOINED her at the door as she retrieved the key from the lock, fingers still trembling.

She stepped inside and flipped on the lights. "What's up? Is everything okay with M and D?" She fiddled with her purse, buying time before facing Ben.

"They're fine as far as I know. Is everything okay with you?" Ben waited for her, hands on his hips.

She frowned. "I'm good. Thanks. Is everything okay with you? You look angry."

"I rush over here because you don't answer your phone or the house phone and find you parking with Ches Windham."

Her mouth fell open. "I was not parking with Ches." Not really. "He brought me home."

"From where?"

"None of your business." She moved into the kitchen, fished the phone from her purse, and plugged it into the charger on the counter.

"Josie. Is he still dating Mallory Padgett?"

"As far as I know, but I haven't asked him."

"Well, maybe you should."

"Well, maybe you can ask for me, *Dad*."

"Well, maybe I will."

She opened the refrigerator and breathed in the cool air. She hated fighting with Ben. A war of words was inevitable with Sam and sometimes with Heath. But never with Ben. A familiar tingle in the tip of her nose telegraphed coming tears. She sucked in a breath and held it for six beats. "I'm sorry you drove over here. My phone died. I was out for a few hours with Ches about library stuff. That's it. Do you want a glass of milk?"

"No, thank you." He shut the refrigerator and pulled her against his chest. "I think you're playing with fire, Josie." The words were quiet over her ear.

"Ben, what's gotten into you? I'm not playing anything. I'm planning fundraisers for the library."

"I know you've said you wouldn't date another B.J.—"

"Exactly. I am so over B.J., and anyway, Ches isn't like B.J."

"No. He's not. He's got a girlfriend. And from all accounts, it's serious."

"Listen to me." She pulled back, slipped her hands to his shoulders, and locked eyes. "I'm not pining for B.J., and I know Ches has a girlfriend."

"Even if he didn't, I've heard he was kind of a serial dater before her. Not thinking you want someone like that either."

"Of course, I don't." She tilted her head.

"You need someone who's a Christian. A gentleman. Someone with a good job."

"Of course, I do." Eyebrows met above narrowed eyes.

"Glad you agree with me because I have someone in mind."

She pushed away from him. "Ben. Stop. I'm not going on another blind date. I told you guys."

"This wouldn't be a blind date. You've met him. At the build a few weeks ago."

At the build? Who else volunteered at the build? The new version of Ches with frayed jeans and a t-shirt highlighting his ripped muscles captured her attention most of the day.

Not good. Not good. She massaged her temple. "I don't remember anybody."

"Yes, you do. He sat with us at lunch."

She racked her brain. She'd sat on one side of Ben with Heath then Sam then Ches in a semi-circle under a shade tree. They'd eaten bagged sandwiches provided by a local church. Three of her students ate in another nearby circle.

Was somebody on Ben's left? Maybe?

"Milo. Milo Johnstone."

"Milo."

"Don't wrinkle your nose like that when you say his name. His parents were hippies or something."

"You mean the guy who sat beside you, sort of in our circle but halfway out? He kept his nose to his phone for the whole lunch. He dropped a hammer so many times, Jerry put him on sweeping sawdust detail."

"Everybody has strengths and weaknesses, Joselyn."

Again, with the fatherly attitude.

"Bennett."

"He's in my small group. He's a nice guy."

Translation. Not cute. What did he look like? Brown hair? Average height? Glasses? "I don't need you to play matchmaker. I can find my own dates."

"One who doesn't already have a girlfriend?"Ben cocked an eyebrow, his eyes cool.

"Ben!" She thumped his forearm. "That's a low blow and uncalled for. I'm not dating Ches Windham."

"Sorry. I'm just..." He shook his head. "I'll stop beating that horse. Milo is a straight-up good guy. He's an actuary."

"An actuary? Even more boring than—"

"He's smart, and he's something of a history buff."

"Oh, really. Don't tell me he's a reenactor."

Ben continued as if she hadn't interrupted him. "So, you two have some things in common, and he mentioned Latta Plantation was having some sort of celebration on Saturday."

"The Folk Life Festival." She nodded. "I've mentioned it to my students."

"Great. I knew you'd want to go."

"Wait." She shook her head. "I never said—Did you make a date for me?"

"Of course not. I'm not stupid."

"Not exactly convincing me here."

"I may have mentioned you teach history. He may have expressed an interest to see you again. I'm asking your permission to give him your number to call about this Saturday."

"This Saturday? Sorry. I already have plans."

"All day? I may have already slightly mentioned that you'd probably love to go. He's excited. It'll be a little awkward if you say no."

"Well, sorry about that, Ben." She socked him again. "I mean, Sam!"

"Hey now. I'm not that bad."

"This is exactly like something he'd do."

"So, what are your plans?"

"None of your beeswax."

"Ches? Are you running with him again?"

"Training. Train. Ing."

"Josie."

"Do not start again." She blew out a frustrated breath. Why wouldn't her brothers stay out of her love life? Her love life. As if it existed. Maybe she should go out again. Maybe a day of history wouldn't be as bad as a night of getting-to-know-you talk over a pasta dish. "Okay. Fine. Give him my number, but do not ever do this again." She pointed her index finger between his eyes. "Do you understand?"

"Yes, *Mom*." He whipped out his phone and punched in a quick text. "There." He slid his phone back into his pocket. "I need to get going." He smiled. "I love you, you know. Be nice when he calls."

"I'm always nice." Her phone buzzed from the hutch. She pinned wide eyes on her brother. "Are you kidding me?" She picked it up and showed him. "Is this Milo? Is this his number?"

Ben stretched a sheepish grin. "I told you he was excited." He rubbed the top of her head. "See you later."

Her heart hammered. The phone insisted she answer it. Why did she let Ben...She closed her eyes and dove headfirst into what was probably a bad idea.

"Hello."

Two hours later, she sat in bed with a stack of to-be-graded tests and a stack of emotions ranging from irritation—at Ben, at herself, at Milo for persisting with the leave-early-in-the-morning idea even after she asked for mid-morning—to regret about no Ches, or rather, no training on Saturday.

He hadn't mentioned it during the afternoon. Did they have a standing date? No, not date. Agreement? He'd complimented her running. Did he think she didn't need more training?

Oh, God. All this stuff with Ches is making me a little crazy. Yes, he has a girlfriend. But here's the thing, okay? I like spending time with him. Fine. I like him, but I know he has a girlfriend. Can't I just enjoy this fun little interlude in my life while it lasts?

Silence.

He laughs at my jokes. He likes the library. Being with him kind of restores the confidence B.J. stole. The tic in his cheek doesn't show up with me. That's a good thing, right?

She squeezed her eyes tighter.

I. Know. He. Has. A. Girlfriend. Help me keep that thought front and center.

Maybe the folk festival would be a good thing. Keep her mind off other people's boyfriends.

STRETCHING out on his bed felt good after two hours of studying leases. Exhaustion cloaked his body, but Ches's mind swirled with thoughts of Josie and their last conversation and that moment they'd shared. If Ben's headlights hadn't flashed on them...

Hold up. Don't go there.

Think about the words. Her words. She didn't pull punches or avoid tough questions. Great traits for a witness. For a friend too.

Yeah, a friend.

What other insights could she share? About his personality? About his life? About anything?

His cell phone rested alongside his tie where he'd dropped them on his way to his prone position. Could he text her and continue where they left off? But texting on Tuesday night wasn't their normal arrangement.

Like they had a normal arrangement.

Except for Saturday mornings, that is. Running and then smoothies, for what? Two, three weeks in a row? Did that make a normal arrangement?

Reclining against three pillows, he grabbed his phone and texted Josie. To make sure. About Saturday.

"Everything OK with Ben?"

He unbuckled his belt while he waited for her reply, slid it from the loops. No immediate response. He tugged the ends of his dress shirt from his waistband, slipped each button through the buttonholes. His phone buzzed, and he smiled.

"Yes. They couldn't reach me on my dead phone or the landline. Brothers."

"They were worried."

"Yeah."

What now? How to bring up—

"Did you get a lot of work done? Are you finished now?"

"Got a lot done. Finished for tonight. You?"

"Grading tests in bed."

In bed. He arm-wrestled that image out of his mind.

"Thanks for taking me to your uncle's. He's great and already emailed me. You were lucky to spend a summer with him."

"You think so?"

"Absolutely. He's talented, smart, proud of you. Loves you too."

Loves me? Yes. Proud of me?

"Got all that from a quick visit?"

"I'm good like that."

"Yeah."

"Don't you agree? About your uncle? He loves you."

"Maybe."

"Don't want to talk about it?"

"What?"

"Your summer with your uncle."

"Long story."

"OK. No problem."

Could he tell her about being sent as punishment to his uncle's? About learning to love and respect someone he'd heard mostly disparaging comments about beforehand? Maybe.

"Details on Saturday?"

The anticipated sounds good didn't show. Nothing showed for two minutes. He shrugged out of his dress shirt, balled it up and tossed it onto the dry cleaning pile on the closet floor. He unstrapped his leather watch band and laid it on his bedside table. A sprinkling of dust covered the lampstand. The cleaning crew was scheduled for the next morning. Remember to leave a check on the counter. His phone buzzed again. He smiled.

"All-day commitment Saturday. Sorry."

His smile slid into a frown. No training? Which meant no Josie on Saturday. He paid no attention to the disappointment swelling in his chest. Was the hesitation because she was in the middle of grading a test? Or because she regretted her commitment? Or because she was trying to figure out how to say *I'm with B.J. all day?* Or because she was trying to—No. Josie didn't operate like that. She was a direct-answer kind of person.

"Got it. Just get your running in. 2 weeks to 5K."

"Yes, sir, Mr. Trainer!"

"One more Saturday before the race if you want to train then."

"Sounds good."

"Sounds good."

His spirits lifted at the prospect of seeing—no, training—Josie one more time before race day. Should he leave it at that? What about asking—

"Good night, Ches."

"Night, Josie."

CHAPTER 11

"So. Mind explaining why we get takeout tonight instead of Josie's cooking?" Sam spooned barbecue from the cardboard bowl onto his plate.

"Ben's doing penance," Josie added slaw to her plate and passed it to Heath. "He should've brought steaks for everybody."

Saturday hadn't been so bad, but she chafed at getting roped into it. Milo was nice and smart. Two positives, right? But...

"Penance? What'd you do and why do we have to suffer with you?" Sam bit off half a hush puppy.

"Eating barbecue is not suffering." Ben threw his brother an irritated glance.

"It is when we could have had a home-cooked meal," Heath added his two cents.

"Part of our weekend ritual is the great food, yes. Thank you again, by the way, lovely sister." Ben's smile and nod had some serious snark."But it's also about the camaraderie we share together around the table." He sipped his iced tea, ignoring Josie's teacher's eyes.

"Laying it on a little thick, aren't you?" Josie scooped up a bite of Brunswick stew.

"Saying I need to do penance after introducing you to a nice guy is laying it on thick. Last night when I called, you said the date went fine."

"It did. Just fine. He's nice. Just nice." Josie dabbed at her mouth with her napkin.

"He brought you flowers." Ben nodded to the fall bouquet center stage on the side counter. "Flowers are good."

Josie sighed. "Here's a secret, guys. Listen up." She laid her fork on the edge of her plate. "Flowers from a special guy are great. More than great. They're wonderful. Flowers from a not-so-special guy, one whose future with you is iffy, one who wasn't on the radar a couple of days before he brings said flowers, one who—"

"Okay, we get the kind of person you're talking about." Heath rested his chin on his fist. "I'm trembling with anticipation about your secret."

"Funny." She leaned on her elbows, made sure she had their attention. "Flowers are great, but sometimes when they come too soon, it feels awkward. Not exactly welcome. Like the guy is putting too much importance on one date. Makes you want to say, 'hey, it's just a day in a park, not an engagement.' You think the guy is trying too hard before he even says hello."

"He brought you flowers, not a ring." Ben snorted, a smirk on his face.

She cringed, remembering the awkwardness when he'd handed her the bouquet yesterday, his big, hopeful smile. Guilt wrapped around her resentment over not running with Ches. "Like I said—"

"We heard you the first time. Would you or would you not go out with him again?"

"Not your business."

"He's my friend. I don't want to see him hurt."

She grimaced. "I'm not going to hurt him. The day was fine.

He was a gentleman. Being at Latta Plantation was really fun. There just wasn't that, you know, that spark between us."

"Oh, brother. I believe that's my cue." Sam glanced at the clock. "Yes, sir. Time for me to roll."

"He's my ride." Heath pushed his chair back and pulled her ponytail. "Wait for the spark." He winked at her, heading with his plate and glass toward the sink.

"That was a quick dinner," Josie questioned Sam's sudden end to the meal.

"Got things to do, Joey. So, we're Skyping with Mom and Dad next week when they get back to mission headquarters from their side trip. Right?"

"That's what Mom emailed."

"Since nobody wants these hush puppies..." Sam grabbed for the breadbasket. "You didn't ask. I'll take some." Heath swatted at his younger brother's hands.

"Take all of it. I don't want any more." She covered the containers with lids.

Ben drained his iced tea. "So, are you willing to give Milo another chance?"

"I mean," She huffed. "I didn't have a horrible time. It was like being with one of you."

Sam raised an eyebrow and stroked his chin. "Ahm, is that a compliment or an insult?"

"If you have to ask..." Heath gathered a couple of bags of food. "Come on. I thought you had stuff to do."

"Later, dudes." He ruffled Josie's hair and sauntered toward the front door.

Ben dumped the remaining ice from his glass into the sink. "So, you're not opposed to the idea."

"I'm not opposed. I'm not champing at the bit either. Who knew you had aspirations of being a matchmaker?" She rinsed the dishcloth and headed back to the table.

He put the glass into the dishwasher. "No. Not me. I just think—"

"I know what you think, and you're wrong."

He crossed his arms in front of his chest and watched her. "I just want you to be happy. You haven't seemed really happy since—"

"I'm fine. I've got a lot on my plate, remember? Don't worry. I'm good. He's nice. If he asks again..."She shrugged. "Fine. If not, fine too. Okay?"

"Right." He pulled her into a hug. "Have a good week, Josie girl." He kissed her temple. At the door, he paused and turned. "Still training for the 5K?"

"I run about three days a week. Why?"

"No reason. Sounds like you'll be ready for the race."

"Don't worry about me. How 'bout you?"

He smiled. "Yeah. I need to step it up. Probably. See ya."

BROTHERS. Why were they so bothersome? So bossy? So nosy?

She checked the kitchen clock. Not quite eight. Ches didn't usually text until after nine.

No, Josie. Don't start checking the time for something that more than likely wouldn't happen tonight. She hadn't heard from him since the Tuesday night texts. Since they didn't run yesterday, he might forget about training next Saturday. No need for Sunday night texts.

She sighed. Think of something else. No tests to grade tonight. Sam fed Winston for her.

Keep busy till bedtime.

She wandered to the living room and plopped onto the piano stool. The *60 Classical Pieces* book rested on top of a pile of other books, right where Ches had tossed it weeks ago. Ches.

She thumped her forehead to release the image of his rendition of "Spinning Song."

Ice cream. Ice cream would be a nice treat for the close of the weekend. She returned to the kitchen, found her favorite bowl, and filled it with two small scoops of moose tracks. And then one more half scoop. Just because.

She flipped through the channels. A show about people with fake tans and straightened hair.

No.

A rerun of a movie she'd seen five times. No. No.

A show about wedding dresses. No. No. No.

A black and white movie with Katharine Hepburn.

Perfect.

She grabbed her yarn bag from the side of the couch and licked a blob of ice cream from her spoon. As the creamy coolness slid down her throat, she unfolded a partially crocheted square.

A classic movie, ice cream, and a crochet project.

Nice.

She snuggled into her happy place on the couch and surveyed the square. A few more rows to complete it, then add it to the other eight completed squares to donate to the yarn shop downtown. Over and under and grab the yarn with the hook. Pull through two loops. Grab the yarn and pull through two more. The rhythmic movement of the hook looping the yarn soothed her. The easy pattern allowed her to concentrate on the movie rather than the next stitch.

Katherine had just spied a lion when Josie's phone buzzed. She startled. The hook dropped, bouncing off the cushion and landing on the carpet. She picked up her phone first.

Ches.

Her heart rate doubled, the crochet calm shattered.

"Are you busy?"

"No. Just crocheting."

"Old lady crocheting?"

Seriously? Flack about crocheting?

"NO! Cool, hip, trendy crocheting."

"Right. Gotcha. Have a good weekend?"

"Fine. You?"

"Fine. Run?"

"This afternoon."

"Good job."

His praise kindled a warm glow in her chest.

"Thanks."

No immediate response. Was that it? Her heartbeat slowed with the dimming phone screen. She reached for the ice cream and felt the vibration of the new text.

"Still need training?"

"Yes."

"Saturday morning?"

"Yes. I'm getting so good you may not be able to keep up. Just warning you."

"I'm warned, and I accept the challenge."

"Good."

Waiting for his 'good night,' she watched the screen go dark. Okay. Back to Katherine and her lion. Another vibration.

"What are you crocheting?"

"Squares for a blanket. Donating them to a yarn shop."

"Cool. Crochet a lot?"

"Yes. Especially in the fall."

"Nice. See you Saturday."

"Be ready to run."

"Be ready to run fast."

"Good night."

"Night."

Smiling, she wiggled deeper into the cushions, her heart as light as a strand of yarn. A few texts from Ches and—no.

No. No. No.

Definitely not good.

Stupid texts should not make her this happy. Shouldn't make her anything at all. They were just information. Information about the next training session. About her crocheting.

Her bouncy heart slowed to normal. Good. Surprise that Ches remembered she needed training had fueled the happy vibe. People like to be remembered. Like Mr. Raymond, her WWII veteran from church, who always reminded her after every St. Patrick's Day or Easter or Veteran's Day card she mailed him. He'd call to say thank you for remembering an old man.

Yes. That was it. She was happy to be remembered. By a very busy attorney with a girlfriend.

Exactly.

DARK CLOUDS overhead hinted at the possibility of a fall shower. Good thing they got their run in early. Ches checked the time. "You're getting faster. You've been keeping up with the running. Good job."

"Yep." Josie looked up from her own wrist. "I can probably shave a few more seconds off my time this week."

"A little competitive, huh?" A shadow of a smile hovered around his mouth.

"I've got three brothers, remember? I have to be." She freed her ponytail from the elastic holding it, shook her head, and gathered the locks into a tighter hold.

Ches blinked and exiled the memory of how soft her hair felt in his fingers. He transferred his gaze to two runners just clearing the covered trail, an eighth of a mile away. "Ahm, yeah. Take it easy this week. You'll be fine at the race. Your adrenaline will be pumping with the other runners. You'll probably make your best time. Don't go too strong this week. Leave some for Saturday."

"I won't be silly, but I think—"

The runners pulled up, stopping beside them. "Josie. Ches. Fancy meeting you here."

Ben. With a vaguely familiar friend who had eyes only for Josie.

"Hey, Josie. Good thing the Folk Festival was last week, huh? We had great weather, but by the look of those clouds, not so much today." The friend nodded to the darkening sky.

"Right." She flicked a tight smile to the one man, leveled granite eyes, those classroom eyes, to Ben. "Do we need introductions?"

"Ches, remember my friend, Milo Johnstone? Milo, Ches Windham."

"From the build. Right." Ches shook Milo's hand and stepped back.

"I didn't know you were running today." Josie clamped her lips into a formidable line and crossed her arms.

"Getting ready for next week."

She tossed her head, nodding to the trail. "Well then, we'll leave you to it."

Ben planted his hands on his hips. "We were thinking maybe you—"

"Because we—" she glanced at Ches, "have a few things to discuss about the race."

Her brother narrowed his eyes.

Josie mirrored her brother's stance.

Ben shook his head. "Call you later, sis."

"You got my number. Bye, Milo. Have a good run."

The two men jogged away. She closed her eyes and grabbed a hank of hair in each hand. Elbows extended on either side of her head, she yanked the ponytail hard, roots stretched taut from her forehead.

"Josie?"

"Wait. I'm counting to ten." She blew out a breath, released her hair, and flopped her arms to her side.

Ches nodded. "Why?"

"My brothers can send me. Ben knew—" She bit off the end of her sentence.

"I'm surmising here, but was Milo your commitment last Saturday?"

She sighed. "Yes. Ben kind of arranged it."

"He set you up? A blind date?"

"He gave Milo my number after pretty much guilting me into saying, 'yes.'"

"Can't imagine that happening. I thought you were the boss."

The teasing comment brought her smile back. "Yes, well..."

"He do that often? Set you up?"

"Never again."

He disregarded the nugget of relief winging in his chest. "That bad, huh?"

"No, not really. It's just...Hey, you're bringing ten runners next week, right? Because I'm running, and you said..."

He furrowed his brow. "What? Okay, sure. I'll hold up my end of the bargain."

"Good." She glanced after her brother. "We had to talk about the race. I told Ben."

"Right. So, we talked about it, and you didn't lie to your brother."

She nodded.

Ches glanced after the runners disappearing into the wooded trail. Should he ask about getting a smoothie? Her shuttered face offered no clues to help him move forward.

"Do you need to get going?" He stretched his arms behind his back.

"No." Was that a hopeful expression lighting her eyes?

He massaged the top of his shoulder. "Up for a smoothie or...?"

One corner of her mouth lifted. "Smoothies sound good."

CHAPTER 12

The green tea smoothie filled only half the cup. Josie wasn't a glass-half-empty kind of girl, but time dwindled, urging her to mention Ches's summer with his uncle. They'd sat at the refreshment kiosk discussing the changing weather, the virtues of a green tea versus a mango smoothie, the number of runners preregistered for the race. Small talk topics, check.

She swirled her straw through the remaining slushy mix. Would he open up with her? He'd been in a funk since they'd finished running. His posture mimicked the wrought iron chair, ramrod straight back, and unyielding presence. Not exactly an invitation for deep conversation.

After the race next Saturday, however, she had no guarantee she'd see him again. If she wanted to talk about his relationship with his uncle, she had to begin the conversation now.

Her pulse kicked into a higher gear. *Okay, God. Here goes. Help me out, please.*

"So...your uncle has already emailed me the names of artists for the crafts fair. He's on the ball. We've chosen the date for the fair too."

"Yeah?"

"Mmm-hmm." She sipped the sweet concoction. "He's got great ideas. I wish he'd serve on the library board with me. I may ask him."

"Is that right?" He scratched his ankle resting on his knee.

"Uh-huh. He's talented too. And—" She swallowed. "He taught you everything you know about wood-working and carpentry, right?"

He gripped his ankle, zeroing in on her gaze with cold eyes.

Don't want to talk about it now? Should she back down? No. Sharing could be a good thing.

She returned the unyielding stare without flinching.

"Yes."

"And you learned it when you stayed with him one summer?"

He narrowed his eyes. "Yes."

Thank You, God, I don't have to face him in a courtroom.

You don't scare me. You don't scare me. You don't scare me.

Act nonchalant. Pretend you're not picking up on the no trespassing vibes. She smashed a frozen chunk with the tip of her straw. "So why did you? Live with him?"

He studied his watch.

Rats. If he left now, the moment would be over. She'd never know the reason for his summer with his uncle.

"You said you'd give details. When we were texting about training last Saturday." She sipped the smoothie and watched him from the corner of her eye.

He folded his arms across his chest. "Speaking of last Saturday—"

She chuckled and shook her head. "No, we were speaking of your uncle." She set the plastic cup on the table. "You make it sound like it's a big secret. Did your parents send you to help him out? Were you in love with someone your parents disapproved of? Did they—"

"I broke into eight cars in my gated community and stole anything I could get my hands on the last day of school in my sophomore year of high school." The words whooshed out of his mouth like a tidal wave. He dropped his foot to join the other and wiped a palm over his face, kept his eyes straight ahead.

"Oh."

"I can't really say why. Anger at my father, for sure. The thrill of sneaking around in the dark, maybe." He shook his head. "I don't know, but from the time the police brought me to my front door, my father never said a word to me."

Ches's breathing came in quick, shallow puffs. "He took care of all the…problems. I don't know how much money he spent to cover it up. Sent me packing to the hinterlands of Gastonia for the summer." He leaned his forearms onto his thighs. "My mother drove me to the bus stop the next morning. They thought riding on a bus and the shame of being exiled to my uncle would humiliate me into shaping up and flying right." He rolled his napkin into a tight ball.

She leaned toward him. "Your dad didn't talk to you?"

He whipped his head toward her, his eyes glittering. "That's the question you ask after hearing my story?"

"I can't imagine my dad not talking to me. Whenever we mess up—"

"You call stealing messing up?" He stuck his thumb through the balled-up napkin, then tore the paper in two.

"Okay, sure. Stealing's wrong, and you knew better, but you were what? Fifteen? Teenagers do stupid stuff. And what did you steal? Money? Maybe a few cell phones. Not everybody had a phone back then. Or laptops either. So you stole some CDs?"

"Ripped out a couple of sound systems."

"Ouch." She grimaced. "Okay. So you went to your uncle's.

And I guess you had to pay for the stolen items and damage to the cars?"

"No." He tore a strip of the napkin, added a second strip to the first.

"Are you kidding me? Your dad took care of that too?"

"I told you he took care of the problems."

She shook her head. "You should have had to repay every one of your victims. You should have had to write apologies *and* hand-deliver them."

He snorted. "You *are* tough." He tucked the shredded pieces of the napkin into his empty plastic cup and replaced the lid.

"That's not being tough, that's being decent. Instead, you got to go to your uncle's—wait. What does 'the shame of being exiled to your uncle's' mean?"

Two maple leaves cartwheeled along the trail at their feet. A bird's call filled the growing silence.

He cleared his throat. "My father doesn't really get along with him." He sank back against his chair. "No, that's not right." He wiped his palms on his shorts. "He doesn't respect my uncle. Thinks he squandered his potential."

She scrunched her eyebrows. "How so?"

"By not going into business or law and making a ton of money."

"Your uncle's a veteran, right? And so talented with wood. He's a quality person. That's a valid life, you know?"

He turned his cup upside down. Flipped it back right side up.

"Don't you agree, Ches?"

He gazed toward the park entrance. The tic in his cheek beat a steady rhythm.

"Ches, you don't agree with your dad, do you?"

He shifted back to her, a haunted look around his eyes. "I used to. I'd heard my father's disdain for his brother all my life. I hated him for sending me there. I was such a—"

She popped up her hand like a stop sign. "Don't say it."

"A pain in the you-know-where for probably the first two weeks. But my aunt and uncle took the attitude I dished out and just kept loving me."

She nodded. "I can see Jack doing that."

"The plan to punish me by making me live with my uncle backfired. I saw what a real family should be like." He looked at her. "Like yours. By the end of the summer, I didn't want to go home. Jack and Heidi pushed me to go back, to honor my father." He let out a bitter laugh.

"You didn't want to go home? Even to see your mother?"

He shook his head.

"So now you live here, close to Jack, but it sounds like you don't see him much."

"No. My father goes ballistic every time he finds out." He brought his other ankle up to rest on his knee. "And he always finds out."

"He okayed your move to Charlotte?"

"Told him it was my best offer. It was. But I applied only to Charlotte firms." He traced his finger along the iron scrollwork of their cafe table.

"Jack's a special person, Ches. I hope you can spend more time with him."

He shrugged and yanked on the tongue of his shoe. Conversation over? Okay. Some of the tension had left him. Good. No more pushing today.

She clasped her empty cup and straightened. "Well, I'm sure you have to—"

"Not so fast. Your turn."

"What?"

He smiled, a lazy, gotcha kind of smile. "Last Saturday?"

A SLIGHT BREEZE carried the scent of warm pine straw, lifted strands from Josie's ponytail and whipped them across her lips. Ches swallowed. He grabbed his cup instead of brushing her hair behind her ears. Did he really want details about last Saturday?

She pulled the wisps from her mouth and arched a brow. "If you were one of my brothers, I'd tell you to mind your own business. Plus, I find it hard to believe you're interested in the details of my life."

He massaged his hamstring. Probably need to ice that later. "I'm interested in why your brother felt the need to set you up on a blind date."

"He didn't 'feel the need.' He just did it."

"Why?" He stretched his legs, crossing his ankles.

She tucked her feet underneath her chair. "Maybe you should ask him if you're so curious."

"Anything to do with B.J.?"

She turned steely eyes on him. He met her stare and waited, counting off seconds. Nine, ten, eleven—

She threw her head back and laughed. Her long neck captured his attention. "Too bad you don't have a sibling. You got the staredown, for sure."

"I'll add that skill to my social media profile. So. He set you up?"

"And stubborn."

"Tenacious has the better connotation."

She narrowed her eyes. "Is this how you win cases?"

"Real estate attorney. Don't really go to court." He raised his brows. "The setup?"

"Why are you so bent on this story?"

He shrugged. "I told you something personal." He relaxed against the back of his chair and threaded his fingers, resting them on top of his mid-section. "Turnabout's fair play."

She tapped her index finger on the wrought iron table. "Okay. I surrender." She tossed her ponytail. "Ben thinks I should go out more, which is a crock. He hasn't been on a date in forever."

"Why don't you date?"

"I didn't say I don't date. I'm just super busy with my students and the library right now. Not to mention keeping my brothers straight."She made a face. "I don't know why we're talking about this."

"Then he's not trying to help you forget B.J.?"

"Who?"

He chuckled. "Cute."

And she was.

"So you went to a renaissance fair?"

"Wrong. The Folk Life Festival at Latta Plantation."

"Sounds intriguing."

"Don't make fun."

"I'm not. I majored in history with an English minor in undergrad."

"Oh." A tiny smile accompanied her nod.

Did that admission impress her? Did it matter? "So, what kind of folklife did you get to see?"

"The usual. People dressed in period clothes offered living history demonstrations like bookbinding, woodworking, and cooking. We ate delicious homemade bread straight out of a brick oven. Lots of vendors showcased their handcrafts like pottery, basket weaving, and needlecrafts."

"Needlecrafts." He grinned. He couldn't help it. "Like crochet? Old lady or hip and trendy?"

She arched a brow. "You have nerve to say that to my face. If you were one of my brothers, I'd smack your head right now."

He stroked his chin. "You could try."

"I would succeed, but I'll use my manners and ignore your comment." She shrugged a shoulder. "Okay. Fine. We saw intricate crocheted and knitted items as well as beautiful examples of embroidery and candle wicking. We also enjoyed a house tour, and several bands played live music of the times."

She delivered her description like an advertisement or a tour guide. He needed more information. Of the personal kind. For better or worse. "So you had a good time."

"Yep. It was a fun day."

His heart did a little flip. "So you're going out with him again." Did he really want to hear the answer? Maybe not, but he had to ask. Sort of like looking at a car accident or picking at a scab. He braced himself for her answer.

"I didn't say that."

His chest loosened a bit. "You're not going on a second date."

"I didn't say that either. I thought we were talking about last Saturday, not what comes next."

"Right."

Exactly right.

What comes next equals none of my business.

Last Saturday didn't fall into his business either, but it didn't keep him from wandering, from asking.

CHAPTER 13

The mirror cooled Ches's aching forehead as he leaned against the fogged glass. The hot shower had erased some of the kinks in his neck and shoulders from three hours of Mallory's company. The soap had eliminated her perfume too. Thank goodness. Now if the acetaminophen would kick in.

She'd been pretty riled about cutting the evening short. She called the office to make sure he was there like he'd told her.

What if she'd asked about Saturday mornings?

None of her business.

He pressed a hand under his ribs, the familiar burning reminding him of his Mexican dinner. Maybe he should have suggested eating at Manzetti's and ordered the potato soup. Probably wouldn't have made a difference, though. His gut seemed to flare up every day no matter what he ate. Maybe the burning had more to do with the company than the food.

Mallory.

He groaned.

They'd made no promises to each other. They had more of an unspoken understanding. They'd begun seeing each other regularly sometime last spring, but they'd slipped into it rather than mutually deciding anything. Accepting a few of her invitations had morphed into their dating schedule. Every Friday and Saturday night, some Sunday afternoons, with weeknights added when necessary.

Very romantic.

Not.

But very practical and helpful for propelling forward his career with the firm.

He wiped the fog away with his open palm and blanched at the burning eyes in the mirror. *What are you doing? Being with her ties you up in knots. Her constant chatter fills the void, but sometimes quiet is good. Really good.*

When was the last time they'd had fun together? When was the last time they talked about more than the firm or her gallery? When did every quirk of her personality begin to grate on his nerves?

He gripped the edge of the bathroom counter with both hands and leaned his forehead against the mirror.

Mallory.

Clearly, she was beautiful, accomplished, intelligent. She completed law school as expected of a Padgett but chose her own way in art instead of practicing. Her art gallery, because of her contacts, business smarts, and social media skills, was becoming a trendy spot for the cool set in downtown.

She maneuvered important dinner parties like hostess of the year, and her ace in the hole, her great grandfather founded the firm.

But she's not Josie.

He gritted his teeth. Mallory's considerable charms had convinced him they were enough to sustain a relationship. But lately… Would this arrangement work for the rest of his life?

He dropped spread-eagle onto his bed, his face planted into his pillow. Sick of thinking about Mallory, he barricaded his mind against the pros and cons of their relationship. Josie's image floated to the front of his thoughts. Better. He allowed a smile to form on his mouth and let the images roll.

Josie relaxing with the breeze blowing her hair, laughing at his stare down attempt, listening to his story about breaking into those cars without judging. And way back last summer, the first time they met when she discerned his need for stress relief and challenged him in her bossy way to do something fun. She could read him even then.

He flipped to his back, grabbed his phone, and found her name.

"Hey."

Shifting to sitting, he stuffed three pillows behind him and checked his email until a text arrived.

"Hey back."

Thirty seconds. Quick response. A good sign.

"Did you go to church today?"

"Of course. Did you?"

"Of course not."

"Why don't you go with Jack?"

"Not my scene."

"Uh-huh. What is your scene?"

"Trying to figure that out."

"Sounds deep."

Nope. Not going there tonight, Miss Josie. How about a new topic.

"Ready for Saturday?"

"Can't wait."

"Love the enthusiasm."

"Then I'll never have to run again."

"Funny."

He grinned at the phone. With a few short texts, the heaviness pressing on him lifted. His gut ceased churning. He closed his eyes.

Thank you, God.

His eyes popped open. A prayer? Where did that come from? He hadn't prayed seriously since? Since who knows? He'd prayed a lot the summer with Jack and then returned to the same old same old at home. Didn't see the necessity.

Hard work and determination. That's what accomplished goals.

Josie. Think about Josie.

"So I don't have to worry about you chickening out?"

"Absolutely not. I'm no chicken."

"True. I knew that. See you Saturday."

"Yep. Don't forget your friends."

"Who?"

"Very funny. The 20 people you're bringing."

"10"

"15"

"You changing our deal? Then what are you adding to the pot? Running the 5K and what else?"

"I hoped you'd bring as many people as possible out of the goodness of your heart. It's for a good cause."

"I don't have a good heart."

"Yes, you do. I've seen it in action."

"No."

"Yes. Building the house, being with your uncle, helping me run."

Heat rose in his neck. A good heart? Not exactly. Except. Jack had told him the same thing several times during his summer exile. But would a good-hearted person despise the trajectory of his life? Would a good-hearted person date someone simply because she may be able to help him achieve a loathed holy grail? Would a good-hearted person have dinner with one woman and text another?

His stomach clenched.

Did he hate where his life was heading?

Yes.

He wiped the sweat from his upper lip.

Finally. He'd admitted he hated where his life was headed. What was he going to do about it? Anything?

What could he do about it? His whole life pointed to partnering in a law firm. What would his life point to if he stepped off the path planned for him since birth?

His phone buzzed.

Josie.

"Good night. See you Saturday."

He wished he could see her now. She could help settle him, make him feel happy. Make him feel peace.

Make him feel.

"Good night, Josie."

WITH THE CONNECTION to her cut, his heart thumped in his chest. His lungs pumped as if he'd just run a set of suicides. He paced in front of his bed, but relief evaded him. He stalked down the hall into his kitchen.

Trapped. He felt trapped in his own house. Trapped in his life. Like an animal at the Asheboro Zoo. They had free rein up to a point, freedom to roam up to the border of their exhibit.

He had freedom too. He chose his specialty, the firm, the kind of car he bought, but those choices were tethered to his father's expectations for him.

Jack.

He sought the clock. After 11:00. Too late to call. But he had to.

If he didn't, he'd go crazy.

Ches gripped the phone to still his shaking fingers. The screen read 11:11. If he called and they were asleep, he'd scare them, make them think the worst.

But how many times had Jack said to call anytime? Did he really mean it?

Yes. Jack never said anything he didn't mean. Did they watch the late news?

No. It's too late. Heidi will be asleep or at least in bed.

Blood pounded in his temples. He dragged shaking fingers through his hair, tugged on the ends till the pain gave him something new to focus on besides the fear rising in his gut. He had to do something, or his chest would explode.

Just relax. Breathe in. Breathe out. Slow down, heart. Relax.

Call him.

He tapped the numbers and blinked away moisture in his eyes.

One ring. Two rings. Halfway through the third ring, Jack answered, sharp concern tingeing his husky voice. "Ches, what's up?"

"I, I'm sorry. It's late. I'll call back tomorrow."

"Ches. What's wrong?" Iron surrounded Jack's words. For the first time in his life, Ches noticed a resemblance between his father and his uncle. His father's voice dripped icicles from steel-coated words meant to freeze out opposition, but Jack's words, firm and strong, coaxed cooperation, confirmed Ches was important to him.

"Where are you?"

"At my place."

Jack released a breath. "So you're safe? You weren't in an accident?"

"No. No. I'm...listen. Sorry I bothered you."

"You're not bothering me." Fabric swished in the background.

Of course, he'd been in bed. Asleep.

"Tell me why you're calling." His words brooked no argument.

"Jack, I. It's..." What could he say? That he was petrified in his own house? That his body felt like it was about to explode? That the prospect of his future filled him with nothing but dread? "I'm trying to sort stuff out."

"I'm listening. Tell me about it."

Could he say it out loud? That he felt like he was going crazy. That he couldn't stand being alone and needed to hear someone else's voice. Someone real. Someone subjective who didn't have an agenda.

What did he think he'd accomplish by calling Jack? He couldn't make it better, could he?

"I think you want to talk, Ches, or you wouldn't have called."

"Yeah. Yeah." Would it be so bad? Admitting it to Jack? Maybe he'd admit he hated the firm. Just that. Admit a little at a time.

He opened his mouth, but the words wouldn't come. If he said it out loud, what would happen? Would everything start to unravel? He leaned against the wall, rammed his phone to the side of his head.

"Okay, Ches. When you're ready. Until then, remember I'm praying for you."

"You pray for me? Still?"

"Of course. Heidi's been praying since I saw your name on the screen. We love you, buddy. We. Love. You."

Ches's insides constricted. He clamped his eyelids together. He would not cry. He hadn't cried since he broke his arm when he was nine. His father laughed at the tears on his cheeks.

"I can be at your place in less than thirty minutes."

He'd do that too. He'd jump in his car and come. Because Jack loved him.

"No. No, thank you. You don't have to."

"I want to."

He slid down the wall, weak. "I'm good. Just talking with

you. What you said helped." The band strangling his chest loosened.

"That we're praying for you."

"Yeah." He covered his eyes with his palm. "The other too."

"That we love you?"

"Yeah."

Silence. "Ches." His voice sounded deeper. "We love you. Don't forget that. We love you, son. Not because of your degree or the fancy job downtown or the shiny car you drive. Because of you, Ches. Because of who you are. That won't change, Ches. Do you hear me?"

"Yeah."

"Do you believe me?"

"Yes."

Son. His own father had never called him son. Never said he loved him. The back of his throat ached. He opened his mouth to thank Jack, but a croak sounded instead of the words. He rested his head on his bent knees.

"When you're ready to talk, I'll listen."

Ches bit the inside of his cheek. Get it together, man. You're fine. Jack and Heidi are praying. He startled. When did praying make a difference to him? Not since that summer with Jack, for sure. "Right. I feel better now. Yeah. I couldn't breathe while ago. Couldn't stand being in my place."

"If you need a change of pace or a new view out your window, your old room's available. Heidi's fingers are itching for some fall baking too. Just FYI."

The image of the moss green room materialized in his mind's eye. A twin bed filling one corner, a bookcase, and desk, a wooden plaque with a Bible verse Jack carved hanging by the door. Once he let go of the chip on his shoulder, he'd spent a happy summer in that room, in their house talking around the kitchen table eating Heidi's cooking. Especially her overnight coffee cake with the crunchy cinnamon topping.

How would it feel to go back now? Peaceful. Yeah. For sure.

A longing for that summer and those good people filled his chest. Made it difficult to talk. He swallowed. "Good to know. I might. Thank you. I'll let you get some sleep now. Good night."

"Good night."

"Jack. I…" He couldn't say it. Not yet.

"Yeah?"

"Thank you."

"Any time, buddy. Any time."

CHAPTER 14

I can do… Josie wiped glacial raindrops from her eyes and gritted her teeth. I can do all things through Christ who gives me strength.

Not fun. Not fun. Not fun. Keep moving. One step in front of the other. Not fun. Keep moving. Hot chocolate after a hot shower. I can do all things—

"How ya holding up?" Ches jogged beside her, perfectly content. Not winded at all.

"Fine."

"You're doing great. You can do it, Josie."

"Stop talking."

"Too bad we didn't train in inclement weather, but you're doing fine."

"Go." Huff. "Away." Pant. This, too, shall pass. Is that a Bible verse? Probably not. Hot shower. Hot chocolate. Her ears ached with the cold. *Christ, please strengthen me.*

"You've passed everybody except the lead group. There's the two-and-a-half-mile mark. You've got time if you want to—"

"Shut—"

"Just sayin'."

Why did he have to mention the possibility of beating more people? Why did her competitive streak wake up on this horrible, no good, very cold, and wet day? She increased her pace. A tad. She felt Ches's glance.

You own the cattle on a thousand hills. God, please give me more energy.

She boosted her speed again.

You are the maker of Heaven and Earth. Make my legs keep moving, please. Did that combination Bible verse and prayer even make sense? Who cared?

She caught the last runner of the lead group and kept up with her for several seconds.

God, You have a strong right arm. Push me with Your arm over the finish line. I promise I'll never sign up for another 5K. Ever. Never again.

She pressed her thumbs against the top of her fists and kicked into high gear. She passed two more women ten steps before the finish line.

The brothers' voices rang above the crowd cheering on the sidelines. *Thank You, God.*

Hot shower. Hot chocolate.

She jogged to a curb out of the way of finish line traffic, but before she could drop to the wet ground, strong arms enveloped her into a tight hug. "Great job, Josie girl." Ben rested his cheek on the top of her head.

Another set of arms grabbed her next. "Joey, you came in third. Can you believe it?" Heath laughed and kissed her temple.

"Third?" A warm tingly feeling bubbled in her chest. Stupid competitive streak, but winning with a third-place showing when her goal had simply been to complete the race? Her sunny attitude returned from wherever it had hidden since the beginning of the race. If she had any energy left, she'd jump up and down. Maybe dance a victory dance.

She stepped out of Heath's embrace and into the final hug.

She sighed against the hard chest. Wait. This didn't feel like Sam.

"You ran a great race. I hope you're not too disappointed with third." Ches's voice whispered near her ear. His arms tightened around her.

She'd hugged Ches. Instead of Sam. She wiggled out of his hold. Where was Sam? Wait. What had Ches said? Disappointed?

"Why would I be disappointed?"

Arms grabbed her from behind. "Way to go, Jo Jo. You let a high schooler beat you, but she's on a cross country team..."

She elbowed Sam's ribs. "I didn't let anybody beat me. I beat everybody else except two really good runners. When do I get my medal?"

"Ahm...are you supposed to get a medal? I mean, you're part of the team hosting this shindig. Wouldn't it be kind of, well, maybe a little unseemly? Leaning toward cheating?" Heath smoothed back his wet hair and repositioned his ball cap.

"Cheating? Are you kidding me?"

She scrunched her forehead. Would it be improper if she accepted a third-place medal when she was the one who chose and purchased all the medals for the winners?

Probably.

But still.

"I came in third. When I was praying the whole way just to finish. Till you—" she pointed to Ches— "told me to go for it."

Eyebrows rose. "I did what?"

Another pair of arms slid a beach towel around her. She glanced over her shoulder. Milo.

"Thank you."

"I brought an extra one. Thought you might like it."

"It's nice. Thanks."

"Ches. There you are." Mallory zigged zagged her way through runners stretching their legs and guzzling sports drinks.

She wore super cute rain boots and a bright slicker whose hood bunched behind her sleek ponytail. She held an umbrella decorated with a classic artwork Josie had coveted on a trendy retail website. Her eyes left Ches long enough to give Josie the quick once over she'd worked at the grant party.

Josie didn't need a mirror to know she looked like a drowned rat. Her hair stuck tight to her head, but because of her hat and the rain, not mousse and hair spray like Mallory's.

"Are you ready to leave? We need to be at my parents' by 11:30."

The tic in his cheek reported for duty.

Josie ignored the proprietary vibe accompanying Mallory. Ignored the sinking feeling in her stomach too. She looked straight into his beautiful blue eyes, probably for the last time, and smiled. "Thank you for running today and for bringing the ten other runners. You upped the cash tally a lot."

"Twelve. I brought twelve extra, so I held up my end of the bargain and then some." He smiled back, or at least the tight movement of his mouth resembled one. "You're welcome."

Right. The bargain. He'd held up his end, and now it was over. Official. No more training sessions. No more Ches.

And she was going to have to give up her medal too.

Rats.

Hot shower.

Hot chocolate.

THE PHONE RESTED on top of Josie's comforter, enticing her to text Ches. She snuggled deeper into the cozy warmth of her bed, luxuriating in the plump softness. She'd spent Saturday alternating between hot lemon ginger tea and hot chocolate, watching movies set in exotic island locales just to thaw out from her early morning romp through freezing rain.

The February-like temperatures hung on all weekend, affording her the perfect chance on Sunday morning to adorn herself in wool from head to toe, including thick wool socks, and tights, covered in knee-high leather boots. Now, reclining in her fuzzy robe and flannel pajamas, she wiggled her happy toes, toasty underneath the covers.

Yes, her toes were happy, but her insides jumbled with discontentment. Would he text? It was Sunday night. He'd texted for the past several Sunday nights.

Six, right?

Her logical brain reminded her they had no reason to keep up their connection now the race was over. He'd helped get the craft fair plans underway, but she couldn't see him being involved with any other library fundraiser.

Still, the rest of her, mainly her silly heart, clung to a minuscule hope that maybe he'd text to check on her. But what if he didn't? She'd finished her novel earlier in the afternoon. She was sick of watching movies. She'd made her Thanksgiving menu and grocery list. The bedside clock showed nine o'clock. She wasn't sleepy. She'd go crazy in the next few hours watching her phone lie silent on the bed.

What if she texted him? Her cheeks heated. She pushed back the comforter to cool off. Chasing after a man wasn't exactly her style.

Oh, sound like Grandma much?

Texting Ches wasn't chasing after him. He probably wouldn't blink an eye at a text from her. He was probably used to being texted by many women.

The exact reason not to text him.

What if he was with Mallory? What if he was in an important meeting? What if…?

Quit analyzing every move. She grabbed her phone and found his name.

"Hey. Recovered from yesterday?"

She hit send and tossed the phone away from her before she could change her mind one more time. She unloosed her robe belt and shrugged her shoulders from the boiling fleece. What was wrong with her? She resembled a turn-of-the-century schoolmarm about to swoon over—the phone buzzed.

Scrambling over the comforter to retrieve the phone, she knocked it off the bed instead. She slid down the side and landed on the pink carpet she'd chosen in eighth grade. Leaning back against the tangled covers, she crisscrossed her legs and read the text.

"Training was so good recovery was a piece of cake."

"Lucky you. I've been freezing since yesterday."

"Must have been a bad weekend."

"No. Finished a novel. Watched four movies."

"No date?"

"Didn't say that."

Milo asked, but she begged off citing her exhaustion from the run.

"So you did have a date?"

"Didn't say that either. No date except for lots of flannel and hot chocolate."

Okay, Mr. Windham. You asked a pointed question. Thank you. That opens the door for me.

"What did you mean yesterday? About being disappointed?"

"Because you came in third."

"Third place was tremendous for me."

"You're really happy?"

What was wrong with him? Why was he so embarrassed about her placement? Forget this texting. She touched the phone receiver icon before she'd realized what she'd done.

Her stomach dropped.

What had she done?

He'd never called her in the whole six weeks of training.

Why did she make that move first? Why couldn't she just keep texting?

He answered after the second ring. "Hey."

"Sorry. I called before I thought. You're not in the middle of something, are you? Is it okay I called?" She squeezed her eyes shut, wincing at how words tumbled out of her mouth, making her sound like a schoolgirl instead of a grown woman with a career.

A beat passed.

"Sure. Why not?"

Did he hesitate before he answered? Yes, definitely. Not good. Not good. Hang up now.

HEARING her voice was the best thing since she'd hugged him after the race. His weekend crashed downhill ever since, beginning with the dude wrapping her in a beach towel and then Mallory showing up to drag him to her parents' house. This call was a definite upswing to an otherwise pit of two days. If his father looked at his phone records, he'd come up with some believable reason to have her phone number listed at 9:30 on a Sunday night. Then again, his father hadn't commented on phone records in a while.

"Listen, sorry I bothered you."

He grabbed the remote. "Wait. Of course, you can call me. I'm glad you did." He turned off the TV and extended his legs to the end of the sofa.

"Really? Because it seems like, well, I mean…" Stop being ridiculous. She took a breath. "I just wondered why you're not happy about third place."

"I didn't want you to be disappointed. I saw how you kicked it up right there at the end. I saw how you wanted it."

"Yeah. I wanted to finish and finish in front of as many

people as I could. I never dreamed of placing. I was too busy praying to make it to the finish line."

"You were praying?"

"Of course. So what's wrong with third? Did I embarrass you?"

"Absolutely not."

"Well then? I don't understand."

He covered his eyes with his forearm. "Josie, in my childhood, third place meant not first. You didn't win. You got beat."

How did she manage to wrangle secrets out of him? First, the story behind Jack and now this. A rush of air sounded in the receiver.

"Ches, I'm sorry about that. Third place to me means if you tried your hardest, you played better, or ran faster, or jumped higher than a whole group of people except for two who probably tried as hard as they could. Third place is a good thing."

"So you're really fine with third?"

"I'm ecstatic about third except for the fact that my brothers guilted me into doing the noble thing and declining my rightfully-earned medal."

"You seriously wanted a medal?"

"It would have dangled from around my neck all day yesterday and accompanied me to church underneath my wool sweater—I do have some decency—this morning."

A deep laugh unshackled his insides, stretched his cheeks. "Who knew you liked a little bling?"

"Most girls like a little bling."

"I'll remember that."

"Yes, well, I guess I should go."

She's hanging up. Not yet. Keep her on the line.

"Hey. Do you have numbers yet? How much did you raise?"

"We had one hundred fifteen runners pre-register times forty dollars. That's forty-six hundred. Plus, we had twenty-four runners register yesterday for another nine hundred sixty. That's fifty-five hundred sixty, but I have to tally the outgoing receipts. Still waiting on a few to come in. Not sure what all the expenses were. We probably would've had more runners register on Saturday if the weather hadn't turned so lousy."

"Are you happy with the total?"

"We've got to earn ten thousand by next September to win the full grant. Our March book sale usually pulls around three or four thousand. I'm not sure what the craft fair will bring since we just earn a percentage of sales. We need to come up with another fundraiser to get us over the top." She made a noise on the phone.

"Did you just growl?"

"Sorry."

"Why'd you growl?"

"I hate fundraising."

"So why do it?"

"I love the library. Somebody has to help it."

Their talk moved from fundraising possibilities to current events to dream vacations before his phone beeped. He checked the screen.

"My phone's about to die. Let me get my charger."

She sucked in air. "It's ten after eleven."

"'Bout to turn into a pumpkin?"

She rewarded him with a chuckle. "No, but...We've talked for two hours."

"Is that bad?"

"No. Just..."

"What?"

"I should go. I have an early call tomorrow."

He didn't want to hang up. He wanted to keep talking. "Is that usual or unusual?"

"Usual. I have to be in my office at 7:30 for my eight o'clock class. So—"

"Wait. Could I ask a question?" He might be making a mistake, but he needed to know.

"You can ask."

"What's the deal with B.J.?"

"B.J.? Right out of left field there. Why are you interested in him?"

"He was hanging around Saturday. Just wondered about your story." She could shut him down right now. Their story wasn't any of his business.

She sighed. "He's not very nice. He broke up with me the day after my parents left for the Dominican Republic. I was already in a funk missing them. He piles on, says he can't handle the emotional place I was in.

"Granted, I was subdued, but I wasn't a sobbing, emotional mess. I was happy for their adventure. If he'd broken up with me a few days before, I could have cried on my mom's shoulder, let her love on me some before she left. You know?"

No. I don't know.

"In retrospect, it's better they left before. She would've been upset leaving me after a breakup. But the thing is, he didn't do it to spare my mom. He did it to spare himself."

"Safe bet your brothers don't have a high opinion of him."

"Yeah. Here's a tip. Don't bring him up in front of them."

"Got it." Interesting personal information. Could she shed light on B.J.'s curiosity in the firm? "Do you know anything about the story he's working on?"

"Not really. Why?"

"Just curious. He's appeared in the same places I eat lunch, talking with some of the law clerks, legal assistants, even parale-gals. Then he shows up at the 5K."

"At the race, huh? Not running, for sure. The pain in the neck." She sighed. "He wondered why the library got a grant when it's been on the city's chopping block for two years. He's wondered about the money being doled out in increments instead of all at once."

"The library won a grant because you wrote a great proposal."

"Exactly what I told him. Thank you again."

The smile in her voice sidetracked him for a second.

"About the other thing, I don't know. Not in charge of that. I thought the money came out of a trust fund." He'd never applied for a grant, didn't know how allocations usually played out. Maybe the firm got a break on taxes if the money was distributed over months instead of in one lump sum.

What does B.J. want? He's a crime investigative reporter. What crime is he hunting at one of the most respected firms in Charlotte?

Nothing. He has nothing. He's blowing smoke. He's trying to—

"So, ahm...I'll say, 'good night,' and grab my beauty sleep."

Her voice brought him back from his musings. "You don't need beauty sleep, Josie."

Silence. "Good night, Ches."

He felt her uneasiness. Maybe he shouldn't have said that last line, but it was true. She had a natural beauty enhanced by her kind, funny personality.

"Good night, Josie."

He should turn in too. His Monday was packed, but sleep would be an elusive friend tonight. Thoughts of a green-eyed blonde already filled his mind, pushing out everything else but her.

CHAPTER 15

The golden-brown turkey rested on a bed of rosemary stems. Josie checked the meat thermometer. Perfect. She pulled the twenty-two-pound bird out of the oven and grunted as she landed the roaster on hot pads. She blew curling wisps away from her flushed face and adjusted the foil tent before filling the oven with the last of the casseroles.

Everything was on time to start the big lunch in less than an hour. She surveyed the room. Almost everyone had arrived. They lounged in the family room with a dog show muted in the background, waiting for football games to start.

Three international students from the college sat together on the couch, eager for their first Thanksgiving celebration. William, from mainland China, had brought a bouquet of flowers. Portia from Twickenham, England, had brought a trifle for dessert, and Ariana, from South Africa, had brought some kind of spicy appetizer shaped into spirals.

She stirred the giblet gravy in one pan and the brown gravy in another. Two different gravies satisfied everyone, including Sam who refused to touch the giblet kind.

"How's it going, Joey? Mmmm. Smells so good in here. Just

like when mom cooks." Heath leaned against the counter and snagged a spicy pinwheel.

"Well, she taught me how." She laid the spoon in the spoon rest."Everything's fine. The last casseroles will be finished soon, then I'll bake the rolls. Everybody's here except Aunt Jewell and the Simpson sisters from church."

Heath swallowed and reached for another spiral."These are fantastic. Can you—"

"I'll ask for the recipe. Don't worry."

The doorbell rang.

"Speak of the devil." Entering the kitchen, Sam grabbed two pinwheels on his way to the front door.

"That's not nice, Sam." Josie wiped her hands on a kitchen towel and pressed the oven light button to check the browning casseroles.

"Hey, glad you could make it, man."

"Thanks for asking me."

Josie dropped the towel. A voice she hadn't heard in several weeks except in her dreams greeted her brother. She stooped to retrieve the towel, the flush in her cheeks having nothing to do with the heat in the kitchen this time. Sam had invited Ches? And he'd accepted?

Nerve endings fired electric alerts all over her body.

Sam sauntered back into the kitchen with Ches in his wake. "Hey, look who made it, Jo Jo."

"I see." Her voice had a breathy quality she attributed to her exhaustion of preparing to feed close to thirty people, not to the surprise of seeing Ches again. With him, the family, the students, friends from church, the count would definitely be thirty. "Happy Thanksgiving."

"Happy Thanksgiving. Thank you for having me." He nodded to the floral bouquet in his hands. "Sam said not to bring anything, so I went with flowers." Mums, sunflowers, zinnias, and roses spilled out of a wicker cornucopia. "But I see you already have some."

"You can never have too many flowers." From the corner of her eye, she saw Ben gape at her. She mentally stuck out her tongue at her brother and took the arrangement, setting it on the side table near the family picture. "Thank you so much."

Ben crammed his hands in his pockets. "We're still waiting for a few people to arrive. We can search for a game while we wait." He nodded toward the family room. Sam followed, stuffing another appetizer into his grinning mouth.

Ches turned to Josie. "You look like you did when you found out you placed third in the 5K. Stunned. You didn't know Sam asked me, did you?"

A good hostess shouldn't admit to being caught off guard, should she? She bit her lip. But what could she say without lying? "Well, ahm. We always have plenty of food. I'm glad you're here." Her crazy heartbeat testified to how glad she felt.

"That evasive but gracious answer tells me the truth. Hey. Sorry for crashing."

She touched his arm. "You're not crashing. You were invited." She smiled. A genuine smile because she was thrilled to see him again. "It's good to see you." Saved by the doorbell. "Oh, there're the rest of our guests. If you'll excuse me, I'll get the door." Nice. Time to recover from the shock. And think of ways to make Sam pay for not giving her a heads-up.

AFTER THE CROWD had held hands and listened to Ben say grace, after the first few guests had begun the line to fill their plates from the kitchen island loaded with delectable dishes, Josie slipped upstairs to decompress. She'd just reclined on her bed and closed her eyes when her bedroom door opened. Ben entered and leaned against the closed door.

"I thought I'd find you up here."

"What are you doing? You're one of the hosts. You're supposed to be downstairs."

He folded his arms across his chest. "A textbook example of the pot calling the kettle black, I believe."

"I'll be back down before the line is finished. I need a few minutes."

"To get over the shock of Ches being here."

She pressed the crook of her elbow against her eyes. "To recharge for a little bit. I've been up preparing food for hours, FYI. And I didn't know he was coming."

"I got that."

She peeked from under her arm. "Did you know?"

"Sam didn't fill me in either. If I'd known—"

"What?" She scootched to sitting and adjusted the pillows behind her. "You would have uninvited him?"

He sat on the edge of the bed. "Of course not. But maybe I'd have pressed Milo to come for lunch. Remember, he's coming later, right?"

"What's the difference if Milo comes sooner rather than later?"

"Josie. I saw the way your eyes lit up, partly with shock, partly with pleasure when Ches walked in. Don't deny it."

"I was excited to see all our guests."

"Josie."

"Ches is turning into a friend. Remember he helped me train and come in third at the 5K?"

He grabbed one of the throw pillows and tossed it at her. "That's such a bunch of you-know-what. You're an athlete. You needed a trainer about like that turkey down there needs a nest."

She stuffed a fringed pillow behind her neck. "Funny."

"Heath and I both offered to run with you, but you declined our help. And you came in third on your own, FYI."

She wrapped her arms around him. "Ben, I love you. Please

don't be worried. We always invite people who don't have a place to go to."

He lifted her chin and pinned her eyes with his. "Do you honestly believe Ches Windham didn't have a place to go for Thanksgiving?"

She broke the gaze. "I don't know. I do know he accepted Sam's invitation, so maybe he didn't." She patted his chest. "Please go back down there. I need a few more minutes. I started wrestling with Tom Turkey at six o'clock this morning."

"And we love you for it." He searched her face for a few beats. "Just be careful. I don't want you to be hurt again." He pushed from the bed. "See you in a few. Don't fall asleep." Ben clicked the door closed behind him.

She slid to her knees and rested her profile against the nubby comforter. Her body glowed with an exhaustion halo. She could fall asleep right here, kneeling beside her bed.

Except ignoring her guests wasn't exactly a good look for a hostess.

Not that she'd ever been able to ignore one of them, for sure. And what was wrong with noticing Ches? Or enjoying his company?

I see his faults and his girlfriend. I don't flirt with him. I'm not trying to steal him away from Mallory. I can cultivate a friendship with a man without getting burned, Ben.

She massaged her forehead.

Oh, God. I'm so tired. I need some help to keep going today.

She sighed and snuggled into the soft folds. Her comfy bed enticed her more than the food waiting on the counter.

Thank You for all the people downstairs. And here it is, God because I know You know it already. Ben was right. I'm happy that Ches came. Really happy. I don't want to be happy because it isn't the happiness that comes from knowing the guest needed a place and we could provide it. This happiness is because seeing

Ches makes me happy. But I don't want it. I don't want seeing Ches to make me happy.

Please change my heart. I know he's dating Mallory, and even if he wasn't, there're plenty of other girls waiting in line.

Laughter bubbled upstairs and reminded her to join the party.

Okay, God. Help. Help. Help. I need strength to walk back downstairs and hide my stubborn feelings. From Ches. And the brothers. And especially, especially from Ben.

THE FOOTBALL SAILED toward Josie who jogged backward, her eyes trained on the spiraling ball. Gaining ground with every step, Sam sprinted in a beeline straight for her.

"Hey, watch out." Ches kicked up his speed to prevent the inevitable crash between siblings.

Sam lunged for the ball. "No, you don't, Jo." He grabbed the ball but lost his balance, crashing into Josie and knocking her to the ground. Her head bounced on the brown grass.

Ches reached her in time to scoop her up and stand her on her feet. "Are you okay?" He kept his arms on her waist to make sure she had her footing again. And because he liked them there with her arms resting on top of his.

She glanced up into his eyes, holding the glance a couple of extra beats. Red splotches tinged her neck and rose into her cheeks. "Yeah." She pushed away from him, brushing off the seat of her jeans. "Sam, what's wrong with you? This is tag football, not tackle." Tears gathered in her eyes but didn't fall.

"If it's too hot in the kitchen..."

"That's a stupid analogy, especially today when I didn't see you in the kitchen at all except to eat." Her voice cracked, and deep furrows creased her forehead.

Ruffled feathers, for sure.

Ben grabbed the ball from Sam. His knitted eyebrows resembled his sister's. "Foul, little brother."

"I was going for the ball. No tackle intended." Sam had the grace to hang his head. A little. "Sorry, Joey. Really. I got a little competitive. Didn't mean to hurt you."

She expelled a quick breath and rubbed the back of her head. "I'll have a stinking headache for a while, but I've had worse from you and survived."

Watching her from lowered lids, Sam let a tiny grin grow from one side of his mouth. "I know you're tough."

"Right. Don't forget it." She glared at him but allowed Sam to kiss her cheek.

Ches dismissed the tight feeling the scene produced in his chest.

Milo turned to the porch. "Someone's phone is ringing."

The familiar ring tone brought him back to his reality. He should have left a while ago, but with the basketball and football and Milo showing up... "Mine. I'll get it. Thanks." He trotted to the porch and slipped the phone into his pocket without checking the screen. He offered his hand to Ben, Heath, then Sam, stopping short in front of Josie. Awkward.

Should he shake her hand? Kiss her cheek like Sam? Give her a thank you hug? None of those options felt right when what he really wanted...

He stuffed his hands into his pockets. "Thank you for your hospitality, Josie. The food was delicious, and I haven't played tag football in years. I had fun." His eyes flickered to the side of her head. "I hope you won't have much of a bump."

"I'll be fine. We're glad you joined us today. Happy Thanksgiving." She smiled at him, and his heart did a funny squeezing thing in the middle of his chest.

With nothing left to say, he made his way to his car, checking the cell screen for the recent call. Mallory. I'm on my way. We'll talk when I get there.

He dropped the phone into the cup holder and shut the door to the smack talk echoing from the front yard.

So that's what Thanksgiving could be like. Hands passing bowls and platters piled with homey kinds of delicious food. Extra chairs squeezed around a laden table. Card tables set up in adjoining rooms. Three or four conversations crisscrossing like a ball in an arcade game. Smiles all around and mirrored on everybody's faces because everybody was happy to be there. To be included with a happy, loving family.

Food and conversation moved to a quick round of his dominating a game of HORSE accompanied by the expected, confused stares and, "What do you mean you didn't play high school basketball? What are you six two, six three?"

He'd perfected his answer that always satisfied but never gave the full story—the story of how he hadn't made his freshman team, so his father forbade him to try again. "Forget about failures. Play to your strengths."

Father, would you be surprised that I can sink a ball from anywhere on the half-court?

More anger, probably. "If you'd spent all that time studying instead of throwing long balls, you'd've graduated summa cum laude instead of magna cum laude."

Yeah. Never enough, right, ol' man? What'll be wrong when I make partner?

He shoved his father's words out of his head. He wanted to cling to the afternoon, not his father's disapproval. The football game. Yeah. Think of the game. Fun until Sam bulldozed Josie.

What a tough cookie. Her head bounced on the ground, and she jumped up to give her brother what-for.

Ches smiled. He merged south onto I-77, leaving the Daniels family behind, savoring the memories.

CHAPTER 16

*J*osie coasted into a parking space in front of the warehouse store. No sign of Lucy yet. She'd be here soon, and they could begin their hunt for whatever her friend needed. If she timed her outing just right, the brothers should be finished hanging the outside Christmas decorations. They'd retrieved the indoor boxes from the attic as soon as they arrived for decorating detail. She dropped her head against the headrest. Those decorations would be hers to deal with all next week.

Next week. No 5K looming over her head. No training with Ches. No Ches. Of course, she'd already lived through the Ches-less stretch after the 5K. She'd become accustomed to his absence when he surprised her on Thanksgiving. Seeing him sharpened a missing-him space in her heart.

No. No. No. Not her heart.

Just, she'd enjoyed his friendship. His attention. She loved the challenge of making the tic in his cheek disappear, the smoothies after running, the texts on Sunday nights.

Yep. She missed him.

She shook her head to empty it of thoughts of Ches. Better to

138

concentrate on the upcoming finals. A rapid knocking on her window bounced her off the seat.

Lucy.

"You scared me half to death." Her pulse clamoring, she grabbed her purse and locked the door.

Lucy giggled. "Got your heart going, huh? You didn't see me pull in right beside you? Come on. Let's get this party started." She linked elbows with Josie and guided her to the front door.

"What exactly are you looking for?"

"I'll know it when I see it."

"Are you kidding?" Josie surveyed the aisles of merchandise sardined on racks and shelves. How many acres did this warehouse cover? How long would it take them to finish Lucy's mission?

"No, seriously. I need lots of goodies for the children's Christmas store at church. I'll figure it out as we go. Plus, who knows what else we'll discover in here." Lucy widened her eyes. "Part of the fun."

A half-hour later, Josie fingered the contents of a bin of piano music. Lucy guided a half-filled cart behind her. "What'd you find?"

"I can't believe this place has piano music."

"This place has everything, but not all the time. You never know what treasures lurk on these shelves. You need some music?"

"Not me." She hadn't planned on buying anything. She'd come to help Lucy, but... "Maybe Ches."

"Ches? He's the to-die-for, over six feet of gorgeous, GQ model man who camped out beside your classroom door and took you to lunch a few months ago, right? The cute one who ran with you. The buff one you keep saying's just a friend, right?"

Josie arched a brow. "Lucy, you do remember you're married, right?"

"Yes, I'm married. Happily too. And the mother of three

wonderful children who preface every phrase with, 'Mommy, Mommy, Mommy,' which at some point soon will render me completely insane. But. I still have eyes. Those eyes still register beauty whether you're talking an oil on canvas or a man in an Armani suit."

"Good to know. And I took him to lunch because he forgot his wallet, remember?" Josie smirked at her friend.

"Yeah, I'd buy him lunch, too, and throw in dinner for good measure." Lucy peeked over her shoulder. "So, you're buying him a Christmas present, huh?"

"No." She shook her head. "Not a Christmas present. Maybe a thank you present. For the 5K." She flipped past several classical books. "He plays beautifully, but he doesn't enjoy it. I thought maybe these..." She pulled a jazz book from the pile along with a show tunes book. Added those to a patriotic songbook. "I think he'd get a kick out of these."

"Jazz? I thought jazz was all about improvising."

"Who knows? Maybe you can learn the basics."

Lucy rummaged through a stack of colorful placemats in the adjacent rack. "I wonder if our craft guild would like some of these. They're only fifty cents each or fifteen dollars for the whole box." She held up a colorful one in pinks and greens. "You can sew 'em together and make things."

"Do you have a place to store them?"

"Right." She tossed it back with the others. "So when are you seeing him again?"

Her breath caught. Should have seen that question coming. "I'm not. I guess I'll mail them to him, to the firm maybe. I don't know his home address."

"Josie, call him up. Ask him for lunch. Be a twenty-first-century woman for once. Let him know you're interested."

"He has a girlfriend. I'm not trying to start anything. This isn't that kind of gesture. It's just a gift. I don't think he has a lot of people who are nice to him."

"So you're buying the man piano books." She made a face. "Piano books. Either geeky or cool. I can't decide which."

"Go with geeky then. I'm not trying for cool."

"Maybe a stand-out-above-the-rest kind of gift if someone wanted to shine above all his other admirers."

"No." She shook her head. "This is a friend gift. No strings. No hoping for anything. Just an I-see-you gift."

"So you don't want him to see you back?" Lucy pushed her cart farther down the aisle. She was good like that when she asked a question that may be pressed too hard. She'd ask then let you reflect on the question, not needing the answer for herself but asking the question to make you think.

What if she did want Ches to see her? What did it matter what she wanted? These books wouldn't change the fact that Mallory camped out in his line of vision. Mallory could secure his holy grail, the partnership.

But...

Maybe these books could remind him to loosen up, to have fun, to do something different. And, yes, maybe they'd remind him of her, a little bit.

"You guys. That cake was supposed to be for dessert tomorrow night. What's wrong with you?" Josie gaped at her brothers huddled around the kitchen table, her package and purse forgotten on the hall bench.

"We worked hard the whole time you were out gallivanting. We're starving and needed a snack." Sam licked his fork and winked at her.

"There's plenty left for dessert, Jo. Chill for a few minutes and read the mail. It's on the counter." Ben wiped his mouth with a napkin.

"Yeah, particularly the heavy white envelope on top of the

stack." Sam slid his saucer toward the cake stand. "How about sending another piece this way, bro?"

Heath sliced a small wedge for him. "Cut it out, Sam."

"What? Just directing her to the important stuff in the mail. Check out the return address."

"Sounds like you've already checked it out. So who's the letter from?" Josie grabbed the stack. Sam was right. An envelope of heavy card stock topped the circulars, catalogs, and her mother's *Southern Living* magazine. A gold-script, embossed *W* adorned the left corner of the beautiful envelope with Windham and a Lake Norman address engraved over it.

Heat prickled upward from her midsection, but she forced herself to remain calm in front of the brothers.

"Maybe some kind of invitation, huh?"

"How do I know? I haven't opened it yet. Have you? Steamed it open and glued it back together, I mean?" She slid her finger under the back flap and unsealed the letter.

"Whoa now. Don't disparage your big brothers. We're honest, hardworking, handsome—"

"Blarney alert!" She separated the contents, laid each separately in front of her.

Ben rinsed off his dessert plate and stacked it in the dishwasher. "What's it about, Josie?"

"An invitation to a reception, for the grant recipients, at the Windhams' lake house."

"Didn't the firm already celebrate you with the grant dinner?"

"Yes, but this isn't the firm. The Windhams are hosting." She fingered the embossed card.

"Why?"

"They didn't give a reason, Ben." She took another look at the invitation. "It's for this coming Thursday night. That's quick. I need to RSVP like now."

"You're going?" Ben leaned against the counter, watching her.

"Why not?"

"It just seems, I don't know. Ches's dad doesn't work for the firm, does he?"

"No. He has some sort of business in Virginia."

"Well, then. Why are they hosting an event for people who earned a grant from their son's firm? Seems like it shouldn't be their business to me. Seems, a little strange."

"Maybe Mrs. Windham wants to have a Christmas party, and this is a good excuse. Maybe they're nice people and want to do something nice for other people."

"Maybe they'll do anything to help their son make partner, including butting their nose into the firm's business." A hard edge crept into Ben's voice.

"Why are you being like this? It sounds like a nice night out. Maybe I'll get a new dress."

Ben glanced at his brothers. "Hey, guys. How about putting those boxes we left on the porch back in the garage?"

"That's code for let them talk, big bro." Sam swatted Heath on his shoulder. "We got to get on the road anyway."

"Right behind you." Heath gave her a one-arm hug. "Don't let him push you around."

"Not a chance."

"Dinner still on for tomorrow night?"

"Sure. And Skyping with Mom and Dad."

Heath left with a final encouraging wink.

Ben leaned against the counter, arms crossed. "I'm not going to push you around, but you know how I feel about you and Ches."

"How could I not know? You tell me every chance you get."

"You don't seem to be listening."

"I hear you. Now hear me. There is no me and Ches. And the invitation is from his parents."

"You don't see anything just a little bit off?"

"No." Should she? Was she blinded by the possibility of seeing Ches at the reception? Would he be there? Did it matter?

Yes, of course, it mattered. Was that why she already contemplated an up 'do over leaving her hair long? An emerald green dress to emphasize her eyes instead of the seasonal red.

She shook her head. "The invitation is from his parents for the recipients. Doesn't mention anything about him." Remember that. He might not be there.

But he could be.

"He's the link between the recipients and his parents. Of course, he'll be there." Ben shoved his hands in his pockets. "Well, what time am I supposed to pick you up?"

"No."

"No?"

"The invitation is for me. No plus one. No 'you and your guest.'"

"You're going to a swanky reception without an escort? One's implied, for heaven's sake."

"Mingling is implied. It's a reception, not a sit-down dinner. Thank you for offering, but, sorry. No."

Ben dipped his chin. "Josie, I hope you're not going to regret this."

"I'm going to a fancy reception at Christmas time for something good I did for my community. What's to regret?"

THE BRISK DECEMBER air jolted her face as Josie exited the post office. The front desk had already closed. What kind of business closes before five o'clock? This branch, for one. Oh, well. She couldn't check *Mail piano books to Ches* off her to-do list. She'd take the envelope on Thursday night just in case he attended the reception.

She headed toward her favorite consignment shop on West-haven Street. A well-dressed man talked into his cell phone in front of a coffee shop. Her heart lurched. B.J.

No, thank you. She turned on her heel to retrace her steps, hoping he wouldn't see her. She didn't have time for him today.

"Hey, Josie. Wait up."

Too late. She gritted her teeth.

"What's up. Haven't seen you in a while." He slid the phone into the breast pocket of his jacket.

"I heard you were at the 5K. Working on a story, I guess, because you certainly didn't run it."

"Yeah. I was just checking out some things, making notes."

"About the library or Padgett, Gibbons, Tyler, & Rose?"

He narrowed his eyes. "What do you know about what I'm working on?"

"Nothing, but I think you just confirmed what your latest story is about."

"I didn't say anything."

"Look, this has been interesting, but I have to get going. Bye, B.J." She turned back toward Westhaven Street.

"I thought you were going—hey," realization dawned on his face. "You don't have to avoid me, Josie."

"Right. I don't have to. I just don't have time to chat today. Got to get to Deja Vous before it closes."

He fell into step right beside her, keeping up with her hurried pace with little effort. "Your favorite store. A Christmas party, huh? With the dude holding the beach towel at the race?"

"None of your business, but no."

"With someone else?"

"If you must know, a reception for the PGTR grant recipients." She waited for a light to change before she crossed the street.

"Another one? They already gave you a dinner, right?"

"Why can't people who are doing good things get celebrated

more than once? And anyway the firm isn't giving this reception." Too late, she realized she'd given out information she didn't want him to know.

"Then who's giving it?"

Short of lying, she couldn't get out of continuing this conversation. "Mr. and Mrs. Windham."

"Ches's parents? Are you kidding? Why? What did they have to do with the grant? With the firm?"

The red awning of Deja Vous appeared in her vision. A few more steps and she'd be rid of him. "Can you for once quit asking questions and entertain the possibility they want to do something nice?"

"No. Not these people."

She grimaced. "Don't be mean."

"I'm not. I met them at a chamber event for about three minutes a few years ago, and that's enough for me. Alicia used to be Alice until she changed her name before she got married. Does that tell you anything? They're—"

"B.J., I'm sure you have your opinion, but keep it to yourself."

"Okay. But let me say this, 'be on guard.' Those people don't do anything nice without an ulterior motive. Something's up. I just wish I knew what." He gnawed on his thumbnail, reminding her how much she disliked the habit.

"I'm sure—"

"Listen to me. These are the kind of people who smile at you while the words coming out of their mouths skewer your heart to the wall. I've seen them in action. With their son."

Her breath caught. Could B.J.'s words be true? Visions of the fifteen-year-old being banished from his home, Ches's pale, tight-lipped face after a phone call with his father.

"Thank you for the heads-up, B.J. I'll heed your warning. Now, I've got to do some shopping."

She reached for the door, but he intercepted her arm. "Josie, we weren't right for each other, but I do care for you. I don't want these people to chew you up and spit you out."

Sincerity flashed in his brown eyes. Surprise probably flashed from hers. "I do believe you mean that. Thank you, but I'll be fine."

CHAPTER 17

a light shining on a parking pad to the right of the lake house beckoned Josie to park beside the lone car, Ches's car. Her heart rate picked up speed. So Ches would be at the reception, and she'd brought the music just in case. Grateful her favorite consignment shop had provided the perfect dress for a special evening, she took a slow breath and slid her mother's black cape around her shoulders.

The first to arrive, she vacillated on her next move. Should she go in? Should she wait? She angled the rearview mirror to touch up her lipstick in the muted light. Nice. She dropped the tube and her key into her mother's evening bag and waited.

Red amaryllis for Mrs. Windham and the manila envelope of piano books waited on the seat beside her. She smiled at the hodgepodge of music waiting for Ches. The books would make him smile, too, right?

Another car turned into the driveway and slowed to a stop beside her. Good. A second followed. Better.

She gathered the envelope and amaryllis, climbed out of her car, and joined Martha from a women's shelter and Lee from a dog rescue and adoption group. Not wanting to be the first at the door, she let the others advance while she slowed her breathing to normal. Her big talk of coming alone to the reception sounded good in front of Ben, but in reality, she wished her hand clutched his elbow instead of her sparkly purse.

The door opened, and Ches stood in the doorway, a tight smile greeting her when his eyes found hers. A stylish woman, probably early to mid-sixties, stepped beside him. Her light blond hair, parted on the side and curling under her ears, framed a face featuring a smile more strained than genuine also. "Welcome, everyone. I'm Alicia Windham. My husband, Lloyd, will join us momentarily." She glanced back inside the foyer. "Oh, well. Here he is now."

A man almost as tall as Ches entered from the adjoining room. The family resemblance showed in the blueberry eyes and the line of the jaw. Rigid posture kept his hands at his sides. A faint smile played around his mouth.

This is the man whose calls produced the tic in his son's cheek. This is the man whose brother welcomed her with a laughing smile, a warm hug. Despite the heated air spilling out of the open door, Josie shivered and squeezed her purse.

"We're so pleased to have you join us tonight. Come in." Her head snapped to her son. "Ches, take their coats."

Transferring the gifts from one hand to the other, Josie slipped out of her wrap as he draped coats over his arm.

"Good to see you, Josie."

Her heart ratcheted up a notch. "This is for you. Open it later." She handed him the envelope along with the amaryllis. "This is for your mom."

Mrs. Windham chatted with Martha.

He smiled. "Thank you. You've made me curious." He tucked the envelope under his free arm. "And thanks again for sharing your family on Thanksgiving. I had a great time."

"You're welcome." She'd tucked the bread-and-butter note he sent in her keepsake box. "It was a fun day."

The corner of his mouth dipped. "Until Sam knocked you down."

Mrs. Windham's brittle voice interrupted their conversation. "Ches, take care of those coats and put the flower...in the sunroom. Then help with the drinks."

The familiar tic appeared in his cheek. "Excuse me."

Note to self. Mother doesn't like flowers or Ches chatting with the guests. Focus on the other recipients. She turned toward Martha to ask the expected question the first week in December. "How was your Thanksgiving?" Martha played along, giving numerous, and humorous, details about roasting her first turkey. Josie listened, nodding and smiling, waiting for Ches to return.

When he stepped into her peripheral vision, she trained her eyes on Martha's freckle beside her left eyebrow, the shadow above her upper lip, the eyelash stuck to the corner of her eyeglass lens.

Good girl. Concentrate on Martha. Don't give in to the urge to watch him all night. Focus on Martha.

"We have a few more people coming. Lloyd, show our guests the buffet table and get drinks." Chimes sounded. "Ah. They're probably here now. Ches?"

Ches answered the doorbell and welcomed George Padgett along with the two remaining non-profit representatives.

George shook hands with Ches and kissed Alicia's cheek. "So good to see you. Thank you for hosting this reception. Christmas parties. My favorite time of year."

Lloyd Windham greeted the last guests and gestured toward the dining room. With a wary heart, Josie followed the man with the perfect posture.

TWO RED CHERRIES speared on a plastic sword floated in a

sparkling amber liquid. Josie smiled into Ches's eyes. "Thank you. Ben says I shouldn't eat these things, but they're so good."

"Maybe he should tell you to eat them. Maybe then you'd stop." Ches smiled back at her.

"That makes me sound—"

"Joselyn, we have red and white wine." Alicia Windham appeared beside her son.

"It's Josie. Thank you, but I don't drink."

Alicia arched a brow. "One glass of wine isn't drinking."

"Mother, Josie's fine with ginger ale."

The older woman expelled a breath. "I was telling George Padgett…" She glanced across the room to her husband, huddled with the owner of the firm. "How sorry I was that Mallory—" she glanced at Josie—"couldn't come tonight."

"She's shopping in New York." Ches touched Josie's elbow. "How about some food?"

"Yes, I know. Now." Alicia took steps toward the table with them. "Had I known beforehand, I would have changed the date. She should be here at your side. Social occasions are very important."

And cue the tic. "Mother."

"You have a lovely home, Mrs. Windham." I heard your message, Momma Bear, but I know how to play nice. Even to rude people.

"It's not our home. It's our lake house."

Not making conversation easy, are you? "Even so. You've decorated it beautifully." A little too impersonal for my taste. Where are the macaroni ornaments, the red and green construction paper chains Ches made in kindergarten? But the chic ribbons and balls nestled creatively in greenery took talent and looked perfect.

"Ches, have you mingled with the other guests?"

"I'm talking with Josie right now."

Lloyd Windham stepped between his wife and son. "I believe

you're Joselyn Daniels, the person who invited Ches to Thanksgiving."

"Josie."

"Yes, we were surprised when he declined our invitation to Thanksgiving." Alicia crossed her arms. A diamond the size of a cuff link sparkled on her third finger.

"Thanksgiving in the Bahamas, Mother?"

"We would have loved for you and Mallory to join us."

Got it. Loud and clear. Every time you mention the missing girlfriend. Ches and Mallory are a couple. Hands off. No trespassing.

Several people held plates, sampling appetizers and chatting. How to extract herself politely from this happy group and link with another?

"Mother."

"The food looks delicious." Another attempt at glittering party conversation.

"So, Joselyn, I believe you teach on the college level." Another attempt denied.

"What was your dissertation topic?" Mr. Windham's placid countenance revealed no animosity, no emotion at all, but something hinted that he suspected she didn't have one.

"I don't have a Ph.D., but my master's thesis is—"

"Don't have it *yet*, right? When do you plan to earn a Ph.D.?"

"I've considered the possibility, but—"

"But what? Isn't that the next logical step?"

"It may be for some, but I haven't decided to—"

"Why not?"

"Father."

Lloyd trained cold eyes on his son. "Ches." He swung his gaze back to Josie. "Joselyn, why not?"

"Frankly, after six years of perpetual studying, I was exhausted and ready for a break."

"Being tired is your excuse?"

"Not an excuse. The reason I didn't pursue another degree."

Laughter rang out from Lee's group. Those people were having fun. Meanwhile, she was being subjected to the third degree.

"I'm sure your other guests think I'm monopolizing our hosts. I'll let you chat with them." She ducked her head, intent on the glass plates at the end of the table. Couldn't face the disapproval or irritation she might see in Ches's eyes for sassing his parents.

Was that sassing or just standing up for herself? Who cared? She needed a break. She reached for a plate with unsteady fingers. What would her mom say?

"I'm going to have to take lessons from you." Ches grabbed a plate beside her.

"What?"

"You put my parents in their place with a kid glove. They're still trying to figure out what just happened."

She glanced at the Windhams, chatting with George Padgett and Martha. "I wasn't putting them in their place."

"You stopped an inquisition with grace. I apologize for them." He popped a bacon-wrapped water chestnut in his mouth, pushed it to the side. "Now I do have to mingle." He held her gaze for another two seconds and joined Lee's group.

The swift lifting of her feelings from Ches's compliment crashed to the floor by his absence.

Do not feel bereft. Do not look after him. Connect with someone else.

"Joselyn." A waft of thick perfume accompanied Alicia.

No, no, no, not her.

"I know what you're doing. Don't round your green eyes at me." Alicia smiled as she tonged boiled shrimp onto her plate.

"I'm here to tell you. Leave my son alone. Stop following him, inviting him to carpentry events, asking for his help with who knows what. Ah..." She pointed her red lacquered index finger between them. "Don't give any excuses." She stretched her smile wider. "Don't say a word, especially to Ches Wind-ham. The ring is practically ordered. The date is being discussed. You are not going to derail a train that's been heading for the depot for months."

Josie raised her eyebrow. A train metaphor? Really? She crushed the napkin in her hand.

"Are you listening to me?" Alicia dragged a shrimp through cocktail sauce. "Set your sights on someone else. Someone better suited to you. My son is on his way to a partnership with one of the oldest and most respected law firms in the southeast. My son is taken."

With that final parting shot, she joined her husband, dismissing Josie.

Josie's heart drummed in her chest. Tears burned her throat. The other guests chatted and sampled festive food, but humilia-tion suffocated her. How was she supposed to finish this fiasco of an evening? In an instant, an epiphany exploded in her brain in brilliant hues.

She didn't have to.

Just like the final time a cashier at a local discount store had brought her to tears of frustration. She'd realized other retail choices existed. She never had to shop in that store again.

She didn't have to stay here either and pretend the Windhams were civil people. She already had the grant. How she behaved at a reception hosted by horrible people had no bearing on the extra ten thousand dollars the library needed to raise. She'd help earn the extra money with hard work.

Relief blossomed and swelled in her battered heart. Calm descended, rounding the sharpness of the embarrassment. She set the plate on a side table. Thanking her hosts for the evening would be a lie. Instead, she headed for the front door and didn't look back.

IF HIS MOTHER'S pained smile didn't clue him in, Josie's white face told him he should intervene with their tête-à-tête, but George Padgett related an anecdote of his elk hunting trip to Alberta earlier in the fall. He nodded to George. "Right." Who knew what he'd nodded to? George segued into a wild game dinner he wanted to host next spring with his hunting buddies.

Ches glanced back at Josie...or where she had been. Where was she now?

George finished his story, and Ches excused himself making a straight shot to his mother. "Where's Josie?"

Alicia surveyed the room and smiled. "I don't see her. Did she leave?"

He narrowed his eyes. "What did you say to her?"

She lowered her voice. "Ches, I don't like your tone." Her voice held a challenge.

Lloyd appeared beside his wife, steel eyes boring into him.

"I don't like the way you treated her." Ches turned away from the disapproving stare, intent on following Josie.

"She throws herself at your every turn." Alicia sipped her wine. "Getting you to help build a house, run a race. Stealing you from our Thanksgiving."

Ches faced his parents, ready to defend Josie.

"You're sabotaging your career." Lloyd's face showed no emotion, a granite countenance poised for a fight, but his words hit home with a harsh whisper.

Ches staggered at the verbal sucker punch. Another dig at his failings as a lawyer. As a son? "Okay." He cleared his throat, banishing the huskiness betraying his emotions. "The truth is out. You think the only way I can make a partner is to marry into it, huh?" He pressed a hand to his stomach and looked at the front door. His father's stare held no power over him tonight. He needed to get to Josie.

Alicia's smile vanished. She shook her head. "Don't even think about it. You have guests."

"Josie was a guest too." He stepped toward the room with the coats.

She grabbed his jacket sleeve. "You will not leave."

"Enjoy the rest of your evening." Forcing a semblance of a smile, he pried her fingers from his arm and finished his mission to retrieve Josie's folder, grabbed her forgotten wrap too.

His father met him at the front door. "Ches, take a minute." The man stood composed, one hand in his pocket, white knuckles gripping the drink in his other. "Stay the course. Stick with Mallory. Make partner, then..." He shrugged.

Ches' stomach rolled at the picture at which his father hinted.

Lloyd sipped his drink. "Think about what you're doing. You'll realize your place is here."

"My place is anywhere but here. Good night, Father."

CHAPTER 18

The remote clipped to the sun visor wouldn't lift the garage door. The fuse must have blown again. Josie parked in the driveway. The front of her dress was soaked from tears she cried from the lake house. Still more dripped as she fumbled with the key to the front door. The lights from the family room weren't enough to illuminate her task. Why hadn't she left on the porch light?

Because she expected to park in the garage like usual. Because she'd been too excited about the evening to think of the ending.

What an end.

A fresh wave of humiliation and hurt rolled over her. She pressed her forehead to the painted wooden door. The cheery Christmas tree scent of the fresh evergreen wreath she'd hung with high hopes on Saturday doubled her misery.

Why was she so stubborn? Why couldn't she have learned her lesson with B.J. and be done with this kind of heartache? She knew last summer to avoid Ches. He seemed arrogant. Aloof. Hard. But then she'd seen the tic in his cheek, a flicker of sadness in his eyes.

The tic and sadness had challenged her, kicked in her nurturing gene. And somewhere in the last few months, the nurturing feelings morphed into something more.

Yes, that's right. Strong, independent thought-she-knew-everything Joselyn Daniels did what she claimed she wouldn't do. She'd let Ches Windham become someone important to her. Someone more important than a volunteer buddy. Someone who starred in a few silly fantasies.

Fresh tears followed the trails on her wet cheeks.

"Get in the lock, you stupid key." She stomped her foot, regrouped, and searched for the keyhole with her left index finger. Found it. Put the key beside her finger and slipped it in just as headlights waved across the front of the house.

She tracked the car as it jerked to a stop in the driveway. A familiar car. Ches. Her stomach knotted.

Oh, God, seriously? I don't have the strength for this, for Ches right now. I can't act like I'm fine. I just want to crawl into my bed and lick my wounds. Make him go away, please.

She focused on the key and the doorknob.

"Josie." He called to her as he slammed the car door.

She turned the key, heard the welcome click.

"Josie, wait. I've got your coat."

My coat?

Mom's cape. How could I have forgotten? Humiliation. Humiliation had quelled every thought but leaving.

Okay, God. He's not going away. Help me through this. Please.

She wiped her face to erase the tears, then turned to face him as he bounded up the steps two at a time.

"Here." He draped it over her shoulders. "Aren't you freezing?"

She blinked. "You're talking about the weather?" She squeezed the doorknob for support.

"I hoped you'd wait for the wrap. I wasn't sure you'd wait for me. You left—"

"Yeah. I'd mingled enough. Thank you for bringing the cape. Good night." She freed the key from the lock and fisted it in her left hand.

"Josie, wait. Please. Let's talk."

She shook her head. "There's nothing to say."

"My parents were rude to you in front of me. I can't imagine what my mother said to you when you were alone."

She took a long breath and held it before replying. "She said the truth in a way I heard it. I finally get it. I need to go in now." Her nails cut arcs into her palm around the key. She had to get inside before she lost control in front of him.

"Get what?"

"What Ben and B.J. keep telling me."

He cocked his head. "What do they keep telling you?"

"That I'm being stupid. That I'm playing with fire." Stop that line of talk or he'll figure out what she'd just discovered. "That your parents would chew me up and spit me out." She made a sound resembling a weak chuckle. "I guess B.J. knew what he was talking about."

Ches's nostrils flared. "B.J." He stepped toward her and framed her face, caught a tear with his thumb. "Don't cry, Josie." He transferred the droplet over her lips, glanced into her eyes then lowered his mouth onto hers.

The kiss lasted longer than a fleeting brush of their lips but not long enough. He broke the connection too soon, trailing his lips to her ear. "I'm so sorry they hurt you. That I didn't protect you."

An apology kiss. Not a real one. Her heart twisted. She pulled back. He held firm, cupping one hand under her hair, the other circling her waist.

He kissed her again, harder this time like she'd wanted him to for weeks.

There. She admitted it.

Every time her stomach flipped when a text came through or every time her breath hitched when he smiled at her, she wanted to be in his arms like this.

Her hands slid up his chest to grab his unbuttoned collar. She pressed against him, matching his kisses. He leaned into her inching her toward the brick wall. His lips claimed her with scorching kisses from her mouth to below her ear, the corner of her eye, and back again. She surrendered to the bliss of being in his arms.

Ches cradled her head, tangling his hand in her hair. She slid the pads of her fingers over the warm skin at the base of his neck, felt his racing pulse.

Something rooted around her ankles. Something cold and wet connected with her shin. She tried to rise above the haze created by Ches's kisses, but his mouth found the hollow of her throat, and she sank again.

Another cold zap dotted her shin. That silly dog was always jealous of the attention. Always wanted...Winston. Winston on their porch. She was making out on the front porch with Ches for the whole world to see. She snatched her hand away from his warm skin and pushed against his chest, breathing as hard as he did.

What was she doing? Acting like every other female who had ever crossed paths with Ches. Kissing him like there was no tomorrow.

Like there was no Mallory.

Dear God.

She couldn't finish a prayer. Couldn't get beyond the fact that Ben was right. She'd kissed another woman's boyfriend. She'd wanted him to kiss her. Heaven help her. She'd wanted to kiss him, and she did. Shame burned in her cheeks.

His arms held tight around her.

"I have to go in." She pushed again and stepped back,

breaking his hold. Her legs gave a warning, and she clutched at the door jamb behind her.

"Don't push me away, Josie."

She hid her mouth with the back of her hand. "You shouldn't have kissed me like that."

"That wasn't all me. You kissed me back."

Would the shame ever go away? "Thank you, kind sir, for pointing that out. Real gentlemanly."

He raked his fingers through his hair. It stood on end. "I'm sorry. I just meant there's a mutual—"

"Stop." He felt it too.

But in the end, it didn't matter. "There is no mutual. You're dating Mallory." Her lips felt like they glowed. She pressed them together.

"Don't bring up Mallory without Milo."

"I'm not dating Milo. We've been out."

His eyes narrowed. "How many times?"

"None of your business. And don't act jealous."

"I'm not acting."

She gave a rueful chuckle. "You're not free to be jealous. You're dating Mallory. You're headed toward marriage and partnership and the gilded life of a Charlotte attorney. And you're not free of your parents either." Her voice caught. She swallowed down a sob. "You do everything by their book even though it's killing you. I can see it if you can't."

She pushed away from him. "Go home."

"You want me just as much as I want you. I can feel it. I know you can too."

"No." *Please forgive me for that lie.*

What he said was true. He knew it. She did, too, but she didn't have to admit it. If she did, she'd fall under his spell again. And as wonderful as it felt to be held and kissed to the point of shaky legs, she had no intention of being another woman for Ches to check off a list and left as soon as his interest passed.

161

She had to get on the other side of the front door. "Please let me go." She moved toward her goal, but her foot caught, propelling her back to his chest. She glanced at the floor. The cape tangled around her feet.

He untwisted the fabric, held it for her, grabbed her hand when she reached for it. "Josie, wait. Please." His eyes glittered with, something, not sadness this time.

"Go, Ches. Go call Mallory."

He clamped his jaw shut, dropped his arm to his side. The tic showed up in his cheek.

Fresh tears pooled and trembled on her lids. She usually made that tic disappear.

Not this time.

CHES WAITED in the silent car watching as lights blinked out on the first floor and came on upstairs. Pushing a hand against his burning gut, he reached into his glove compartment for a bottle of chalky tablets. He threw back several and chewed, the minty flavor warring with the memory of that salty, first kiss.

That kiss.

Those kisses.

He swiped his face. Needed air. He pressed the on button, and the engine responded. He let down the window and pulled in long, cold draughts. He should leave. She was inside, safe. He'd heard the click after she mumbled goodbye, locking him out.

Why did he kiss her? What outcome did he expect? That a woman like Josie would enjoy kissing a man who by all accounts in the gossip rags was as good as married?

But she did enjoy that kiss. She denied it, but he felt her reaction, her response as she grabbed his collar, molded herself to him, yielded to him.

His mind jerked back to the beginning, to the Park 'n Go.

She intrigued him from the first ride to the drop-off. He recognized the possibility of trouble but couldn't resist asking for her every time he left on a trip. He thought by not knowing her name, he'd keep a handle on the attraction. He could enjoy her presence, her funny take on life, the way she made him feel, but he'd keep his life sailing toward his goal.

Then she'd shown up at the grants banquet. What a vision she was in that blue dress with her hair draping over the low back. He slammed his eyes shut against the bittersweet memory.

Jack might have called her reappearance a godsend. Was she? When he thought about her, just her, he could see Josie as a gift. He'd told himself they were friends.

Weren't they? He enjoyed being with her, looked forward to the library meetings, their runs together, their Sunday night texts. Yeah. All of it.

But...add Josie plus Mallory plus the firm and his career...the gift idea changed into a complication. Lloyd and Alicia made that perfectly plain at the reception with their hurtful words and actions.

He'd had a hand in hurting her too. If he'd resisted her, said hello at the grants dinner and let that be it, he'd have avoided dragging her into his mess. She wouldn't be upstairs crying right now. He should have stayed with her at the reception, ignored Alicia's orders to mingle. He should have protected her from his parents. He rammed his palm against his gut again.

The manila envelope lay in the passenger seat. He'd grabbed it along with her wrap before he left the lake house. He ran his finger under the flap to break the seal. A note fluttered out and landed on the floor as he emptied the contents.

Piano books? Jazz. Show tunes. Patriotic songs. He smiled, remembering playing her piano before the build all those weeks ago. He stretched for the note on the floor and flipped on the dome light.

Ches,

Thank you for helping me place third in the 5K even if I couldn't keep the medal!

I found these books in a bin at a warehouse store. I couldn't believe it had piano music. I remembered how shocked you were at our music collection and thought you might like these.

Don't waste your talent playing music you don't like.

Enjoy!

Josie

Her words sounded breezy and hopeful and kind. Just like her. His chest contracted. Breathing became a chore.

The idling engine changed sounds, waiting for him to make a move, but dread kept him motionless. Would this be the last time he'd back out of her driveway? Probably. Wretchedness filled the car and pressed down on him.

Don't waste your talent playing music you don't like.

...or working at a job you hate. A bitter laugh sounded in the stifling car.

Her goodbye sounded resolute, final, but he couldn't think about the end tonight. He'd text her, try to explain.

Explain? There was nothing to explain except that he'd been selfish. That he didn't mean to hurt her. That he… What? He just needed to see her again. It couldn't be over. Not like this.

His phone buzzed. He read the screen.

Mallory. He sent the call to voice mail.

Not dealing with anything else tonight.

CHAPTER 19

*L*ess than three hours of sleep didn't help a body look or feel her best. Josie hesitated with the mascara wand inches away from her spiky lashes. Mascara wouldn't hide the swollen lids. Would it draw more attention to her puffy face? She'd already decided not to irritate her scratchy eyes with her contacts.

Thank goodness she'd changed the plastic frames of her early college days to a more stylish pair last spring. Not that upgraded glasses could conceal the telltale signs of a cryfest, but maybe they'd camouflage the ravages on her face. She added blush and lipstick and tugged on a cheerful sweater set, hoping the bright colors would put forth the I'm-fine lie.

Sipping hot, black coffee on the way to work, she promised herself she'd be fine. Maybe not today. Maybe not even by the first of the year, but she'd be fine. Realizing she walked with clay feet and could succumb to a cute face and some attention disconcerted her. Clearly, she hadn't learned her lesson, wasn't stronger or smarter than who she was with B.J.

She was strong to a point, however. Six texts had come through her phone last night. One from Ben thanking her for the *I'm home* text. One from Sam wondering what was on the menu for Sunday night.

And four from Ches.

She'd resisted the urge to open them. She didn't want to read that he was sorry. That he shouldn't have kissed her. That Mallory was coming back from her trip. That he hoped she had a nice life.

Oh, you silly girl, Josie. Why did you ever think you could be friends with a man like Ches and not want more? What a fairytale you spun around him this fall. "He's helping me with the library, Ben. He's helping me train for the 5K."

Right. You enjoyed every minute with him even though you knew he had a girlfriend.

Even though he has a girlfriend.

Her heart contracted.

New tears pricked behind her eyes.

Ben was right about playing with fire. B.J. was right about the Windhams. Why didn't you listen to them? She squeezed the steering wheel.

Remember this crying hangover, Josie. The pounding in the brain, the scratchy, swollen eyes. She'd remember this stinging humiliation over the weeks ahead while she nursed her battered view of herself. She'd fooled herself into believing she was immune to Ches's charms, but she'd regroup and be ready if she ever saw him again.

Besides the crafts fair in February their paths would probably never intersect. He might attend to support his uncle, but probably not. If he did, though, she'd be ready for him in two months.

A siren sounded.

She glanced in her rearview mirror at the flashing blue lights. Her stomach hit the floorboard. *Seriously, God?*

Checking the side of the road, she exited the street and pulled far off the edge. She rolled down her window, killed the engine, and placed her hands on the steering wheel at twelve o'clock. Focused on breathing in and out.

The policeman peered into her window. "Good morning, ma'am. How are you?"

An honest answer? Probably not a good idea. "I'm fine. Thank you."

"Please let me see your license and registration."

She retrieved both and handed them to the officer. "I saw your parking sticker for the college. That where you're headed?"

"Yes, sir."

"Late for class?"

"No, sir."

"What're you studying?"

"I teach history."

The policeman studied her face, then the picture on her license. "You're wearing glasses today. You okay this morning?"

Nothing that dishes of ice cream and time won't heal. "Yes, thank you."

"Well, ma'am. This section of road is thirty-five, not forty-seven."

"Right. Thank you." She addressed the knot of his tie.

"That's twelve above the limit."

She read *Bryant* on his name tag. "Yes, sir. I'm sorry."

"You seem distracted this morning. Are you sure you're good?"

"Sorry, sir. I'm fine."

He handed her pieces of identification back to her. "Ma'am." Silence.

She lifted her eyes to his aviator sunglasses. He pushed them to the top of his head. "I need you to pay attention, ma'am. I'll give you a warning today but be careful. Got it?"

"Yes, sir. Thank you."

He walked back to his cruiser while she listened to the heartbeat in her ears.

She rested her forehead on the steering wheel. No ticket.

Thank You, God.

With trembling fingers, she picked up the travel mug and tipped it to her mouth. Coffee leaked from the mouthpiece all over her sweater.

Grand. Just grand.

She pulled tissues from the box on the floor and sopped up the splotches of black liquid. She blew out a stream of air. Counted to fifteen. A chat with a police officer. A dousing with coffee. Way to begin a happy morning.

Careful to abide by rules of the road, she arrived not late, but later than her normal time and had to park at the far side of the parking lot. A whiff of coffee reached her nose, reminding her of the dotted stains marring her sweater. Maybe she'd have time to sponge it with water.

As she blinked her eyes to adjust to the light in the hallway, a figure outside her office door pushed away from the wall. A big, tall figure in a power suit.

Ches.

Really, God? The police. Coffee. And Ches, too? What about my two months? Not on my A-game here. Help me out. Please.

She pulled off her glasses, stowed them in her satchel, and moved toward the blurry shape waiting for her.

Vain girl.

CHES WATCHED recognition appear on her face. Surprise turned to determination.

"Josie."

"Ches, what are you—"

He clenched his fists in his pockets. "You won't answer my texts. I have to talk to you."

"Well, this isn't the time or place."

"Your first class starts at eight o'clock, thirty minutes from now. I won't take that long."

"There's nothing to say."

He reached for her elbow. "You choose. In the hall or in your office, but we have to talk."

She stepped back with widened eyes.

"I'm sorry." He dropped his hand. "I didn't mean to sound threatening." He pressed his lips together, paused for a second. "Please talk to me. Just a few minutes, Josie. That's all."

Her eyes, swallowed by puffy lids, bore into him. That he and his parents hurt her fractured his heart down the middle.

"I'm sorry for the way my parents treated you last night."

"You told me once not to apologize for something I didn't do. Don't apologize for them." Her voice was flat, devoid of anything relating to the normal Josie.

"This is different from broken sunglasses."

She led him into her office, dropped her satchel into her swivel chair, and turned to him with a sigh. "Ches."

"You look so sad, Josie. I don't want you to be sad because of me or my parents."

"I'm sad because I was stupid. I thought I knew better than everybody else, and I didn't listen to their warnings." She straightened her desk calendar. "I'm sad because I enjoyed our friendship, and I'll miss it."

His stomach twisted. He didn't want to lose her. "I don't want our friendship to be over either."

"Seems like it has to be. Friends don't kiss like that, especially if one of them is seeing someone else."

"Josie."

"For the record, I don't usually kiss another person's boyfriend. I deluded myself that what we were doing was okay, but every minute you spent with me was time away from Mallory."

"Not true."

"You might be used to dating that way, but I'm not."

He jerked his jaw. "So that's what you think of me?"

"Plus, your parents—"

He pounded his fist on her desk. She startled. "It doesn't matter what my parents—"

"Oh, but it does." She nodded her head. "It really does, Ches. I think your parents are the reason you're a lawyer."

He braced himself as a stillness descended in her office. The truth was coming.

"Remember when you asked me about my first impression of you, and I told you I thought you were arrogant?"

He remembered all right. How many car rides had they shared mostly in silence last summer? Precious time with her wasted.

She gathered two colored pens from the desk, gripped them until knuckles turned white. "Arrogance is different from confidence. When you were working on the build, I saw a natural, real confidence that had nothing to do with power suits or a fully-loaded car or how many times your picture made the gossip column. The confidence had everything to do with your abilities. That's why within thirty minutes Jerry left you to work on your own."

She let out a sad laugh. "You gave as good as you got with my brothers too." She pushed a stray lock from her face. With a shaking hand.

"I'm sure you're a good lawyer because you're smart, but you always seem so uncomfortable in that role." She tilted her head and smiled a half-smile toward the door behind him. "You were comfortable building that house."

He stepped toward her. "Josie."

She rolled the chair in front of her, shaking her head. "You are so much more than your father's opinion of you or his idea of what you should be." She met his gaze for the first time since the hallway. "I hope you find what makes you happy."

Growing voices sounded from the hallway.

"I've seen you happy a couple of times but not much. Misery rings your eyes right now." She took a breath, pushed it out. "That's what I hope for you."

He shoved his hands in his pockets. If he didn't, he'd pull her into his arms again, try to make her wish come true.

Or was it his dream? "Are you happy, Josie?"

"I'm going to be."

"That sounds like a decision." The conversation was winding down. His time was running out. His heart, slamming against his chest, knew it too. He yanked at his tie so he could breathe. It didn't work.

"It is. Like love's a decision." She pinched a fuzzy dot from the top of the chair.

"So you decide to fall in love with someone?"

"No. I said love's a decision, not falling in love. You can't help who you fall in love with."

DID those words just come out of her mouth? What was wrong with her?

Completely certifiable.

She could attest, however, to the truth of the inappropriate statement.

Josie glanced at her watch. Fifteen minutes till American History I.

Why did she bring up love? In this conversation. With Ches. Stupidity still showing, girlfriend. Quit talking. Get him out of here. She needed every one of those minutes to regroup if she planned on teaching an exam review coherently.

"Bye, Ches. I have to get ready for my class." Which really meant repair the damage from this surprise visit.

"Then this is it?"

She opened her door and stepped to the side.

"For the record, I don't normally kiss another woman while I'm dating someone else." He paused, cupped her cheek. She stiffened, and he dropped his hand. "Bye, Josie."

The door clicked behind him. She sank into her chair with her face in her hands, dragging in slow, long breaths with the scent of coffee. Great. She'd forgotten the spilled coffee. The door opened again. "Ches, I—"

"Nope. Just me." Lucy stepped into her office and leaned against the closed door. "I saw him loitering by your office about seven-twenty when I got here. Should you be at home? You look awful."

Josie groaned. "Thanks so much. Just what I wanted to hear, especially now." Swollen eyes, minimal makeup, coffee-stained sweater. A perfect look for Ches's last image of her.

"If you looked in a mirror, you knew it already."

"You're still my friend, right? Because it doesn't—"

"Absolutely. Ready to talk about it?"

Josie checked her watch again. "There's nothing to say and no time anyway."

"There's plenty starting with why your eyes look like they've been stung by bees, why that man had to see you before work, why—"

"Okay. Okay." Say it out loud. Maybe it would help. "His parents raked me over the coals, as they say, last night. He kissed me although he's still dating Mallory. End of a sad story."

It didn't help.

"And he shows up to see how you're doing. He could have called. He cares for you, Josie."

Josie held up a hand to stop Lucy from continuing and to stop her heart from fluttering hope. "Don't start. I'm not taking his calls or texts. There's a way to block a number from cell phones, right?" She didn't want to see more texts from Ches.

More importantly, she didn't want to see when he stopped

texting and moved on. She gathered her books and pen. "I've got to make tracks if I want to arrive before Lewis rolls into class."

"Lunch. My treat. We're not finished." Her friend gave her a tight hug, then disappeared into the hall.

Yes, we are. Josie had enough energy and focus for the review classes, not for fielding well-intended questions from Lucy. Maybe some other time, but not today, friend. She reviewed her schedule, confirmed all morning review sessions, and determined to cut short her workday. She'd be out of here before the lunch rush.

And staring at a long, lonely weekend.

A TEXT BUZZED CHES'S phone. Mallory. He grimaced and ground his molars. In all his impromptu planning for the weekend, calling the office, calling Jack, packing an overnight bag with who-knows-what, he'd forgotten to text Mallory.

Telling, eh? Not sharing weekend plans with the girlfriend. Is she my girlfriend? She acts like she is. All of Charlotte thinks she is.

What do you think?

That question halted him. Dragging his eyes from corner to corner, he scanned his old room at Jack's, listening for a repeat but none came. Good. He didn't want to answer that question. Didn't want to think of Mallory when his mind was full of Josie. Her warm body molded against him last night. Her haunted eyes this morning.

He scrubbed his face with his palm. He had to stop thinking about Josie. If her goodbye sounded final last night, her words this morning left no doubt where she stood. "I hope you find what makes you happy."

Josie didn't play games. She said what she meant. She served truth and didn't sugar coat it either.

Stop. Thinking. About. Josie. He picked up the phone and read the message.

"Can't wait to see you! Had a great time in NYC!"

"Sorry. Something came up. Out of town till Sunday."

Charlotte will stay in Charlotte this weekend. He needed quiet to think. He turned his phone off and tossed it onto the twin bed.

CHAPTER 20

The sourdough roll warmed Josie's hand. She pinched off a bit and laid it on the bread saucer, pinched another bit and placed it beside the first one. Was this evening a mistake?

"Are you planning to feed some birds later?"

"What?" She met Milo's smiling eyes across the white tablecloth.

He nodded to her bread plate. "Your bread. Pretty sure you're supposed to eat it yourself."

She laughed. "Sorry. I was thinking about something else." Pay attention to the here and now, not to what might have been or never was.

"I gathered." He dabbed a piece of roll into the olive oil and spices in a dish between them. "You caught me by surprise with your invitation to dinner." He dabbed off the excess oil, then popped the bread into his mouth.

She'd caught herself by surprise, but she needed a decoy conversation for her brothers. Maybe details from tonight could head off the third degree regarding the reception fiasco. Thank goodness Milo was available and willing.

"Oh?"

His statement sounded like the beginning of a serious conversation. She didn't want serious. She wanted a distraction. Was tonight a bad idea? Probably.

She'd hoped with Ches out of the picture, she'd be able to focus on Milo's positive characteristics. His many positive characteristics. But a thought nagged at her conscience. Was she using him? She already planned to pay for dinner. Would that be enough penance?

"A happy surprise, I hope." Change the subject. "Do you know what's good here?" She scanned the menu.

"Josie, you're a really nice person. I enjoyed Latta Plantation. You're a great cook too."

Uh oh. Where was this line of conversation heading? An invitation to his family Christmas? A date for New Year's? You brought this on yourself, Josie. She set aside the menu.

"Your brother's a good guy too. I'm enjoying getting to know him through the *Bible* study." He rotated the olive oil saucer with his index finger and thumb.

"Right. He's mentioned the same."

"I think we both had fun at the folk festival, right?" He shifted in his chair, scratched the back of his neck.

"Right. I enjoyed Latta Plantation." Oh, no. What was happening? She bunched the napkin in her lap.

"So, we have things in common."

"Well, we enjoy history."

"Yes, we do, but..." He sipped his water.

Her breath hitched. "But?" A but at this juncture could be good.

"You can tell me if I'm picking up wrong signals, but..."

What kind of signals was she sending off? She checked herself. A modest but stylish outfit. A polite but reserved hello when he picked her up. Her signals were good. She needed to take control right now. She leaned forward. "Milo, it's true. We do have things in common." Like what besides history?

A waitress settled a bubbling casserole in front of a man seated near them. The scent of tomato sauce and cheese drifted to their table. Milo watched the waitress remove used dishes.

"But just because people have a few like interests, well, they shouldn't base a whole dating relationship on one or two things they have in common."

His gaze swung back to her. "Precisely."

"Well, what exactly are you—"

"Josie, you're smart and attractive, but..."

She'd scream if he didn't quit hesitating. "But what? Milo, just tell me."

"We've had fun together," he moved his spoon a quarter of an inch to match the knife beside his plate. "But I have fun with a lot of people."

Relief winged its way through her heart. She released the strangled napkin and smoothed it over her lap again. "Oh. Does that mean, you...don't feel a spark?"

He met her eyes, a tiny smile hooking the corners of his mouth. "Right."

A frown knitted her brow. "Then why did you agree to tonight?"

"Maybe give it one more shot? Just in case." He shrugged. "Plus, I didn't want to hurt your feelings. Or Ben's. He's always singing your praises."

She balled her fists in her lap. Ben. He would hear from her and hear but good. She considered the man across from her. A lightness swirled alongside relief in her chest. She burst out laughing. "Milo, I think we could be good friends. I'm so glad you agreed to come. And so glad we had this talk. I needed a fun evening."

He smiled a lopsided smile. He seemed less burdened too.

"Then that's what we'll have. A fun evening between friends, right?"

"Right."

He pointed to her bread plate. "Now eat your breadcrumbs and decide what to order."

"Will do."

"OKAY, boys, even with this wool blanket, my toes are beginning to feel numb. I'm going in. When you decide to give up, come watch a sappy movie with me. I'll have popcorn ready too." Heidi hiked her blanket higher around her shoulders and slipped through the sliding glass door.

Ches wiggled his toes. Still good. He sipped the homemade hot chocolate and leaned back into the glider on his uncle's back porch. His breath fogged in front of his face and faded into the black backyard.

"That's a heavy-duty sigh. Ready to talk about it yet?" Jack abandoned his rocking chair and joined Ches. The glider swayed toward the new weight.

"What?"

"Don't treat me like that, Ches." Jack's voice sounded quiet, firm. "If you want to sit out here in silence or sit and talk about how pretty the stars are tonight, fine. I'll follow your lead, but don't act like you don't know what I'm talking about."

He stretched his work boots in front of him. "You get here in the middle of a Friday, a workday, pick at your food like Heidi's a horrible cook, which we know she's not, and work all day helping me organize my woodshop and clear some flower beds. Plus, you eat headache medicine and antacids like candy." He scratched the side of his nose. "You're here for a reason. I'm thinking our time's short, buddy."

Ches jerked his head toward his uncle.

Jack sipped his hot chocolate, not meeting the stare. "I'm not throwing you out. Stay as long as you want, but that bag you brought can't hold too much stuff. I'm figuring you'll leave tomorrow. If you want to talk about what's going on, we got tonight and tomorrow. Or not."

He pointed at the sky dotted with millions of tiny white stars. "Yes, sir. There's the Big Dipper."

Ches pressed his lips together. "I don't want to talk about constellations."

"Okay." Jack rested his mug on his knee.

"Thank you for letting me come."

"You're always welcome here."

Ches nodded. He knew that. He loved it here. He loved Jack and Heidi. He was stupid for staying away just because of his father...

"How do you know if you're heading in the right direction?"

Jack chuckled. "You go for the deep ones, don't you?"

"You're happy, right? I know you are. How did you know years ago you were on a path to being happy?"

"Ches, you know who I am, what's important to me. You already know I pray about—"

"Right, and after you pray, do you get a sign? Do you hear an announcement? How do you know?"

"God answers people in different ways."

"That sounds like such a—"

"Son, let me ask you some questions." Jack slid an arm along the back of the glider. "When you think about your future with the firm, do you see all kinds of possibilities? Do you get excited about the prospects? Do you look forward to how you can contribute to make the firm even better than it is now? Is that what you were talking about, whether or not law is for you?"

Ches pressed his palm against his stomach. "Maybe."

"Or what about Mallory, that's your girlfriend's name, right?

How does she fit into your future? Besides being a ticket to partner?"

Ches stared at the wooden floor slats, counting the cracks.

"Yeah, I've heard talk. Not a very flattering way to regard the person you're supposed to spend the rest of your life with, though."

Ches rubbed his thumb over the Hurricanes emblem decorating his mug, hardened his mouth.

"So what do you think of a future with her? Do you look forward to spending time with her now? Do you think about having a little girl with her eyes? Does she know you're talented with a hammer and saw? What would she think about your carpenter skills?"

"I—"

"Do you race to the phone to share your day with her or tell her something funny you heard on the radio? How do you think she'll handle trials? And, believe me, you'll have trials. How about this? What's her favorite ice cream?"

"Jack, I." Ches gave up and focused on forcing air out of his lungs and sucking it back in, a monumental effort with the weight pressing on his chest. "If I break up with her, I'm done in that firm."

Panic shredded his insides.

"There are other firms, other ways to make a living as a lawyer. Do you want to work with people who play favorites instead of rewarding talent and hard work?"

"I've spent six years working toward being a partner in Padgett, Gibbons, Tyler, and Rose." Despite the frigid fall air, sweat broke out on his upper lip.

"Better six than thirty-six. Realizing you're in the wrong place, I mean." Jack rubbed his chin. "Ches, I just gave you what some call Christian counsel. I pray for you every day, prayed hard since you've been here. I want God's best for you." He sipped his hot chocolate. "I've given you a lot of questions to think about, and while you're thinking, know this. You are the son I never had."

Jack's voice thickened. He cleared his throat. "Let me give you something else. Your dad couldn't get into law school."

Ches whipped his gaze to Jack.

"He tried several times. Instead of acknowledging maybe law wasn't God's path for him—" Jack shrugged—"he turned bitter. Ended up with an MBA and made a pretty nice living for himself in business. When you came along, he put all his deferred hopes on you. You were his revenge on the gods that ruined his chances in law. He lives through your pursuits. Pushed you to be what he couldn't." He shifted in the seat.

"Think about this question. Are you going to live his life for the rest of yours, or are you going to live the one you were meant to live?"

Which one was he meant to live? The one he'd spent his life preparing for or what? His stomach knotted. Thinking of something else felt like jumping off a cliff. "You make it sound so easy."

"Son, we live in a fallen world. Nothing worthwhile is easy, but bank on this." Jack reached over and clutched his shoulder. "I will help you any way I can."

Ches set the mug on the floor and covered his face with his hands. Is this what it felt like to die? Heart racing. Lungs scrambling for air. His gut burned like the fire Jack lit in the fireplace before dinner.

Jack spread his hand in the center of Ches's back. "God in Heaven, Ches needs peace and wisdom and discernment. Open his eyes to Your path for him. Give him the courage to step onto it."

The glider swayed as Jack rose. Two rough hands encircled his head and then, a kiss. "I love you, Ches."

He squeezed his eyes as tight as he could, banking the tears determined to leak.

CHAPTER 21

*J*osie stuck the stamp in the corner of the last Christmas card. Fifty cards in one afternoon equaled a good accomplishment, right? One hundred and fifty more to go and she'd have fulfilled the promise to send out the cards in her mom's stead. She rolled her shoulders and stretched her arms above her head.

Snack time. Ice cream?

Gliding into the kitchen, she heard the doorbell peal. Surprise halted her mid-step. Had she forgotten a Sunday commitment? Redirecting to the front door, she noted a woman's figure through the beveled glass, a head with light blonde hair. Her stomach clenched.

She clutched the doorknob for an extra moment, resisting her curiosity before facing Ches's mother.

"Mrs. Windham."

"Joselyn," she stepped over the threshold without preamble. "I've come for my son."

Josie frowned. "Ches isn't here."

Alicia slackened her posture. "Well, there's a positive." She repositioned her purse, hiding antique brass buttons on her jacket. "Tell me where he is."

"I have no idea where he is. Call his girlfriend."

Mrs. Windham's mouth tightened. She averted her gaze to survey the family room, raking her eyes over the boxes of Christmas cards strewn on the couch, a crocheted afghan bunched on the recliner.

Josie leaned back against the door. Mallory didn't know either. Interesting. Should she offer the woman something to drink, a seat in the living room? Her mom would, even after Thursday's pointed conversation.

Conversation? More like a lecture.

"Mrs. Windham, would you like a cup of tea?"

"Please don't play the perfect hostess with me. I'm not here on a social call."

"I'm not playing. My mom taught me how to treat guests."

Alicia narrowed her eyes. "Is that a veiled dig regarding Thursday night? Maybe your mother should have taught you how to thank a hostess before leaving in a huff."

She jerked away from the door, lifting her chin. "She taught me to make guests feel loved and interesting and worthy."

"I gave a lovely reception with delicious food and beautiful decorations. If you can't appreciate—"

"From the moment I arrived—as an invited guest, I might add— you and your husband belittled my beverage choice and education path, embarrassed me with your not-so-subtle references to Mallory, and attacked me with your neon hands-off signs around your son."

Mrs. Windham raised her chin. "So, you do remember what I told you about Ches and Mallory. They will be married. And you're right. He is my son, and I know what's best for him."

"Oh, really. Do you know how talented a carpenter he is? Do you know—"

"A carpenter?" She grimaced. "He's a talented lawyer. He

has a sparkling future." She tossed her head to reposition her hair. "I'm not talking about this with you. It's none of your business."

"You're the one who came to my house. You're making—"

A slap stung her cheek, the force rattling her head. Shock held her in place for an instant. Her injured pride ached for revenge. She grabbed the seam of her sweatpants to keep her hand from connecting with Alicia's face. In all the years of skirmishing with her older brothers, she gave as much as she got. Heart pounding, she held firm this time.

Tears of hurt, shame, and frustration gathered, ready to show her vulnerability. Do not cry in front of this woman. Tingles skipped over her cheek. Would she have a bruise? She blinked and persevered in measured tones. "You say you know your son. Have you noticed the sadness shadowing his eyes?"

"I don't have to listen to this from you of all people."

"Another insult, I believe." She reached for the door. "And I agree. You can leave." Was she really throwing Alicia Windham out of her house?

The older woman hesitated at the threshold, her hands strangling the purse straps. "You expect me to believe you haven't seen Ches since Thursday night?"

"I haven't seen him since Friday morning."

Alicia's eyes widened, and all the perfectly applied makeup couldn't disguise the sneer marking her face. "Of course, I should have—"

"Shame on you, Mrs. Windham." Despite Josie's attempt at control, her voice rose. Heat rose to the tips of her ears. She checked herself. "He came to my office." She gestured to the doorway.

For a split second, before the older woman stalked through the doorway, Josie recognized a faint resemblance to her son, the same sadness hovering over her eyes.

Josie closed the door and turned the deadbolt. She slumped

against it, taking stock. Despite Alicia's verbal digs and physical abuse, Josie wasn't bleeding or nursing broken bones. Her heart still beat a ragged rhythm, but she wasn't crying, didn't even feel like crying. She didn't feel anything except relief for the woman's exit...and sorrow for Ches. If that scene illustrated his childhood...

A longing for her own mother seized her insides with a fierce grip. Now, tears popped in the corner of her eyes. She missed her mom. And her dad. She'd have to pull it together, or she'd be a mess when Skype time came tonight.

Hmm. A thought teased her. She glanced through the archway at the kitchen clock. Not quite time to assemble the homemade rolls for the second rising. She sniffed and smelled a faint scent of the crockpot just beginning to permeate the house. Why couldn't she? Of course, she could. She was grown, as they say. She didn't have to wait for her brothers. They could call at the regular time, but she missed her mother now.

She raced to her bedroom and powered up her laptop. Her feelings had turned a one-eighty. Anticipation thrashed sorrow. Her pulse switched to a happier rhythm as she banished all the Windhams to the back of her mind. She clicked the correct icons and waited for her mother's lovely face to fill the screen.

THE OVERNIGHT BAG thunked on the floor of Ches's car, echoing what he felt like inside. But he'd had Sunday breakfast and lunch with his aunt and uncle. It was time to go back to his real life.

Heidi grabbed him and squeezed. "I'm so glad you came, Ches. Please come back. I have tons more recipes to cook for you."

Ches chuckled. "I'll have to up my workout this week just to stay in my clothes. Wait. That didn't sound right. You're gonna make me gain weight."

Heidi rewarded him with a laugh and a kiss on his cheek.

"She'll try for sure." Jack patted his flat stomach.

"You still look Army strong."Ches offered his hand, but Jack bear-hugged him too.

His uncle spoke into his ear. "Our door is always open. The phone is always on. We'll help you. Anytime."

Warmth constricted his heart, spread throughout his body. "I know."

"Don't be a stranger."

Ches fixed his eyes on Jack's. "I won't. Not anymore."

"I like the sound of that."

"Me too." Heidi rubbed his upper arm and patted it one last time. "I'm sure you'll be busy at Christmas, but if you have time, swing by. I'll have the rest of my cookies baked by then."

"More than the six kinds we sampled this weekend?"

"She's halfway to her twelve different batches." Jack slipped an arm around his wife's waist.

"Let me know another favorite, Ches. I'll add a batch of those too."

Charlotte was a half-hour away, but it felt like another world. In fact, it was another world, and he was a different man there. Trepidation tapped on his shoulder. He didn't want to go back. He wanted to stay with these decent, loving people and continue licking his wounds, talking with his uncle.

He climbed in the driver's seat, shut the door, and rolled down the window.

Jack rested crossed arms on the window track. "Listen to me. Nothing has been done that can't be undone. People change directions all the time. You're young and smart. We'll be praying for discernment for you. And for courage."

Ches's eyes flew to his uncle's. "Courage?"

Jack nodded.

Yeah. Courage. Sounded right.

"I'll see you soon." Ches meant that. He wouldn't let his

father dictate his visits with Jack anymore. What about every-thing else in his life? Would he continue to let his father dictate the rest of his life?

Courage. Exactly the thing he'd need if he decided to live his own life.

He pushed against his stomach as he headed his car for Charlotte.

JOSIE RAISED her face into the hot water and let the pouring shower spray pound her skin. Her throat ached with unshed tears, but she refused to go to school in the morning with swollen eyes again. If she stayed under the water for five more minutes, then dried her hair for a few more, it'd be bedtime. She could cross this day off her calendar if she was one of those people who crossed days off.

She didn't ex days—too much like wishing your life away—but this day would be one to mark through. Definitely.

Thank goodness for the call to her mom without the brothers in tow. Talking with her, not about manners-challenged, scary Mrs. Windham, or how Josie had completely fallen for the wrong man again, just talking about her mom's projects and Christmas cards and cookie recipes had been a balm to her spirit.

Unfortunately, after the hang-up, depression hit hard. She missed her parents. She wanted them home for Christmas. This would be the first one without them. Being almost twenty-seven didn't matter at Christmas. She wanted to lay her head on her mom's shoulder and not worry about swollen eyelids because her mom could fix them. She could fix all of it.

She turned off the water and pushed a towel into her eyes.

Her brothers' banter had helped some, but they, picking up on her melancholy vibes perhaps, had tempered their usual rowdiness and stayed longer, helping with stamps and return address labels.

She also thanked God for the number blocking function on her cell. Now she wouldn't torture herself listening for texts or calls. She could concentrate on other things.

Oh, joy.

CHAPTER 22

The jangling phone pierced the quiet of the office. "Josie Daniels. May I help you?"

"I certainly hope so."

She sighed into the receiver. "B.J., why are you calling me at work?"

"I was afraid you wouldn't answer my call on your cell, and the receptionist said you have office hours now."

Smart. She wouldn't have answered. "Office hours are for students." She colored in the D on her desk calendar.

"Do you have a student now?"

"No, but—"

"Great. I just have a couple of questions."

"This is also planning time."

"It's final exam week. All planning's been done."

She scowled. "What do you know? I'm grading papers."

"I won't keep you. I promise. I just wanted to follow up on the reception."

She lowered her eyelids wanting to shut out that night for good. "This isn't—"

"Please, you can help fill in some blanks."

B.J. saying, please? "I don't understand how?"

"Call me curious."

"I call you nosey."

He grunted. "I heard you left early."

Her pulse picked up speed. How did he hear that? How was that newsworthy? "It was a floating kind of thing. A reception. Not a sit-down dinner."

"Uh-huh. I heard Ches left early too."

She switched the phone to her other ear. "B.J., why is this news?"

"Mallory has been seen out on the town, alone. That hasn't happened since they started dating. Just wondering why."

"Are you writing for the gossip column now? Not enough crime to keep you busy?"

"When I write a story, I get all the angles."

Angles that somehow included her. "Well, I can't help you with any of the angles. I went. I came home." She knocked on her office door. "Someone's knocking on my door." Someone in the form of herself. "I have to go."

"For real? That's the oldest trick in the book, Josie."

"Bye, B.J."

Was it true? Was Mallory enjoying Charlotte's nightlife by herself? Could that mean...? Stop. It means what it means to them, but it doesn't mean anything to anyone else.

Ches could stop seeing Mallory and still not be free. Not be free to be happy or live his own life. The piano books. Had he looked at them yet? Would he feel free enough to play the music?

The feelings bouncing between his parents and Ches at the reception skewed toward ice rather than warm and cozy. More like strained and distant. If Ches broke up with Mallory, his mother, for sure, would disapprove.

Would she blame me? Pay me another visit?

Unfortunately, Ches followed his parents' requests. More like orders. He'd rarely visited Jack whom he clearly loved because his dad didn't approve.

No, breaking up with Mallory would not be the path for Ches.

She shook her head.

Enough thinking about Ches. She glanced at the stack of exams spread like a fan on her desk. Her heart slipped down near her lap. Twenty-three more exams to grade before tomorrow.

She'd stop on the way home for frozen yogurt.

With lots of chocolate chips.

THREE. Four. Ches counted the rings, began composing his message when Mallory answered on the sixth ring.

"Thinking I was gonna have to leave a voice mail."

"And I thought I would've heard from you last night. After you got home."

Calling her would have been the boyfriend-thing to do, but last night he didn't feel like doing the boyfriend thing. Didn't feel like it most of the time lately. Last night he wanted to process the conversations with Jack. He wanted to regroup and be ready for the week. He wanted to pray.

Tonight, he needed to see Mallory. To talk about stuff. To talk about the future. Their future. If he didn't feel a connection with her, maybe she didn't either.

"Yeah. I had a lot of catching up to do."

"No time even for a text?"

"I said, I was really busy."

"And yet, not too busy to text someone else that you were back to the real world."

His gut clenched. "What do you mean?"

"Well, let me read it so I'm exactly right. Here we go.

"Thanks for the weekend. I needed it. Now back to the real world." Want to explain?"

He stifled a groan. Mallory got the text meant for Jack. He raked his hand through his hair. "I—"

"And don't lie. I deserve the truth."

"I've never lied to you." As the words left his mouth, a conversation with Jack about lying by omission crossed his brain. He closed his eyes. "I visited with my uncle and aunt near Gastonia. That's it."

"But you felt you needed to get away from the real world? I guess I'm included in the real world?"

Did her full lips have a smirk or a pout? Lately, she sported either one or the other, certainly not an honest, open smile like—He rubbed his forehead. Stop going there. "I was calling about dinner. Do you feel like Italian tonight?"

"I'm busy tonight."

Going to make this tough, huh? He gritted his teeth and pushed ahead. "I understand. I'm free tomorrow if you are, but the rest of the week—"

A sigh came over the phone. "Ches, what's going on with you? You've been distant for weeks. I thought we were simpatico, you know. I thought we enjoyed being together."

He worked his jaw. "You're right. I haven't been myself lately." Maybe he'd been his truer self. "Let's talk it out, okay? When's good?"

Seconds ticked by. "I can make tonight work."

THE CARDBOARD CUP of frozen yogurt numbed her hand. Josie secured a napkin around the cup and switched hands.

"Mmm. This is so good. Aren't you glad I horned my way into your self-pity session?" Lucy licked the purple plastic spoon.

"Remind me why I agreed to share my yogurt time? Especially since you're bent on irritating me."

"Because you bailed on me last Friday. Because you know I love you. Because you want to tell me why you were so distracted all day. Because you want to hear straight answers."

"I don't remember asking any questions. I pretty much understand what's going on."

"Then you need a sounding board."

"You just want to hear the gory details."

Lucy's eyes widened. "Are there gory details?"

Josie sighed. "No. It's just a lot going on. I've got fifty million essays to grade. B.J. is being a pest. I miss my parents." She smoothed annoying strands away from her face.

"First off, fifty million? You have less than fifty. You can do it. Second, is B.J. trying to get back together?"

"Absolutely not. He's got some story going on about a law firm, Ches's firm. He keeps pumping me for information."

"He's a crime reporter, right?"

"Yeah, he's been like a dog with a juicy bone all fall. At first, I thought he was barking up the wrong tree." She hesitated, but Lucy ignored her pathetic attempt at humor. "But he keeps asking questions. Ches even said—"

"You don't think Ches..."

"No way. He may be Mr. Hot Shot Lawyer, but he's not a criminal."

"White-collar criminals wear nice suits."

"Lucy."

"I'm just sayin'."

"Ches is a nice guy."

"He's a nice guy who led you on."

"He did not lead me on. I led myself down the path to disaster. I knew he was dating someone. I knew there was no chance for anything more than training sessions and library meetings. That's what makes me so angry about this whole mess.

"I walked in with my eyes wide open. I thought I could handle it. Be friends with him and not expect or wish for anything more. I should have prayed for direction and protection. I thought I was smarter after the B.J. debacle." She took a long breath. "Seeing myself as a weak cliché is hard to take."

"You're not weak or a cliché either."

"Falling for the guy you can't have, the good-looking guy who has a girlfriend and simply wants to help a girl run is a cliché. A pathetic cliché."

"I'm glad you can admit it."

"You're agreeing I'm a cliché now?" She crunched an almond sliver.

"No. Agreeing that you've fallen in love with him."

She squirmed under Lucy's scrutiny. "I—"

"Yes, you did."

Josie closed her eyes. True. She was in love with Ches. That's why her breath caught every time she saw him. That's why she savored every library meeting, every Saturday morning run, every Sunday night text. Lucy detected her true feelings. Were they obvious to him? To his mom? She gritted her teeth.

"What else is going on?"

"What do you mean?" Josie dug her green spoon into the treat, scored chocolate chips and a mango bit covered in cappuccino yogurt.

"You're not telling me something. Come on. What is it?"

"His mom dropped by yesterday afternoon."

Lucy leaned forward. "She came to your house. Are you kidding me?"

"She was looking for Ches."

"And she thought you'd know?" Lucy raised an eyebrow. "Hmm."

"Here's something else. Seems Mallory didn't know either."

"Oh." Surprise rounded Lucy's mouth.

"Don't worry. I'm not speculating on that news. I'm working hard to climb out of the pit I created for myself."

Her tongue longed to spill the rest of the encounter with Ches' mom. What would Lucy say if she mentioned the slap? She licked her lips, tasting the words, imagining their sweet release.

No. She clamped her mouth on the empty spoon. No need to rehash that humiliation too. Forget about it and move on.

Lucy arched her brow. "You know, my cousin's next-door neighbor has been seeing someone she met online for several months now. Sounds serious. Have you—"

"Did you not hear me? I'm climbing out." She shook her head. "Not ready to fall in again. Okay?"

"I know it's too soon but meeting new people could be a good distraction. Lots of people need dates for Christmas parties. You'd get to dress up."

"I have plenty to distract me. Frankly, I don't know if I'll ever be ready for online dating."

"Right. I hear ya, but I know at least five people who—"

"Lucy. Not interested."

"Got it." Lucy tossed a wadded napkin into her bowl and covered Josie's hand with hers. "Are you going to be okay, sweetie? I've been teasing you, but you know I love you. I don't like seeing you hurt."

"I know. I'm good." Or she would be at least. "I have fifty million essays to keep my attention tonight."

HALF THE ANGEL hair remained on Ches's plate. Going with a light choice instead of steak hadn't helped settle his churning stomach. The silent conversation searing his brain added fuel to the usual gastro-discomfort and took a back seat to Mallory's chatter. Grateful that nods and half-hearted smiles had sufficed for his end of the table talk, he sipped some water, readying himself for the topic he needed to broach.

"Still working on that or do you want a box?" Their waitress smiled, inclining her head to his pesto-covered noodles.

"I'm finished. No box. Thank you." Relieved to be rid of the food, he slid the plate toward her.

"And you, ma'am?"

Mallory dabbed the corner of her mouth with her napkin. "Yes. Take it away. We'd like the raspberry tart. With a scoop of vanilla gelato."

He cleared his throat. "We need to talk."

She tilted her head. "About syncing our calendars with all the Christmas events?"

He dragged his palm over his jaw. "Not exactly."

A hard look flashed before she lowered her lids. Two bright spots highlighted her cheekbones. "What exactly do you mean, Ches?"

"Mallory." He took a breath. "I've been going through some stuff."

"What kind of stuff? What's wrong?"

He studied the tablecloth. Where to start?

She positioned her chair closer to the table and leaned in. "You've been acting weird for weeks, all moody and disengaged. I gave you some slack because law can be relentless, exactly why I chose a different route after law school."

"I know I've been distant for a while, but it's not just because of work."

She locked eyes with him. Some emotions fleeted across her face. Hurt? Sadness?

Guilt pinged in his gut. The phantom emotion vanished with her narrowing eyes.

"Oh." She chewed the side of her cheek. "This is a breakup dinner?"

He took a breath. "You and I—"

"Because think for a minute. We're right in the middle of the holiday party season. I've already RSVP'd for us." She swished a hank of hair behind her shoulder. "No shows won't be a good look, especially at the firm's party. My grandfather will be expecting us."

Was that a threat? A reminder that she could help him attain the goal of a partner. An ache thumped at his temple.

"It won't look good for the firm or my gallery. People love a love story, especially at Christmas. Think about this. We're two weeks away from Christmas and three weeks from New Year's Eve, the biggest party in Charlotte. I've already bought my dress and shoes."

"Mallory."

"Look. I've noticed your moodiness. I gave you passes when you were aloof when you canceled or shortened dates. I hoped it was only stress from the job. You're a decent guy. Please, let's—"

"You really want to be with someone who—"

"Ches." She pressed her lips together for a moment. "Let's finish the next few weeks together. We'll go with our eyes open, like a business arrangement." She fiddled with her wine glass. "Tamber Miller has already whispered questions in her gossip column about why I partied with the girls last Saturday night."

The waitress set the dessert plate between them along with clean spoons.

"Why *did* you go out Saturday night?"

She lifted a shoulder that peeked out of a black sleeve. "I went out to have fun, to be with friends, enjoy people who wanted to be with me. I had done the sitting-at-home thing, hoping you'd change your mind on Friday night. Do you blame me for wanting something different on Saturday?"

He deserved that. And more in all honesty. "Did you think I'd—"

"I didn't know what to think." She jutted her chin toward

him. "We've been dating for months, happily so I might add, until this fall. And then you disappear last weekend without any kind of heads up. So I went out to have some fun. No problem." She made a face. "But Tamber Miller had a field day with the news."

Guilt crept over his shoulder, took up residence. For years, he'd been grasping the partner plan with a death grip. Had been mostly content until a possibility of something different wafted into his mind. New dreams germinated. He'd grown distant and left her hanging several times as options that didn't include the law firm filled his fantasies. Mallory and he had entered their relationship with like minds. He'd been the one to doubt the understanding, to change the playing field. He owed it to her, to be honest.

Mallory dragged a spoon through the gelato and sliced off the tip of the raspberry triangle. She slid the dessert plate toward him, shaking her head. "I don't want any of this."

Something they could agree on. He pushed the plate aside.

"You're under a lot of stress. Responsibilities at the firm are heating up. The holidays. Your parents are in town. I understand.

"But here's the other thing. I've been wooing Bo Rochester for eighteen months. He's had works in New York, Pittsburgh, and Atlanta. Having him show in my gallery would be a huge coup for me. He's going to be at the New Year's Eve bash downtown.

"Remember when we met him last summer? He liked you. You'd help me out a lot if we could schmooze with him because AdVo down in Third Ward is after him too."

Nothing. He felt nothing except a desire to finish this conversation and leave. He rolled his fork over, tines pointed down. "Listen."

"Please, Ches." She softened her eyes and smiled a tentative smile. "Let's table this conversation until after the holidays. Let's meet our obligations, save the firm bad press, and maybe score one of the hottest artists in his generation for my gallery."

Was this plea for real? He rolled the fork back to the original position with one hand and pushed against his midsection with the other. The raspberry tart would have to wait until another time, preferably when thoughts of food didn't accompany stomach pain.

"I won't add to your stress. We'll just attend some parties together. Help me out. Please?"

He worked his jaw. He hadn't expected this turn in the conversation.

As much as he hated continuing the farce, he didn't want to humiliate her with a breakup in the middle of what society called the happiest time of the year. This mess wasn't her fault. She hadn't changed in the past few months, but he had. He'd begun to listen to... What? His stressed-out stomach? His talents and interests? His uncle's so-called Christian counsel? All of the above?

Okay, Mallory. Fine, he'd do what he could to help her out, but come January...

Play music you enjoy.

Exactly what I plan to do, Josie.

CHAPTER 23

The heavy ball nestled in the palm of Josie's left hand. She wiggled her fingers in the grip holes. A steady rhythm resembling happiness beat in her heart. She took a deep breath.

Happiness felt good.

"If you roll another strike, Heath will give you one hundred dollars."

Heath sputtered his cold beverage and wiped his mouth with his sleeve. "Speak for yourself, bro."

"Thanks a lot, Sam, for trying to ruin my mojo." She lowered the ball in front of her stomach. "Just to let you know, it won't work."

"Put your money where your big mouth is. You've rolled three strikes in a row. Roll another one and," Sam looked at his brothers, "we'll give you one hundred smackeroos. Waddaya say, boys?"

Heath cocked his head. "Do you even have twenty dollars in your pocket, Sam?"

"I can pay my share." Sam moved closer to Josie. "You

must've been practicing on the sly. I didn't think you'd bowled since, maybe one of our birthday parties. Keeping secrets?"

Josie smirked. "Wouldn't you like to know?" She set the ball back into the tray to rest her arms.

Heath clasped his hands high above his head, turned his neck left then right. "And why'd you get to come to boys' birthday parties anyway?"

"You could've come to mine."

Sam pretended to huff. "Do I look like I wanted to go to a Cinderella birthday party?"

"Really want me to answer that question?" She flexed her fingers.

Ben raised his palm to stop the bickering. "Go ahead. Show us how to do it, Jo Jo."

"Wait."Heath leaned back from the scoreboard. "I've heard only one side. What do we get if she misses?"

"You get a home-cooked meal every Sunday night till Mom and Dad come home." Josie bent over the ball tray and retrieved her lucky ball.

"I'll take that deal." Ben chomped on a chip dripping with melted cheese.

"Wait a minute. She already cooks, and we didn't—"

"I did, and I'm the oldest. Roll the ball, Josie girl."

She moved near the foul line and raised the ball again, her eyes focused on the middle pin. How in the world had she rolled three strikes? Crazy. Did imagining B. J. or Mallory or Mrs. Windham's faces on the pins help? She smiled. Certainly didn't hurt. Whatever worked, and tonight was exactly what she needed.

Who cared if most other people in Charlotte were attending swanky parties to welcome in the New Year? Being in a bowling alley with her brothers suited her to a T. She squinted at the center pin. She swung the ball backward as she stepped to the foul line, released it as her toe stopped short of the line. The ball rolled straight in the center of the lane from the moment it left her fingertips. She watched until it was three-quarters home and then turned her back to it. She listened for the crash, her eyes glued to her brothers' reaction.

She laughed out loud as they pounced on her with hugs and high fives.

Midnight would have nothing on her four-stroke party.

THE BURNING in Ches's gut increased ten-fold since they entered the ballroom a half-hour ago. He'd chewed tablets just before picking up Mallory. Not time for another dose. He set his drink on a waiter's tray, not trusting himself to keep it upright or intact. Could he really squeeze hard enough to shatter a ten-ounce glass? Would he find out tonight?

He glanced at his watch. With the ramping pain, he'd never make it to midnight. He shoved out a steady stream of air, imagining the pain leaving his body at the same time.

Nope. It didn't really work.

A waitress working the crowd with a tray of hors d'oeuvres glided past him. The smell of prosciutto-wrapped scallops nearly made him retch. A sweatdrop trailed down the middle of his back.

He sucked in another breath through clamped teeth and held it as a phantom dagger lacerated his insides. Managing to stay vertical, he scanned the room. Where was she?

Number one priority. Find Mallory and leave before he screamed in front of Charlotte's most beautiful movers and shakers. He wiped the moisture from his upper lip with the back of his hand.

A familiar laugh indicated her location. She entertained a group of two men and a woman. Familiar faces, but their names? Who cared if they were the mayor or the owner of the Panthers.

He threaded through the crowd of sequins and bow ties. He clutched her elbow.

"Oh, you've found us." Her smile turned up the corners of her lips but didn't light her eyes. They flashed like cold rocks.

He leaned close to her ear, steeling himself against the onslaught of her perfume. "I need to leave."

She stiffened. "Excuse us, please." She offered her back to the group and hard eyes to Ches."What do you mean, need to leave? Bo Rochester isn't here yet."

He wiped his palm across his mouth. "I mean if I don't leave right now, I'm going to scream bloody murder and not care who hears it or how it's written up in tomorrow's paper."

"You don't have to be—" Mallory stepped sideways as Ches lurched forward.

Pain seared his stomach and doubled him over. Ches grabbed the arm of a passing waiter for support, knocking his empty tray to the floor. He pinned his gaze on the waiter. "Get me to the lobby." Sucking in streaks of air, he ground out the words.

The fresher air in the lobby cooled his sweat-drenched face.

"What do you need, Ches?" She held her arms in rigid lines by her side.

Pain sucked every other thought from his brain. He ran his tongue over his lips, pushed out more air. "I need to get to the ER."

"Now? Before midnight?"

"Sorry. Didn't check my watch."

"I'm sorry. I'm not good with medical stuff."

He appealed to the waiter whose arm he still grasped. "Ambulance, please." He shook his head. "I can't drive."

"Are you serious, Ches? What about an Alka-Seltzer or something first?" She glanced back at the doors they'd just exited.

He shook his head. "Sorry I can't—" He braced himself as jagged pain racked his insides. "Go enjoy the rest of the party."

The waiter led him to an alcove with a bench. "I'll get an ambulance. Hang tight, sir."

Cradling his mid-section with one forearm, Ches retrieved his phone from his inside pocket with the other hand and punched redial. Mallory followed behind but divided her attention between him and the doors to the ballroom.

Jack answered on the first ring. "Happy New Year!"

"Ah, Jack."

"What's wrong? You don't sound like yourself."

He forced out another shaky breath. Nausea gripped him. "Meet me at Presbyterian?"

"On my way."

ENTERING the kitchen after her mid-morning shower, Josie wrinkled her nose at the pungent aroma of black-eyed peas cooking in the crockpot. Never her favorite, the peas nonetheless made an appearance on the traditional New Year's table, along with some sort of leafy green vegetable and a pork dish to bring good luck and money in the months ahead. The brothers had voted for barbecued pork chops this year. Lunch preparations would commence as soon as she had more coffee and completed the daily crossword puzzle.

A picture on the front page of the style section caught her eye before she found the crossword. Scenes from Charlotte's last night of the year filled most of the page with few captions. Last night pictures already? Working on New Year's Eve—rough assignment. Not able to make her hands turn directly to the puzzle section, she scanned every picture for a sight of Ches.

Nothing.

Her eyes revisited the snapshots searching for Mallory. Still nothing. Maybe they attended an out-of-town party.

Maybe it doesn't matter.

For related stories, see page 7C.

Despite her admonition to herself to leave it alone, she flipped to 7C and skimmed the articles. Her eyes seized his name. Jackpot. Flutters rose in her chest.

Golden couple Mallory Padgett and Ches Windham left before they could welcome in the New Year with other Grand Ballroom partiers. Wondering minds want to know why? Could this signal the merger of Padgett and Windham we've all been waiting for? Or could the early departure validate swirling rumors that trouble is brewing at Padgett, Gibbons, Tyler, & Rose?

Tamber Miller. Pot stirrer extraordinaire. Rumors about the firm? Had she teamed up with B.J. now?

Charlotte people are breathless to solve the mystery, Mallory! Tweet me to set up an interview soon!

Ending the article with a call to tweet her? Josie grimaced. Tamber must be frustrated to put out an appeal in the paper. If B.J. had been covering the Padgett-Windham story, he'd have known why they left early and where they went. The grimace transformed into a smile.

Complimenting B.J.? Good for you, Joselyn. You're growing up. You've moved on.

She nodded to herself. B.J. was definitely a good reporter. Just not a good boyfriend.

Before turning to the crossword puzzle, she glanced back at the pictures on the front page. Sometime in the near future, all indications pointed to an engagement announcement, a merger of Padgett and Windham.

She drew in a long breath and held it. I can be ready for it.

I will be ready for it.

Be happy, Ches.

CHAPTER 24

*D*rops of medicine or fluids or both dripped down the clear IV tube into Ches's arm. Admitted to the hospital on New Year's Day. Foreshadowing of the next twelve months perhaps? Wonderful. He stifled a groan so as not to disturb Jack and Heidi asleep in two reclining chairs.

Jack and Heidi. They'd arrived minutes after the ER staff had wheeled him into a room, concern tinting their smiles. They insisted on staying. Heidi proved her point, wielding a satchel she'd packed with overnight items. Jack sealed the deal by asking the nurse for an extra chair and two blankets.

Thank goodness for them. Last night had been one roller coaster ride of pain, humiliation, and panic. Seeing their faces, knowing they prayed for him, loved him...

How many times had a nurse or an orderly addressed them as his parents? His parents. He smirked to himself. Celebrating in the Bahamas? No, that was Thanksgiving. The week after Christmas found them in Denver for a week of skiing before ringing in the New Year.

Thankfully, Jack had resisted calling them. What could they do besides chastise him for not staying healthy? He didn't want to deal with this ulcer or whatever it was as well as his parents.

A knock sounded just before the door opened to admit a doctor. Jack and Heidi woke and stood, Heidi covering a yawn. Jack massaged his lower back.

"Good morning, Lloyd."

"Call me Ches." He moved his arm and felt the twinge of the IV needle.

"Ches." The doctor nodded. "How are you feeling today?"

"I've been better. Last night was worse." He shifted in the bed to sit up straighter. He didn't like the height disadvantage.

The man nodded, scanning the first page of the chart. "You were admitted last night—or this morning I should say—experiencing severe abdominal pain and..." The doctor checked the notes. "Coffee ground emesis."

Ches winced remembering Mallory's scream when she saw the black vomit splatter on her stilettos just as EMT workers entered the hotel lobby last night. Not exactly a great picture for a girlfriend. To be honest, the sight had terrified him too.

Remember to reimburse her for the shoes.

"The admitting doctor noted extreme pallor as well."

"It *is* winter. I haven't been working on my tan."

The doctor by-passed the weak attempt at humor. "Pale skin can be evidence of anemia." He tapped his pen on the top of the chart. "We've got you stabilized, so this is what we're going to do. A gastroenterologist will come in for a consultation soon. We'll schedule an endoscopy to take a look at what's going on in your stomach. It's probably a bleeding ulcer. If it is, we can cauterize the ulcer right then. We'll also do a biopsy."

"A biopsy?" Heidi's eyes rounded. "I thought biopsies were for—"

"Yes, ma'am, but ulcers are also caused by bacteria. We'll check for that with the scope. We'll keep you on fluids today. Any questions?" The doctor closed the chart.

"When can I go home?"

"If all goes according to this plan, probably tomorrow. We'll see." He tucked the chart under his arm.

Jack moved toward him extending his hand. "Thank you, doctor." He turned to Ches, arching his back. "Well, it's good to know something, to have a plan."

"Now that we have a plan, why don't you two take a break? You're probably starving for breakfast. Take Heidi out for a fancy brunch."

"Trying to get rid—"

Both men turned toward Heidi's gasp. "Nothing." She waved her hand in front of her. "I just remembered the crockpot full of black-eyed peas."

Ches released his groan this time."One saving grace of all this. I don't have to eat black-eyed peas today. Doctor's orders. A liquid diet, remember?"

Jack chuckled. "Yeah. Looks like you might need some New Year good luck, though."

"Not luck. Prayers." Heidi sat on the edge of the bed and gathered his hand into hers. The gesture, unusual for their relationship, communicated love and family and healing. He turned his hand over to clutch his aunt's.

"Now we know what's going on…" Jack took a breath. "Let's call your parents."

"Jack."

"They need to know."

"Jack's right, Ches. They'll be upset if you wait to tell them."

He cocked his head at his aunt. "You have to know that's false, Heidi. They're at the front end of a ski vacation in the Rocky Mountains. Anyway, honestly? I don't feel like dealing with them." He swiped his palm over his face. "I feel like a truck ran over me or something. I just want to lie here and…just lie here. Do nothing. Not even think." He closed his eyes. The vomiting scene repeated in his mind. Heard Mallory's dry heaves. Mortification swelled again.

"Got it. Anybody else? I can make the calls." Jack raised his leg behind him and rotated his ankle.

Ches stared at the ceiling. "The office. It's closed today, but it sounds like I may not get in tomorrow."

"Of course not. For Heaven's sake, Ches. You *may* be released tomorrow. You might not make it in for a couple of days." Heidi tugged at the sheet on his chest.

Jack typed into his phone with one finger. "Who else?"

Ches shrugged.

Jack scrubbed his whiskered chin. "Mallory?"

"Not exactly the hospital kind, Jack." He shook his head. "I'll text her later."

Jack glanced at Ches with a questioning look then down at his phone. "Is that it? Anybody else? Your friend, Josie, might appreciate—"

His heart seized at her name. "No." He shook his head. "Nobody else."

THE LADLE DRIPPED pea juice onto the blue and white tablecloth. "Great. A black-eyed pea stain on mom's tablecloth." Josie glowered at Heath as he added peas to his plate.

Another negative mark on this beginning of the year. A broken water glass, resulting in a sliced ring finger. A stopped-up drain, which was an easy fix, but still. Scorched Brussels sprouts, her new take on the leafy green vegetable portion of the traditional meal. Her brothers, however, saw the stove mishap as a gift from God and munched on raw, baby carrots instead.

"It'll wash out."

"You mean I'll wash it out."

"A tad touchy, Josie girl." Heath studied her from across the table.

"Hey, where's the bowl of tomatoes and vinegar and sugar and stuff that goes on top? You can't make me eat these peas without that tomato stuff." Sam scanned the table then pointed a questioning gaze at his sister.

"I'm not making you do anything except clean up. Don't eat peas. Don't have good luck or earn any money this year. I don't care. It's as simple as that." She crossed her arms. "The tomatoes are in the fridge. I forgot to set out the dish." She stared at Sam until he ambled to the refrigerator.

"Forgetful and irritable this morning. You must have had a late night." Ben wiped a streak of barbecue sauce from the corner of his mouth.

"Very funny. You know exactly when I got home." She rested her chin in her hand. The food didn't entice her one bit.

"Who knows? You could have had a January rendezvous after you kicked your brothers to the curb." Heath tossed Ben a roll. It sailed right by her nose.

"Cut it out, boys." But they were right. Her attitude bordered on dreadful this morning. Her brothers livened the table, teasing, playing, enjoying the meal. She had much to be thankful for, no right to let the heaviness suffocating her ruin time with them.

"Sorry, you guys. I'm in a foul mood. I hate it. I don't want the rest of the year to be this way." She fidgeted with the band-aid on her finger. "So many things went wonky this morning."

"Wouldn't have anything to do with the coverage of all those swanky parties last night, would it?" Ben broke his roll in half. "Sorry, you didn't go ring in the new year with Charlotte's brightest and best."

She ignored the twinge pinging her heart and raised her brow. "Of course not." The memory of New Year's Eve coaxed a fledgling smile. "I had a blast last night, feeling the bowling ball in my hands after so long. Oh, and especially feeling the twenties and tens provided by my dear brothers celebrating my expertise with the pins." She tapped her cheek with her index finger on her uninjured hand. "What should I buy with all my moolah?"

"Remember who taught you everything you know," Sam added more roasted potatoes to his plate. "Maybe I should charge a training fee."

"Dad. Dad taught me to bowl. You were busy with the birthday party, remember?"

The boys worked their magic for the rest of the meal and cleaned every dish and counter at the end. They perched her on a kitchen stool and let her shout commands. Her mood continued to rise exponentially with every order. By the time they left, she felt lighter than she had all day.

But as the quiet of the empty house settled around her, melancholy slipped back on top of her shoulders. The whole of the New Year stretched in front of her. It seemed empty too.

She wished she'd get a text from Ches and thumped her own forehead for that thought.

She wished she could see Ches again just to make sure he was fine. Another thump.

She wished she had some sort of distraction so that every thought didn't circle back to Ches.

CHES SCRAPED at the bandage covering his IV puncture, ready to be finished with all reminders of the past two days. Ready to be back at the office, but did he still have a job?

What a way to begin a new year.

Keys jingled at the door before Jack and Heidi entered his house carrying a few grocery bags.

"We're back with plenty of provisions. Now your refrigerator won't look so sad." Heidi laughed, the smell of a cold, winter's day clinging to her parka.

"You two are spoiling me." His pleasure at their company, their help, surprised Ches. He liked the fantasy that these two people were his parents. He hadn't corrected a single nurse who called them his mom and dad.

His real parents were MIA. Happy to hear that Ches was on the mend, they decided to finish skiing in Colorado. Jack's face, a bright red during the abbreviated conversation last night, betrayed his emotions.

"You're finally letting us, so I'm getting in as much as I can." Heidi rubbed her hands together. "It's really dismal out there. We could turn on your fire and make it cozy in here if you like."

"I'll get it." Ches moved to the fireplace and switched on the gas logs. Cozy and his house didn't exactly go together, but maybe...

"What about chicken soup for dinner? I make a killer soup."

"You make a killer everything, Heidi. Soup sounds great."

She grinned and kissed his forehead. He didn't cringe or writhe away. Making her happy felt good. Her affection for him, in the form of a hug or a kiss or good food, felt good.

Jack returned from the kitchen, folding cloth grocery bags. "Hey, what's this?" He pointed to the arrangement of cut fruit on the table.

"Oh, that." Ches shifted in his recliner. "A gift from Mallory."

"That's her gift for someone who has an ulcer?"

"In her defense, I'm not on any diet restrictions. Doc said to eat whatever appeals to me."

"True, but...she didn't even come to the ER with you."

"I let her off the hook. She's not really a medical kind of person."

"But as your girlfriend..."

"She's technically not my girlfriend anymore. We had an arrangement through the holidays, and now the holidays are over."

"Honey, it's none of our business." Heidi tugged on Jack's arm, worry evident on her brow. "Enough about her." Heidi knelt beside the recliner. "But, how are you?"

"About our parting? Relieved. It's been months in the making."

She searched his eyes and nodded. "I believe you. I am, too, relieved, I mean."

"Me too." Jack loosened his grip on the bags. "Well, this opens the door for—"

"For what comes next, not who comes next." And just like that. Even though he didn't want her to, even though he tried not to think about her, Josie appeared in his mind's eye, smiling, waiting. He let Jack and Heidi retreat into the kitchen to prepare the soup, and for the first time in a long time allowed himself to remember the first day at the Park 'n Go.

She was feisty trying to deny the tip. Bold, telling him to do something fun yet compassionate over his broken sunglasses.

His mind jumped ahead to the grant party and her blue dress that nabbed his attention in the middle of the crowd. The vision of her had petrified and thrilled him at the same time. His two worlds collided, his real world of the firm and his fantasy world of the Park 'n Go girl. That night he discovered depth to her beauty, intelligence, and passion for a cause.

Other pictures of her flipped through his mind—hammering nails, placing third in the 5K. He wanted to linger in the image of her in the second right after their first kiss before she reamed him for kissing her, but his traitorous mind skipped to the haunted, swollen eyes the last morning in her office.

He fisted his hand, hating himself for hurting her.

Soft laughter and murmurs floated in from the kitchen along with chopping sounds and the noise of the exhaust fan over the stove. The scent of boiling chicken drifted by the recliner. Chicken soup. Could he eat?

More importantly, could he go through with the idea fermenting in his brain since that morning in Josie's office?

No, the idea had knocked around his brain before then, but he'd refused to acknowledge it. The morning he saw the magnitude of her hurt, the idea dragged up a recliner and stretched out, claiming a permanent spot.

Christmas parties and concerts and dinners gave him a reprieve. The illness afforded him extra days to contemplate the consequences of future actions.

But crunch time approached. His rising pulse attested to the fact.

Could he really go through with the idea? Could he really quit the firm, not be a Padgett, Gibbons, Tyler, and Rose attorney after all these years? After all the sixty-hour weeks? After three years of law school and four years of undergrad? Everything pointed toward the exact spot he found himself in right now.

Everything about him was tied to that label. The car he drove. The suits he wore. Even his so-called girlfriend had been centered around the firm. He rubbed an aching temple.

How long before Mallory's influence affected his place in the firm in a negative way? Should he act first or wait for George Padgett to share with him that the firm was going in a different direction or no partnerships were available at this time or a simple, "Thank you for your time and expertise. Good luck with the rest of your life."

Raising the footrest, he shifted in the recliner, the pounding in his head intensifying.

Focus on the positive as Jack would say.

But what did his positive look like?

CHAPTER 25

*J*osie surveyed the library's multi-purpose room filled with tables and booths. Exhibitors worked on displaying their crafts. Uniformed Boy and Girl Scouts carried crafts to designated places, earning volunteer hours.

She checked the time. Eight twenty-five. Five minutes till the last round of crafters arrived to set up their tables. Thirty-five minutes until the craft fair opened to consumers.

Please, please let this be a success for the participants and the library.

"Good morning, Josie."

She swiveled to the warm sound of Jack's greeting. "Hey." Her eyes darted behind him before she could stop them. Her heart rate stuttered with the anticipation of possibly seeing Ches today. She could do this. She could say hello, exchange pleasantries, and move away to chat with other people.

Really. She could.

She tipped the corners of her mouth. "How are you? It's so nice to see you again. I'll show you to your table." She glanced behind him again. "Do you need some help with your carvings, or do you have someone?"

"He's not here."

She clutched her clipboard to the tightness in her chest. "Oh, I didn't mean, I mean..."

He squinted his eyes and dipped his head. "Josie."

She sighed. Busted. "Sorry. I did wonder if he'd come to help you today. He was interested in the library and the grant." She stopped, clamping her mouth shut. That's right. Interested in the library and the grant. Not her.

Ignore the sinking feeling. Focus on Jack. "Okay. I guess you do need help." She turned toward the information table. "We have several groups volunteering today. Maybe—"

Jack touched her forearm. "Josie, he's had a health problem. He's still taking it easy for a couple more weeks."

She startled, the breath escaping her. "Is he okay? I didn't know. I would have—" What? Visited him? Maybe not. Probably not. No. No, she wouldn't have, but she would have prayed for him.

"Right. Not many people found out. He's fine now. He had a little scare on New Year's Eve. Ended up in the ER with a bleeding ulcer."

"Oh, no." New Year's Eve she bowled strikes with her brothers. Ches languished in the ER.

Jack nodded. "He's doing really well. My wife loves preparing healthy foods for him. He's been letting us make sure he's following doctor's orders."

Heidi cooked for him. No mention of Mallory. Or his parents.

Stop. Stop. Stop thinking on that path. As much as she wanted to hear every detail about Ches, she couldn't keep talking about him. The words would fan into flame the embers she'd worked so hard to extinguish.

She didn't want to think about Ches. It still hurt. Last fall when they planned this event, she assumed Ches would be here to help his uncle. A tiny part of her hoped he'd show up today, but the bigger part of her, the still-wounded heart, needed more time to heal. She'd pay for this conversation tonight when she replayed every word.

Over and over and over.

"Well, that's good to hear." She cleared her throat, dropped her gaze to the clipboard. "So. About this morning." She searched the hand-drawn map of vendor booths. "Where are you supposed to be?"

He shuffled his feet. "Josie." His quiet voice commanded her attention.

Contrition panged her heart. "I'm sorry." She swallowed down the hurt in the back of her throat. "I didn't mean to change topics so quickly. I sounded a bit harsh, I guess."

He studied her, shifting the box of carved items on his hip. "You're fine. I think I understand. Let me say this though. Don't give up on my nephew. He's a good man."

She gave a rueful laugh. "I know he is. That's my problem." She squeezed his hand. "Please tell him I hope he has a quick recovery." Nice. Friendly concern. Now return to the business of the morning. She checked her clipboard a second time for Jack's booth.

Jack rubbed his chin. "Looks like you can tell him yourself."

Josie dropped her pen and bent to retrieve it. She rose to lock gazes with a set of blueberry eyes. No, no, no. She chastised her body as it reacted to his presence. Speeding heart rate. Difficulty breathing. Signs of a heart attack maybe? Or a stroke? Could someone call an ambulance and wheel her away from an encounter she wasn't ready for?

She did not want to be affected by Ches anymore. In fact, she wasn't affected by him. The shock of his appearance affected her. Jack had told her he was sick. She envisioned him wrapped in a blanket on a sofa. Yet, he strode toward her in a cobalt blue sweater with a shawl collar and black jeans, looking very healthy, and happy, and beautiful.

"Hello, Josie. Looks like you've got a good start to the craft fair."

CHES TRANSFERRED his coat to his left arm and shook hands with Jack. "I thought you might need some help." He spoke to his uncle, but his eyes bounced back and forth to Josie. Her hair was pulled back from her face, but loose curls cascaded down her back. A moss-green sweater and brown corduroy pants softened her all-business stance as she clutched the clipboard in front of her.

"We're ready for a good day thanks to Jack." Her eyes skittered between his chest and his uncle. After the initial glance, she averted her gaze from his eyes. "I was just about to show him his table. This way."

That's it? No, hello, how are you? No, how's your year going? She said she couldn't be friends. She acted like an acquaintance. Cordial, but aloof. Is that what they were now? His chest knotted at the thought. He stuffed his hands in his pockets to dry his sweating palms.

An empty table waited near the main door to the room. "What do you think, Jack? Is this spot okay?"

He set the box on top of the table. "Perfect. Everyone who comes in will have to step right by my table. Great location. It pays to know people." He tipped his head to her. "Thank you."

She smiled at Jack, then turned to Ches. "Your uncle mentioned your trip to the ER on New Year's Eve. I hope you're recovering well."

"I am. Thank you. Jack and Heidi are seeing to it."

Jack waved his hand. "You two catch up. I left a couple of

things in the car. No, I don't need help." The older man left with a smile on his face.

Ches faced Josie. "You look great."

She looked away and hugged the clipboard tighter.

He regretted saying something not related to crafts or the library. He cleared his throat and started over. "You've got a crowd of vendors. Perfect. Looks like the fair should be a success."

"We'll need buyers, too, for real success."

"The library receives only a percentage of the profits, right?"

Surprise lit her eyes. "Yes. That's right."

"I remembered."

She glanced away. "So, this event is more about community goodwill than raising a lot of money."

He dragged his teeth across his bottom lip. He didn't want to talk about the library. He wanted to talk about her, about her Christmas, about how she was doing. With her holding the clipboard like a shield and eyes darting every place but his, meaningful conversation might be difficult. "Goodwill is good. You still have other events, right? Like the chocolate tasting?"

"Yes, and the antique evening. We'll get to the goal eventually."

"I have no doubt, Josie."

"Yes, well, I—"

"Look. I know you've got a big day going, but maybe we could talk later, maybe catch up as Jack said." He watched the hesitation rise in her face. "You know, when you take a break. Not long. Whenever you get the crafters settled and the helpers doing their thing."

She chewed on the corner of her lip. Was she remembering the last time they talked? A weight clunked between his lungs. What else could he say to persuade her?

"Okay. Give me a little while and..." She glanced at her watch then around the room. "We could talk later."

He smiled. Relief rushed through him, releasing his shoulder muscles. She didn't shut him down. That had to be a good sign. He'd take it as good, for sure. "Great. Okay. See you later then."

THE SECOND HAND swept over the twelve for the second time while Josie stared at her watch. Nine forty-seven. The vendors were busy with a steady stream of curious shoppers. Everything ticked along smoothly. Everything except her heart. Her heart banged against her ribs like a toddler on a set of drums.

She'd checked on every vendor to make sure no one needed anything. Every vendor, that is, except Jack. She'd avoided his table and his nephew since the surprise this morning. Calming her nerves at the sight of him had taken most of her concentration, and now it was time to take a break and have that talk with Ches.

Or not.

Maybe he was just being nice. Maybe he was just piggy-backing on what Jack had suggested, catch up with each other. Maybe he just came to help Jack and not to see her. He was being kind.

That's it.

They'd said hello. He was doing fine. They didn't really need to catch up. She slipped out of the main room and headed down the hallway.

"Hey, Josie." Ches called from behind her.

She stopped and sucked in a breath.

"Is it break time yet?" He smiled at her. "Looks like every-body's off to a good start."

"Yeah." She nodded. "Looks good."

"I smelled coffee. Jack said it's for the crafters and helpers, right?"

"We have a break room with snacks and coffee down this

way." She gestured toward a room at the end of the hallway.

"Great. Ready for a cup?"

"Sure." She'd order decaf. Her system didn't need caffeine with Ches beside her.

They sat at a small table with hot drinks in hand. "So, it's been a while."

"Yep." Fifty days to be exact. Fifty-one days since he'd kissed her and fifty days since his visit to her office. Fifty days should be enough time to build up a strong defense, right?

Then why was her pulse pumping madly in her wrist? She tugged at the fuzzy edge of her sleeve to cover the traitorous beat. Stop thinking about all the other stuff. Take the offense. "I'm glad you're on the mend. A trip to the ER? That's kind of frightening."

"Once I realized I couldn't fix whatever was wrong with me, it was more of a relief."

"Well, frightening for your family. I'm sure your mom—"

"My mom was in Denver skiing. Jack and Heidi stayed with me."

Mallory? What about Mallory? Not my business. Not my business. Think of something else.

"A bleeding ulcer, right? Does that mean you're watching what you eat?"

"I'm not restricted to special foods if that's what you mean, but I am trying to de-stress my life, take better care of myself."

"A great New Year's resolution. Good for you. I resolved to eat less ice cream."

"Less? Not cut it out entirely?"

"I'm not a martyr."

Ches threw his head back and laughed at her joke. The three other people in the break room looked their way and back at their coffees.

Stop. Stop. Stop heart from soaring at his laugh. She'd pay

for these fifteen minutes with Ches. Too bad about the resolution. She'd probably break it wide open tonight.

"It's so good to see you, Josie."

No. No. No. We're not doing this today. She made a production of pushing back her sleeve, centering the watch face on her wrist, checking the time. "I really need to get back to the vendors."

"Wait, Josie." He caught her arm. "The vendors are fine. Please stay a few more minutes." He slid his hand back to his side of the table. "I'll be good, not make you uncomfortable. I promise."

Too late. The discomfort ship sailed the moment Jack started talking about Ches.

"Did you have an estimate of people in mind for today?"

"No, and the foot traffic looks a little light this morning. I hope it picks up for the vendors' sakes. Hey, you should call Mallory to come by." What kind of stupid suggestion...?

"I don't think so."

"Yeah. You're right. Not exactly her scene." Good. Missed that bullet.

"True, plus I'm not seeing her anymore."

No. No. No, heart. Settle down. It doesn't matter. It does not matter. "Oh, well. I'm sorry."

"I'm not. We parted fairly amicably on New Year's Eve."

Her eyes locked with his. "When you got sick?"

"Yeah. She doesn't do medical emergencies."

"She doesn't—" She shook her head. Not her business. Her mind spun with questions demanding to be asked, but she couldn't go there. She bit her lip closed to keep more stupid questions from popping out. Say something else. "I'm sure your mom—"

"My mother has nothing to do with this."

"Gauging from the last time we spoke, she might answer differently."

"When she ambushed you at the reception."

"No, at my house."

His eyes narrowed. "She came to your house?"

Why did he look so angry?

"Yes. On that Sunday after the reception. Looking for you." Heat rose up to her neck again with the memory. Her cheek tingled where Mrs. Windham's hand had connected.

"I'm sorry, Josie. I didn't know. I was at Jack's."

"No problem. It's just, your mom practically had the invitations printed. She must be devastated."

"I haven't told them."

"You haven't told your parents?" Why? Did he want to try out the breakup before he mentioned it to his parents? Did he hope they'd get back together?

"Josie, I'm not like you and your family. I'm not close with my parents. The only reason they knew about the ER is Jack called them. I didn't."

Not being close to her family? She couldn't fathom it. "Oh. Well, that's probably good, not telling them, I mean. You can work things out, and your mom doesn't have to get upset."

He leaned across the table. "There is nothing to work out. Mallory and I never talked about marriage. That was my mother's fantasy. I have another dream." His gaze didn't waver.

Nope. Nope. Nope. Not going there today.

"But you're still living your dad's dream."

"I'm still with the firm if that's what you mean."

She nodded.

"I'm trying to figure everything out. You said some wise things to me last fall. I'm trying to apply what fits in my life."

What? What did she say last fall? Her heart cranked faster than when he surprised her this morning. Did he mean he was making changes in his life, his career, based on their conversations after running? During library planning sessions?

No. No. No. She couldn't be responsible for major life changes.

"Ches. Wait a minute. What did I say? When did I say it? And what do you mean applying what fits your life? What are you doing?"

"I'm considering life apart from Padgett, Gibbons, Tyler, and Rose."

She gaped at him. His parents would be furious. Would Mrs. Windham pay another visit to her house? She swallowed. "Seriously?"

"Seriously."

"That's a major big change. You've worked your whole life for the goal that's almost in your hand." She moistened her lips. "Are you sure you're not just tired? I remember how tired I was after grad—"

"Josie, I've been working toward a goal, yes, but people change goals all the time."

"Not based on something I said." How could she fix this? She could feel another slap, maybe two this time, on both cheeks. Would she be able to stop herself from landing a slap of her own this time? His mother would be...

"I'm not basing my change on solely your words. Jack's been helping. I've watched your family—"

"Oh, for heaven's sake." She waved away that idea and knocked into her coffee cup. Ches caught and righted it.

"You've known us for a few months. Wait until you see the real Daniels come out."

His eyes lighted. "You mean like bickering and teasing, knocking you flat at Thanksgiving."

"Very funny. I mean don't put changing your life on my shoulders."

He frowned. "I thought you'd be pleased for me to make changes."

"Well, of course. I told you I want you to be happy, enjoy the piano, loosen up, but—"

"Are you still seeing Milo?"

She scowled. "Milo doesn't have anything to do with this conversation."

His mouth tightened. "So you are."

"It's none of your business."

He bent toward her. "What if I want it to be my business?"

What was happening? A quick talk of catching up had turned into, what? The pounding in her ears filled her brain. She couldn't think. His words didn't make sense. Ches sounded like, like he...

"I'm sorry. Clearly, I'm upsetting you." He leaned back in his chair, dragging his coffee with him.

"Ches, you're not upsetting me. I'm just not used to people taking my advice."

"You teach college students."

"I meant my brothers. They rarely listen—"

"So, you think of me as a brother."

"Absolutely not." The reply shot from her mouth. Did she answer too fast? Begin damage control...quick. "You can't live your life for your parents or for anybody else. I can't be the reason—"

"You're not the reason. I've been heading this way for months. My body tried to tell me. If I'd listened sooner, maybe I wouldn't have ended up in the ER. Look, let's table this conversation for now. That panicky look on your face tells me you've had enough."

"I'm not panicking. I just don't want to be held responsible for you throwing away your bright future."

"My future seems anything but bright if it's shackled to the firm. I won't hold you responsible."

"Maybe you won't..." She flattened her palm over her cheek. "Then who?"

She sought the doorway. "I have to check on the vendors." Her gaze swung back to him and stuck on the top toggle of his sweater. "I'm glad you're doing well, but please don't do anything rash. I wish you'd pray about what you're doing."

"I have been."

She met his blue eyes and held the gaze for several delicious moments until two giggling Girl Scouts burst through the break room door. "That's good, Ches. I'm glad." She allowed a tiny smile to light her face and left him for the vendors.

CHAPTER 26

*R*emembering the soft surprise overtaking the panic on Josie's face spurred Ches to what he had to do the following week. *Yes, Josie, praying again is thanks to you and Jack. And I'm going to need lots of prayers for the next hour or so.*

He'd invited his parents to lunch at the Red Door Tavern, one of his favorite places. Clyde, the perennial lunch customer, sat at the bar with an unlit cigarette between his index and middle fingers. His mother suggested the Tower Club, twice, but this meeting belonged to him. He wanted to begin it the way he planned to end it—by his lead.

A waitress set his parents' favorite drinks at the empty places and a glass of ginger ale with two cherries in front of him. The reminder of Josie teased a smile from him, fortified him with the knowledge of her prayers intertwining with Jack's and, yes, with his own too.

The prayers were working. God was seeing him through the tough meetings this week. He splayed his hands on the white tablecloth. Steady fingers, no trembling. His heartbeat a calm tempo. Just like when he delivered his notice to Padgett. The man had been receptive but distracted, digging through files on his desk and in his top drawers.

Clyde moved to the jukebox, dropped some coins in the slot, and punched keys. Strains of "What a Wonderful World" filled the pub. A movement at the door caught his eye. His parents hesitated at the hostess's podium and acknowledged his raised hand with identical nods.

"I can't believe we're eating in this place." Alicia settled into the chair Lloyd held for her. "We could be at the top of downtown Charlotte, but instead we're down in some basement speakeasy kind of place with cheesy music." She shuddered and sipped her Bloody Mary.

"Hello to you, too, Mother. This place has character. I love it."

Lloyd swirled the contents of his glass. "How long has this been sitting here?"

"Our waitress brought it thirty seconds before you arrived. And, Mother, this tavern makes great salads and my favorite sandwich. Do you know what that is, by the way?"

Alicia narrowed her eyes. "Are we here to talk about your dietary habits? Are you still having ulcer trouble?"

Ches tipped his head back. "You just answered my question with a question, the classic diversion technique. My favorite's the club, Mother. Except for avocado instead of mayonnaise and basil leaves instead of lettuce. Oh, and I like the bacon chewy, not crispy. They know how I like it here. I don't even have to order it." He sipped the ginger ale. "But, no. We're not here to talk about food. I was just curious."

"What exactly are we here for?" Lloyd opened the menu.

"My future."

Both heads jerked to attention. "If we're celebrating your partnership, we absolutely should have gone downtown."

Lloyd lifted his glass. "Congratulations, Ches."

"Hold that thought, Father."

"For Heaven's sake, Ches." She scanned the room."This place? And where's Mallory? She should be here too." She pushed back from the table. "Pay for the drinks and let's go. I'm sure we can still get a table at the club."

"Sit down, Mother. We're not leaving. We're not here to celebrate the partnership, and Mallory isn't coming."

Wanda, his usual waitress, came for the orders. "She'll have the spinach salad with the dressing on the side and no croutons. He'll have the ham and cheese on rye. No butter. No condiments."

"And Marco's already working on yours." Wanda smiled and collected the menus.

"I didn't get to look." Alicia reached for a menu.

"You always order a spinach salad, Mother. I'm trying to expedite things."

"Are you in a hurry?"

"I'm ready to share what's happening in my life."

"Share?" She unwrapped the utensils, fluffed the napkin over her lap. "Have you joined a cult?"

"No, but you might say I've rejoined life."

Lloyd sighed. "Spit out what you want to tell us already. All this new age-y speak is—"

"I've resigned from the firm."

"Are you kidding?" Lloyd bent toward the table and lowered his voice. "What's the matter with you? Have you gone ape—"

"Lloyd Windham." His mother's raised hand and no-nonsense voice checked the end of his father's sentence. "Ches, you mean you're thinking about it. You wouldn't do anything so stupid." Alicia fingered the abstract shapes comprising her bold necklace.

"Thank you for the vote of confidence, Mother, but I resigned this morning."

"The deed's done? Clearly, you've taken a better offer."

"No. Currently, I'm unemployed."

"You should have discussed this with us. We're your parents." Lloyd spoke through clenched teeth. A faint red crept along his neck.

Despite his belief he was doing the right thing, despite the prayers, the old fear of disappointing his parents rocked his fledgling peace. Ches's heart and lungs came to life, pummeling his insides.

God, I need that peace back. Trying to walk Your path here, not theirs.

A few ginger ale bubbles knocked against the double cherries. "You don't have to remind me, but I'm glad you remembered."

"I don't like how that sounds. What does that mean?" Alicia removed the celery stalk from her drink. "What did Mallory say?"

"She didn't say anything. We broke up weeks ago."

Alicia's gasp turned heads. "No. No, you're just taking a break." She sifted through her purse and found her phone. "Oh, poor Mallory. She must be devastated."

"Not poor Mallory. I heard she's been seen with the new running back for the Panthers."

"An athlete?" Alicia found her phone and swiped the screen with a French-tipped finger.

"Back to the issue at hand." Lloyd threw down the remainder of his drink, signaled for a second. "Since we paid for your degree, we deserved some sort of warning before you threw away your future."

As expected, dishing the guilt. He kneaded the muscle in his thigh. "You paid for my undergraduate degree like many parents do, not my law school tuition."

The law degree belonged to him, bought with his own money as well as scholarships, his own sweat, and hard work. "I didn't tell you before because I didn't want to give you a chance to guilt me into changing my mind. Not that you could. I'm standing firm in my decision."

Lloyd groaned. "You sound like Jack."

"I'll take that as a compliment. Mother stop texting at the table. Here's your salad."

Alicia moved her hands to the side so that the waitress could serve the meal. "I'm texting Mallory." She dropped the phone into her purse, gold initials on the flap winking in the muted light. "Oh, this just reeks of that Joselyn girl. I'm sure she's at the heart of it."

"You're wrong. And I'd appreciate it if you'd stay away from her. Don't go back to her house." He nodded at his mother's questioning gaze. "Yes, she told me—"

"Of course, she'd try to win your sympathy." Alicia sniffed. Red bloomed underneath the powdered blush on her cheekbones. "Well, did she tell you she provoked that slap?"

Ches stilled. Fire leaped in his gut, spreading down his limbs, fisting his hands. Lucky for his parents, they were in a public place. "She never said a word about a slap." He leaned forward and banded his fingers around his mother's wrist.

Her mouth dropped open.

"Listen to me." He waited for her eyes to rise to his. "Do. Not. Ever. Seek Josie again. Do you hear me?"

"Don't talk to your mother like that, Ches."

Ches slid his plate away, the imagined scene between Josie and Alicia turning his stomach. The slap explained her panicked look when he mentioned leaving the firm at the craft fair. He signaled to Wanda.

"I'm done here. Enjoy your lunch. It's on me."

THE STRETCHING exercises completed his Friday afternoon workout. Ches reached into the cool refrigerator for a sports drink and downed it with a few swallows. Running had been essential to releasing the fury brought on by his mother's revelation about the slap.

She slapped Josie. He cringed.

He needed to see Josie, to apologize, to beg forgiveness, but how could he look her in her eyes? How could he ever make it up to her? Blood pounded in his ears as anger rose again. He checked himself. He'd figure it out. Don't ruin the running high.

Yeah. Running five and a half miles, a solid workout. And after a day like today, resigning from the firm and dealing with his parents, releasing the stress was paramount to the new healthy path he determined to take.

His stomach seized at the idea of resigning from the firm. Jack had cautioned him about resigning without having another job in place, but he had three interviews next week. His confidence in those interviews, his solid bank account, plus the peace covering the resignation confirmed his decision to move forward. Once he'd decided, why wait?

George Padgett had rejected the two weeks' notice as anticipated, so now he was free. Free from the shackles of living for someone else. Free to live his own life.

He tossed the empty bottle into the recycling bin and tapped his phone. No messages. Nothing. He'd hoped to hear from Josie. But maybe it was too soon. Maybe she'd text tomorrow. Or maybe he'd try to text her again in a bit.

Maybe she'd unblock his phone at least.

Right now, he needed a shower. He reached for the ceiling. A couple of vertebrae popped in his back. Nice stretch. The doorbell rang. He wiped his face with the bottom of his t-shirt and ambled to the front door.

CHAPTER 27

*J*osie closed the front door with her foot as she sifted through the Saturday mail. The brunch with Lucy had been just what she needed, a time to hear about the antics of preschoolers and first graders, tooth fairy visits, and little league basketball games. Lucy also asked good questions about the craft fair and Ches.

Talking about Ches with Lucy felt good. Sorting out the conversation, discussing the nuances made her feel hopeful, not depressed or anxious or silly. Lucy'd suggested unblocking his number from her phone. Maybe.

She dropped the mail onto the countertop, including a small, intriguing box wrapped in brown paper. She hadn't ordered anything online lately, and her birthday was months away. The Charlotte return label gave the street name but no sender name. The postmark showed it had been mailed on Thursday. Traveling from Charlotte to Charlotte took two days? She shook the box and heard...something.

She rummaged in the kitchen junk drawer, happy for a diversion from thoughts of Ches. Today marked a week since the craft fair. Every day this week, she'd replayed their break room conversation. Every day this week, she'd wondered if he'd text, but she didn't remove the block from her phone.

Wondering was one thing. Knowing for sure he hadn't texted was another.

She cut through the packing tape and revealed the small box along with a note. OPEN BOX FIRST was printed in bold, black letters on the outside of the note. She opened the box and pulled out cotton stuffing. Three pennies. Three wheat pennies clustered in the middle of more cotton.

Lines formed between her eyebrows as she unfolded the note. She scanned to the end of the words.

Ches.

Her hand shook.

I discovered you collect wheat pennies the first time we had lunch. I'd like to take you to lunch again—and pay for it this time. Ches

She smiled. He was asking her on a date. Goose pimples raised on the back of her arms. She smoothed messy hair behind her ear. Should she unblock his number?

Uh-huh. She should unblock his number.

She grabbed her purse for her phone and texted thank you before she could talk herself out of it. She'd make coffee while she waited for a reply.

A knock sounded a half-second before her three brothers pushed through the front door.

"We told you to keep the door locked." Ben's voice held an edge to it.

"I just walked in."

"You do realize your reply doesn't make sense."

"What's up? I'm not cooking until tomorrow night." All three here in the middle of a Saturday? Something was wrong.

Her insides froze. "Is it Mom and Dad? Tell me. What happened?"

"No. No." Taking her arm, Ben guided her into the family room. "Mom and Dad are good. Come sit down."

She dug in her heels. "Tell me now. If it's not them, then—"

"I got a call while ago. Ches has been arrested."

"That's not funny."

Ben raked his hair back from his forehead. "Nope. Not funny, but true."

She wound her arms around her waist. "How do you know? Who called you? Why was he arrested? When?" Not Thursday. He'd mailed her pennies on Thursday.

"According to B.J.—"

"B.J." She spat the word out of her mouth, hating to say his name. "B.J. called you? That's rich."

"Come on. Sit down." He led her into the family room. "B.J.'s been working on an embezzling story involving the firm. He thought you'd want to know but probably not want to hear it from him."

She frowned at Ben. Since when did B.J. care about her feelings? Since never. "Embezzling? This is so stupid. Ches didn't do it. Where is he? He's not still in jail, is he? His parents posted bail, right?" She sat on the edge of the couch, hugging a pillow to her chest.

Think. Think. Think.

"As far as I know, he's still in jail. They've kept things quiet so far, but it's coming out. It'll be in the paper tomorrow."

Ches would be branded as an embezzler. How could she fix this? Heath sat on the ottoman, his hands on his thighs, watching her. Sam sat on the hearth with his hands clutched between his knees, his eyes on the floor.

"You don't believe this, do you? Because I can tell you right now. He's innocent." *Oh, God. What should we do?* She searched the carpet for answers.

Help Ches. Help Ches. Help Ches.

"We'll get all the details." Ben's hand on the back of her neck felt like a lead weight. She shrugged it off and stood.

"He is innocent." Her heart pummeled so hard it used all the space in her chest, no room left for her lungs to work.

Heath rose and took her in his arms. "He's a good guy, Jo Jo. We liked him on the build and at Thanksgiving." Sam joined them, rubbing circles on her back. Ben completed the family hug with his arms around all three.

She squeezed her eyes tight and silently yelled at the forming tears to stay in place. This was crazy. Ches in jail? He'd just mailed wheat pennies to her, for Heaven's sake. Who comforted him, supported him? What was he doing right now? She couldn't breathe.

"I'm calling Jack."

THE WINDHAMS' front door appeared more intimidating than on the night of the reception. Grateful to have Jack and Heidi standing with her this time, Josie watched Jack ring the doorbell and knock three times. Heidi's arm encircled Josie's shoulders. The two had bonded instantly when Josie called and discovered they were on their way to his brother's house.

"We should have told him we were coming." Heidi peered into the glass panel flanking the entry.

Jack pounded on the door again. "He hung up on me before I could tell him."

Heidi reached for his arm. "He was probably hurt that Ches called you and not him."

"Now's not the time to be—"

The door swung open to reveal Alicia Windham, her features brittle, her posture like an arrow. "Please stop pounding on my door, Jack." The bottom edges of her tan cardigan hit her leather belt at different levels, a missed button at the top was the culprit.

\

"Where is he? Still here or did he go get his son?"

"He's in his study. Ches wants you. He called you, remember?" Her naked mouth pinched together, a stark contrast to the perfect countenance welcoming the reception guests two months ago.

Jack pushed beyond her, ignoring her huff. "He's going to Ches, or he'll regret it till the day he dies. I'll drag him if I have to." He called down the hallway. "Lloyd. Get in the car. We're leaving." He disappeared into one of the distant rooms.

"Alicia, you have to make him go." Heidi planted herself in front of her sister-in-law.

"I don't have to do anything. Ches made his choice." She patted a blond wave at her cheekbone. "He's humiliated me beyond comprehension." Her chin trembled for a split second before she quashed it with a snap of her jaw.

"You're humiliated? You can't believe he's guilty." The words tumbled out before Josie could stop them.

Alicia narrowed her eyes and stepped around Heidi. "You. Don't speak to me about my son. I blame you for all of this anyway." Alicia folded her arms around her waist and took a breath. "I don't know what I believe anymore. Ches isn't acting like himself. He's doing crazy things."

Heidi reached for Alicia, but she rejected the offer of comfort. "Crazy things like what?"

"Breaking up with Mallory." She glanced at Josie. "Don't tell me you didn't have a hand in that." She wrung her hands, devoid of jewelry except for one gold band. "Resigning from the firm."

Heidi placed her hand in the middle of Josie's back. "I've been with Ches most of January. He seemed fine to me."

"Oh, is that a slam against me, too, because you were here when Ches got sick and I wasn't?"

"Of course not. I was thankful for the time to be with my nephew. He's a great human being."

"Don't you think I know that? He's my son."

"But you're doubting—"

The door to the study opened, and Jack pushed his brother into the hallway. "It doesn't matter who he called. We're both going down there."

Lloyd shrugged on a coat. "I can't believe you thought I had that much money just lying around."

Jack pulled him along by his bicep to the front door. "Let's go. We'll stop at some ATMs on the way."

"Wait." Alicia's frantic eyes flicked over the group. "I have some money upstairs." She ran up the stairs and returned in less than a minute with a clutch in her hand. "Here." She flung the bag to her husband.

Lloyd caught it with both hands against his chest. "What's all this?"

"My just-in-case money."

Lloyd's face hardened. "Just in case what?"

She returned his look with a scorching one of her own. "Just-in-case-my-son-needs-to-be-bailed-out-of-jail money. Take it. And call Baxter. He'll help us. He has to." Neglecting to say goodbye, she turned from them and retreated up the stairs.

CHAPTER 28

"*He* loves my chicken soup, and he has most of what I need. Good. I'll improvise the rest." Heidi closed the refrigerator. She opened a cabinet. "Also, he loves brownies with ice cream. Sweet, here's a box of mix." Heidi glided around Ches's kitchen like it belonged to her, comfortable, at home.

Josie felt like a boy at a middle school dance, crushed toes in new shoes, praying for the night to end. She felt like a spy. She crossed her arms not knowing what to do with them, not wanting to touch anything. At the same time, she wanted to look at everything, see more of the real Ches, discover the private side he enjoyed at home.

Exactly. Private.

Precisely why she felt like an interloper. He hadn't invited her. He wouldn't want her here. Who would want to be seen after a night in jail?

She'd driven Heidi to Ches's house while the men rushed downtown. She planned to leave immediately, but Heidi insisted she come inside. His house, a craftsman style two-bedroom, faced Queens Boulevard, a coveted neighborhood in Charlotte.

Cozy and comfortable, the house avoided pretense or a hot-shot-lawyer pad vibe. It was beautiful.

"You know, Ches redid this house by himself. The hardwood floors, the kitchen cabinets, the painting. He bought this house for a song and turned it into a place that just shines. Don't you think?"

"It's beautiful, for sure." The house was gorgeous, but something didn't feel right. She considered the room with the TV. The walls. Perfectly painted but completely blank. No hanging pictures. No framed pictures on side tables. No knickknacks. Nothing personal.

"Take a look at the floor in the living room, the pattern around the edge. He did that too."

Her eyes followed the intricate pattern in the wood to an upright piano hugging the inside wall. Music books covered one end of the bench, the books she'd given him. One book, open above the keys, showed "The Stars and Stripes Forever". A patriotic selection. Nice. A sudden chill brought her up short.

An invitation to lunch wasn't necessarily an invitation to check out his personal space. She had to get out before Ches caught her. She faced Heidi. "Hey, you've got things under control here, so I think I'll shove off."

Heidi dropped an eggshell into the trash. "But I thought you'd stay and see Ches."

Josie smoothed a hand along the counter. "Honestly, I feel a little strange being here without being invited."

"He'll want to see you."

"I'm not so sure of that." Did she want to see him after a night in jail, knowing people assumed he was a criminal? Would he look defeated or defiant?

"People need to know they have support." She opened a drawer and extracted a paring knife. "You saw the piano books, didn't you? The ones you gave him? He's played some for us. He's really talented."

"I saw them. I'm glad he's using them."

"He's told us a little about you. That's saying something, especially when getting hello out of him used to be a major accomplishment."

Josie chuckled. She knew that Ches, for sure.

Heidi turned down a burner under the boiling chicken. "This ulcer has been a blessing in disguise. It's helped him make decisions he's been moving toward for a while."

"Hmm. God turned a curse into a blessing."

"Exactly." Heidi smiled. "I knew I liked you. Could you cut up those carrots, please? Jack mentioned your parents are short-term missionaries."

She hesitated for a moment, torn between a request for help and a desire to flee before Ches found her in his house. Obeying her people-pleaser personality, Josie took her place beside Heidi chopping and slicing, describing her parents, sharing about her brothers, and ignoring the chant in her mind to leave, leave, leave.

CHES OPENED his front door to delicious aromas emanating from his kitchen. Home at last. Thank God.

"Jack? Ches? Is that you?"

"Just me."

Heidi flew from the kitchen, wiping her hands in a towel. She grabbed him before he could throw his keys in the basket. He didn't move, not comfortable with the hug, but Heidi squeezed hard till he surrendered to the love and support she offered. He rested his chin on top of her head and closed his eyes. *Thank You for Heidi and Jack and home.* "It smells wonderful in here."

"We've been cooking up a storm."

"We?" He lifted his head to see Josie rounding the corner, a blush tinging her cheeks. Heat rose in his own neck, his scruffy neck. He cringed. Two days' worth of stubble shadowed his face. He released Heidi and yanked to straighten his shirt. The shirt he'd worn to run five miles yesterday afternoon. And sweated in.

At least it wasn't the orange jumpsuit.

Thank You, God, for that blessing.

He ran his hands through his hair, hair that hadn't been washed since yesterday morning. Nice look. What was she doing in his house? Humiliation mushroomed in his chest and swirled up to cloud his brain. What was Heidi talking about? Food?

"Josie even made a banana chocolate chip bread with the spotted bananas on your counter. See, I knew the flour I bought for your pantry was a good idea." Heidi kept an arm around his waist and closed the gap to Josie. "Say hello to Josie, Ches. She's been such a help today."

"I'm sure. Thank you for helping." Helping what? Why was she here? In his house. Cooking with Heidi. Looking like it's the last place she wanted to be.

Not that he could blame her. His picture would be on the front page of the newspaper tomorrow if it wasn't already. Who but family members would want to...? No, not all family members.

Heidi glanced behind his shoulder. "Where are Jack and Lloyd?"

"Jack's taking him home." He gritted his teeth. "I declined to use Baxter, his lawyer. I want to call Peter, a friend from law school, instead."

Josie hugged her arms around herself. "Everything's pretty much finished, so I guess I'll be on my way."

"Oh, Ches." Heidi tapped his chest with her palm. "Make her stay. She's been trying to leave since she drove me here."

"I'm sure she has things to do." Leaving would probably be best for her, but the embarrassment had subsided, settling into the familiar feeling hanging on him since the policemen knocked on his door late yesterday afternoon.

He wished she'd stay. He'd love to spend time with her for a while, talking about the last two months, going for a run, enjoying a smoothie. Normal Saturday things. But today wasn't a normal Saturday. Not by a long shot.

"No. She doesn't have anything to do. She finished grading last night. She said something crazy about not being invited here."

Ches intercepted a look between Josie and Heidi.

"Invite her while I check on the oven." Heidi hugged him to her one last time and headed for the kitchen.

"Never knew Heidi was so meddlesome." He rubbed his chin, the stubble reminding him of his appearance. He swallowed a groan. "Listen. I understand. You don't want to be here. Who would?" He laughed, but it sounded bitter. "My parents don't. Thank you for helping Heidi."

"I enjoyed cooking with her. It's just, being here without you knowing felt…" She shrugged. "A little weird."

"Weird left the building yesterday beginning with my arrest and continued with an overnight stay downtown, and I don't mean at the Marriott." He sighed. "Yeah. Weird graduated to humiliation, shame, disgrace. Pick your synonym." He scraped his hand over his eyes. "I can imagine how the paper's going to spin this sordid tale. Sorry, you have to see me like this."

"I've seen you look grubby before."

His head snapped to attention, heat rising again.

"At the build, remember? I know you can rock a five o'clock shadow."

Something in his heart shifted, felt lighter than a memory. Mallory declined to go to the hospital, never visited when he was sick, yet here Josie stood, smiling at him, a suspected embezzler. Emotion choked his throat.

"More like a thirty-six-hour shadow." He scratched the

stubbly growth and sighed. "I'd even started praying again, Josie."

"Well, don't stop. Now's the time to pray and pray hard. Without ceasing."

"I don't even know what to pray." Weariness blanketed him.

"Pray to be exonerated, for the truth to come out. Pray for strength to get through what's coming. Pray for peace."

"You're good at this." He studied her for a long moment. "You don't believe I'm guilty?"

She shook her head. "Of course not. You're innocent."

What had he done to deserve her faith? What had he done to deserve Jack and Heidi's love and constant help through the last month? Nothing. In fact, for most of his life, he'd been cool toward them, aloof to the point of ignoring them. He didn't deserve their love or their help either. But Heidi was cooking for him again, and Jack had posted bail and dragged his father downtown with him.

"Thank you." His voice caught, and he cleared his throat. "Please stay, if you can. Don't leave because you think I don't want you here."

She glanced at the front door.

"I understand if you're uncomfortable and want to leave. I don't blame you. But...I'd really like for you to stay. I'm going to take a shower." He chewed the corner of his bottom lip. "I hope you'll wait for me."

"Okay."

A tiny bit of tension eased from his shoulders. Her smile could almost make him forget the shame of the last few hours, the anger and hurt toward his parents. "Promise?"

"I'll stay."

SHE'D PROMISED to stay with him and did through the meal with

Jack and Heidi. They managed to make him smile several times and actually laugh out loud twice.

Yep, Josie kept score. She'd hoped for three, but she'd take two laughs, especially when his eyes crinkled. Those crinkles lasted for brief seconds before the familiar sadness hijacked them and outlined his gaze.

When he'd accompanied her to her car, he reached for the door, paused then leaned his back against it instead, his eyes glancing off hers then dropping away.

He scuffed the toe of his docksider. "I'm glad you were here when I got home. I mean, now I am. When I first saw you, I was..."

"Angry?"

"Of course not. Try humiliated."

"But why? You didn't do anything wrong."

He swung his head toward her and narrowed his eyes. "You say it with such confidence."

"Confidence is easy when you believe it. I was worried you'd be irritated to find me in your space."

A quick breeze blew a loose curl over her shoulder. He captured the ends between his fingers. "I like it when you leave your hair down." He reached for her shoulders, slid his hands down to capture both of hers.

"I guess we were both wrong, about being in my space, I mean." He held her gaze for a long moment, then transferred his attention to the edge of the yard. "This isn't how I planned my new year, my life. When I resigned yesterday morning, I expected to head toward a bright new future."

The frustration in his voice twisted her heart.

He bit off a harsh laugh. "Wrong."

"Keep believing in your bright future. It's coming, Ches. You'll be a better person, a stronger person because of this trial." The words sounded optimistic. She meant them. He had to believe them.

The tic appeared in his cheek. She hated that tic.

Before she could talk herself out of it, her arms encircled his waist. She rested her head against his chest, listening to his heartbeat. For five full seconds, Ches remained stiff. With surprise? With discomfort? With embarrassment? She held on through whatever emotion seized him until he relaxed and enveloped her in his arms.

His sigh sounded like victory.

She could have stayed wrapped up in him, breathing in his clean, soapy scent and letting the warmth of his body protect her from the chill of the winter's evening as long as he needed her, but a neighbor turned on a car somewhere down the street, the sound breaking into their cocoon of silence.

He'd asked her to stay through dinner, and she did. She'd do whatever she could for Ches including calling B.J. on a Saturday night. She hit his numbers on her phone and set her jaw.

Please make this an easy call, B.J. Please help me out.

"Josie, this is a surprise. Not. I kinda figured I'd hear from you."

"Oh, yeah? Well, you were right. What can you tell me?" She held a pen to paper, ready for any tidbit that could help Ches.

"Nothing. You can read it all in the paper tomorrow."

"Is it a big story? Is it horrible?"

"It's the cover story. It's big because it's the Padgett firm, because it's an embezzling story, and because frankly, now Ches is involved."

"What do you mean, 'now Ches is involved'?"

Silence.

"B.J., you've been working on this story since last fall, haven't you? Do you mean you weren't investigating him then too? Do you mean *now* like it's new news?"

"Josie, you don't know what you're talking about."

"Then tell me."

More silence.

"If you ever felt anything for me—"

"What you're asking—"

"I'm not asking you to betray a source. I'm just asking, I don't, I just need to know something." Panic dripped off her words in the silent room. Did it travel over the phone lines too?

B.J. made a sound on the phone. "You got it bad, Josie. I told you—"

Patience thinned and snapped her voice. "I'm not interested in what you told me. I'm interested in what you can tell me now. About this story."

"Josie."

"Don't whine, B.J."

He grunted. "I know better than to do this, but okay. I've been working on the story on and off for a long time. A couple of years ago, I got pretty close to answering a lot of questions, questions that had floated about the firm for years. Then, all of a sudden, my two leads took jobs way out west, one in California, the other in Washington state. No firing. No scandal, just two people moving on to greener pastures."

"So?"

"The story dried up, and I bided my time and kept my notes. Rumors started again last summer." He muttered something under his breath. "But here's the thing. Nothing ever pointed to Ches. His arrest yesterday took my team by surprise."

A nugget of hope planted itself squarely in the middle of her heart. "Surprised you? But they arrested him. You don't just get arrested for rumors. What points to him now?"

"Enough to get him arrested. Some powerful people work at that firm."

"Exactly. Powerful people who can manipulate all kinds of things. You know he's innocent too."

"I never said that. My sources say lots of stuff has his name on it."

"He is innocent. B.J., please keep his picture out of the paper."

"I have no control over layout design."

"That's a different song than you used to sing. I thought you had control over everything at the paper."

"You just won't let it go, will you?" He shoved out a breath. "I was trying to impress you then, Josie."

Oh. That was new news right there. She persevered. "Impress me now. Keep his picture out."

"I can't promise anything."

"Please, B.J. They'll put his arrest photo on the front page, and then when his name is cleared, as much as it ever can be, the apology will be on page sixteen."

"Harsh indictment of the press, Josie. And you're still asking me for help, right?"

"You know it's true. He'll be forever linked with this story, but it'll be better for him the faster the real embezzler is caught. Please, don't let this be the end of your investigation. Please, keep looking for the truth."

"That's what I do."

"I know." A strange peace enveloped her. Nothing had changed for Ches in reality, but B.J. thought something was up. He'd get to the bottom of it. "Thank you."

Thank You, God, for B.J. Please help him uncover the truth.

A prayer for B.J.? Crazy, but it felt right.

She plugged her phone into her charger and dropped onto her bed, exhausted with the day's events. The emotional fatigue surpassed any physical tiredness she'd experienced before. If she felt spent, how was Ches doing?

Was the brunch with Lucy only twelve hours ago? It seemed like eons. Ten hours ago, she'd thought Ches was someone who might be interested in her, someone who remembered an autumn lunch and added to her wheat penny collection. Now, he was someone accused of embezzling.

Her phone buzzed. A text. She moaned. Her bones protested moving. Could B.J. have more information for her already? Probably not voluntarily. Ben knew she'd left to meet with Jack and Heidi, but he didn't know she'd seen Ches. She'd forgotten to check in. He was probably beside himself with worry. Such a dad.

She forced herself off the bed and plopped beside the outlet. Stretching out on the floor, she punched the text icon.

"Glad you got the pennies."

Ches. She scrambled to sitting, her heart beating a cut-time rhythm.

"I'm excited to add to my collection. Thank you."

While she waited for Ches to respond, she texted Ben an I'm-home text so he wouldn't call or come over to check on her. She wanted to concentrate on Ches.

The response was immediate.

"Glad you unblocked my number."

Ouch. She cringed.

"Sorry. You needed to focus on other things, not me. Are you settled at Jack's?"

"Yeah."

"It was a good idea to go there."

"You think?"

"Get away from reporters. Let Heidi cook for you. They love you."

"Yeah. It'll be good to be here for a few days."

"It's smart to stay there."

"Not cowardly?"

"Absolutely not. You don't want to be watched by reporters till the next news story breaks."

No response. What was going on in his head? How could she turn the conversation away from the news story?

"Thank you for being at my house today. And for staying. Sorry you had to see me like that."

"You had a rough patch. It's not the end of the world."

"Rough patch? I was arrested. Fingerprinted. Had a mug shot taken."

"You're innocent."

"Thank you. It'll be in the paper tomorrow."

"You're innocent."

"I won't be after people read the article."

"You are innocent."

"You are fantastic."

"No. Just smart."

"And a good runner, and a good cook, and a good person and beautiful."

Her breath caught. How to respond? So are you. In a killer suit or in wrecked jeans or even after a night in jail.

"Clearly, you're sleep-deprived and seeing things."

"I wish I could see you. I don't think I can sleep."

"Try. I'm praying for you."

"Thank you. Don't stop. Please."

"I never did."

"Thank you."

"Good night, Josie."

"Night, Ches."

They were texting again. She felt light as a feather. Her full heart banished the anxiety and fatigue from her body. Ches wanted her to pray for him. He was praying again. B.J. would find the truth.

He had to.

CHAPTER 29

*T*he receptionist answered another call as Josie waited at the newspaper office's front desk for B.J. She tapped her toe and adjusted her watch. Ten minutes of waiting. Come on, B.J. What's keeping you?

Was surprising him at work really a good idea? It seemed like a good plan at midnight when sleep eluded her. A perfect, simple plan. Visit B.J. at his office, chat about the case, somehow get a chance to take a look at papers and notes on his desk. Find important information to free Ches and begin a happily ever after.

Her breath caught at the thought of a happily ever after with Ches. She shoved the crazy, way-too-premature thought from her mind.

Time for business now.

A man in silhouette entered the hallway and moved toward her. B.J. He slipped his phone into his shirt pocket, sporting a closed, tolerant expression on his handsome face. "What's up? Why aren't you teaching?"

Her lips formed a straight line. "Are you the work police now? I took a sick day."

He scowled at her. "You don't look sick."

"Thank you. But I am sick, sick of knowing someone's been falsely charged with embezzling."

B.J. rubbed the side of his nose. "Your boyfriend."

"He's not my boyfriend." She fiddled with the clasp on her purse.

"You wish he was."

"We're not dating." She glanced at the receptionist who stared at her computer screen. "Could we go to your office, please? I'm here for information. What's going on? What have you found out?"

"You're changing the subject, but I noticed you didn't deny my statement."

Folding her arms in front of her, she glared her best teacher's eyes at him. "B.J." She jerked her head toward the hall. "Your office?"

He clasped her elbow, led her to a conference room, and shut the door. He held out a chair on the side of the long table. "Have a seat. Let's keep our voices down, shall we? And for the record, we talked Saturday night. Give me some time, all right?" He sat with one thigh on the table, leg dangling from the knee.

"Wouldn't it be more private in your office?"

"I share space with a few others." His eyes cut to the door. "This room is private."

"Okay. How can I help you find the information we need?"

He chuckled and folded his arms. "Oh, so now you're Nancy Drew?"

"I offer to help. I get an insult." More like a compliment. Nancy Drew would have gotten into his office and somehow found the clue on B.J.'s desk. Josie couldn't get passed a sterile conference room.

"Thank you for the offer, but no thanks. You do your job. I'll do mine." He eyed her from the end of the table. "Although...I do need to interview him, and he's not at his house. Won't answer his phone. Know anything about that?"

Josie met his stare full-on, but heat creeping up her neck betrayed her. She arched a brow.

"Stop trying to be nonchalant, Josie. The blush is giving you away. You know where he is, right?"

"I'm not here to talk about Ches. I'm here to find out why you think he's innocent and how you're going to prove it."

"Right now, Ches is the case. He's been arrested, and I want to interview him. Can you make it happen?"

She slapped her palm onto the table. "Tell me what you—"

He jackknifed toward her and lowered his voice again. "I already told you more than I should have over the phone. I'm not saying another word about it." He straightened, smoothing his tie. "If you really want to help, get me an interview with Ches."

She chewed the side of her cheek. "You think an interview will help?"

"It wouldn't hurt."

She lifted wary eyes to him. "Can I trust you?"

The shock on his face registered hurt too. "Josie."

She rubbed her forehead. "I'm sorry. That was uncalled for. It's just—"

"You really like the guy, huh?" He pinched the crease in his pants. "I wasn't a great boyfriend, but I'm good at my job. I want to get to the truth just like you do. Help me do that." He reached across the table, palm up. "Talk to Ches about an interview. Please?"

Her shoulders sagged. "I've read your stuff. You're a good reporter." She didn't like admitting it out loud, to him of all people, but it was true. "Thank you, by the way, for burying his picture in yesterday's article."

"I called some favors. Several, in fact. Wasn't sure it was going to happen." He shrugged. "Thank you." Hope flickered in his brown eyes. "You'll ask him?"

"I'll ask. That's all I can promise." She hoped she wouldn't regret this visit with B.J. If it helped clear Ches's name, it'd be worth every minute. "And you'll keep looking for the truth?"

"As always."

"Are you free to talk?"

The text buzzed Ches's phone right after lunch. Excusing himself, he headed for the swing on Jack's front porch. He punched her numbers and smiled at the immediate sound of her hello.

"This is a nice surprise. What's up?" A call from Josie definitely put the day on an uptick. He pushed his toe to start swinging.

"Ahm. I have to tell you something, but I don't know..."

What did the hesitation signal? A sinking feeling thudded in his gut. "You can tell me anything. What is it?"

"I went to see B.J."

Her old boyfriend. The sinking feeling tightened. Did this mean they were getting back together? A top crime reporter compared to an unemployed, out-of-jail-on-bail lawyer. No comparison. He sucked in a breath and held it. Waited for the day to crash around him.

"And he thinks you're innocent."

His breath exploded from his mouth. Definitely not what he expected her to say. Score one for the reporter.

"But he wants to interview you."

"I've seen his messages." He pressed his thumb between his eyebrows. "I doubt Peter will okay an interview, and I just don't want to talk to anybody, Josie. That's why I'm with Jack and Heidi."

"He's on our side. He's researched this story for years, and nothing ever pointed to you until last week. What's special about last week?"

"I gave my notice."

"That's right."

"I knew there was a reason he kept sniffing around." He sighed. "Josie, you said, 'our side.' I appreciate your help, but you—"

"You want me to butt out. I've overstepped my bounds. Sorry."

"No. Are you crazy?" Rising from the swing, he moved to the porch railing, the chains clanging behind him. "The fact that you want to be on my side, which isn't looking too cushy right now, means more to me than I can express." Sudden emotion clogged his throat, preventing more words.

He wasn't normally an emotional guy. Lately, however...He concentrated on the stark beauty of the dormant woods on the far side of Jack's house, breathed in a faint trace of wood smoke in the cold air.

"Ches, of course, I'm on your side. I know all these charges are bogus. We need to let B.J. help the cops prove it."

"B.J., huh? Your ex-boyfriend."

"Ex is an important part of the equation. We agreed he's a better reporter than a boyfriend."

"Glad for that. What about Milo?"

"Stop with Milo for Heaven's sake. He was two dates, nothing more."

"Anybody else I need to know about?"

"No. My plate's pretty full with students, the library..."

The smile in her voice elicited one of his own. "Is that a hint you're not interested in exploring something new with someone else? Because I was thinking, since you're free and I'm free—"

He slammed his mouth shut. For twenty seconds, he'd forgotten the trajectory of his life and felt like a man flirting with a beautiful woman. He might be free of romantic entanglements, but he was definitely not free. It might not be for a long time. "I'll talk with Peter, but I'm not promising anything."

"Ches. I was teasing you when I said my plate's full. I can absolutely make room—"

"I shouldn't have started talk like that. You can't get tangled up in my drama."

"I'm already tangled up, I think." Her voice sounded soft and quiet, a little hesitant.

How could he backpedal from the conversation he'd started? How could he spare her feelings? "We probably need to sit back and see how all this plays out."

Silence filled the phone.

"Let me get this straight." Was that spunk in her voice now, a little irritation? "We're going back to no texting or talking on the phone?"

The bleak days of December and January flooded his mind. No contact with Josie. The desolation accompanied him everywhere, an unwelcome, persistent companion. Could he endure a desert time like that again? With what he might be facing? He didn't want to. But could he drag her into the mess of his current situation? Was it fair to her?

An image of Josie in his arms before she left on Saturday floated before him. She'd felt so right with his chin resting on her soft hair. He closed his eyes and tried to imagine the subtle scent of something sweet clinging...

"Ches, are you still there?"

"I'm still here."

"So am I. Let me be your friend through this, and then we'll see what happens next. Okay?"

He sighed. From the time he first saw this woman, she intrigued him. He recognized her specialness. He didn't know how she'd affect his life, but he knew every time she teased him or challenged him or goaded him, she pushed him to a better place.

What had he done to deserve a friend like her?

As his brain processed the word friend, his heart protested. He wanted more than friendship with her. But more would have to wait. "So, you're saying let's just be friends?"

She chuckled. "I'll take that. And you'll call B.J.?"

"I'll check with Peter. See what he says." He didn't want to, but if Peter agreed, he'd meet with B.J. For her.

"And we can call or text each other, right? We're on the same page, right?"

"Right. The same page."

"Good. Okay. Sounds good."

"Sounds good."

He slid the phone back in his pocket. Would she feel the same way a few months from now?

God, thank you for sending this woman into my life. Please help me not to hurt her again. Please let me have more. More with her…more of her.

CHAPTER 30

a knock sounded on Josie's open door.

"'Sup, Ms. Daniels?"

Josie swiveled in her chair to greet the gruff-voiced student and met Lucy instead. "What's with the fake dude voice?"

"What's with the sick day? Are you all better this morning?"

"Not quite, but I'm here. Thank you for taking two of my classes." Josie closed her grade book and arched her back for a good stretch.

Lucy leaned against the door jamb, empathy radiating from her. "I didn't do much. Just got them started in the library as you asked me to."

"Yeah. Well, I appreciate you. Anybody give you any trouble?"

"Nothing I couldn't handle." Lucy breathed on her nails and shined them on her sleeve.

"Were they bad?"

"Just teasing. They were fine. Tell me. How are you?" Lucy's joking evaporated, replaced with concern. "I read the article."

Josie blew out a breath. "You and everyone else in Charlotte I'm guessing."

"The front-page picture showed the firm's building, not Ches's face. It was buried in the middle of section A."

"Way to look for the silver lining." Josie gave her a double thumbs-up.

"There's more positive. The article also mentioned embezzling rumors stalking the firm for years, maybe ten. Long before Ches joined it." Lucy sank into the extra chair at the edge of the desk.

"True. People who read the whole thing will get the whole information, but those paragraphs closed the story. Still, the headline trumpeted EMBEZZELING and Lloyd Chester Windham, IV's name shines right in the first sentence."

"B.J. and his team did a good job of not trying him in the newspaper. They stuck to facts, didn't feed the fire with speculation."

"I agree, but he didn't have any control over social media, did he? That buried picture has been shared tons of times. And did you read any of the comments? People are horrible. They're so mean. Give people a computer, and they become brave. No, not brave. Bold. Audacious.

"It's like some kind of weapon. They shoot vitriol all over the place. Who cares about the truth? It's just fun to rip people to shreds."

Simmering anger pounded against her breastbone. She wanted to hit something. Or someone. Her knuckles gripped around a purple pen, turned white.

"And most of the time, the meanest ones have never heard of commas, periods, or spell-check." Lucy tugged on the pen to free it from Josie's fist and laid it beside the grade book.

Her words wielded the intended diversion. A laugh waylaid the building anger.

"You're right. Thanks for reminding me." Josie flipped her hair over her shoulder. "It's just so frustrating. And unfair. He's innocent."

"Switching gears a little bit. What does all this mean for the library?" Lucy raised her eyebrows.

Josie shook her head. "Not following."

"The grant money. The firm doled out the money in install-ments, right?"

Josie's pulse rate accelerated. The library. She hadn't thought of it once since the bad news hit. Her mind had been consumed with Ches.

The library had received the first installment at the grant dinner. The next installment was due January fifteenth. After a week passed with no check, Sharon, the head librarian, called the firm. She'd laughed when she said, "to shake loose our check." The second check arrived days before the craft fair.

Did that delay in releasing the library's money foreshadow future problems with the final installment? Would the firm be able to pay out if the library, no, when the library raised the rest of the money by September?

Minor problems, for sure, compared to Ches's. But what was the status of the library's money? Should she call the firm? Maybe not the best time, but she'd have to know at some point. Was there a protocol to follow in something like this? Would manners.com have the answer about the waiting period before contacting a law firm with embezzling problems regarding money promised in a grant?

Would calling now seem too unseemly?

"Hello, I've heard about what's happening at the firm. Sorry about your troubles, but when can the library expect the last installment of the grant money?"

She closed her eyes to the tests on her desk clamoring to be graded and vacillated between worrying about the library and worrying about Ches.

Quick knocks brought her out of her musings. "Come in. It's open."

Lucy angled to make room for the visitor.

A double bouquet of daisies burst through the door followed by a delivery lady dressed in a shirt bearing the logo of the downtown flower shop. A few sprigs of baby's breath rounded the bouquet, and a cornflower blue ribbon completed the arrangement.

Valentine's Day. She'd forgotten until most of her female students appeared with variations of red blouses and t-shirts. One male student wore a red bow tie and received the attention he'd hoped for.

Stop beating so fast, crazy heart. Ches did not send flowers for Valentine's Day.

But he could have.

"Ooh, beautiful flowers. Lucky you."

She tipped the delivery lady and read the attached card.

Thank you for taking care of us. We hope these flowers are the good kind. We love you. Ben, Heath, and Sam

Her smile dimmed, but she forced the corners back up. Her favorite flowers from her favorite brothers. A sweet, sweet thing. She was blessed beyond measure to have them.

For the brief second, she'd thought Ches sent them, her heart had beaten triple time. Now her buoyant mood slipped a bit, which was crazy. She and Ches weren't dating. He had no reason to send her flowers. He had more on his mind, a lot more than ordering flowers for a friend.

"My crazy brothers. Aren't they sweet?"

She refused to let her sinking emotions ruin a beautiful gesture from the boys who had her heart first. She touched her nose to a petal and thanked God for blessings in the form of big brothers.

And the possibility of new blessings with someone special.

JOSIE SET the vase on the counter, let the mail fall from under her other arm, and used both free hands to examine the package she'd found in the mailbox.

The return address read Gastonia. Jack and Heidi live in Gastonia. Another box from Ches? She grabbed the scissors and cut through the tape. The four-by-six box kept its secret well. It gave away only a slight thud when she shook it. No more wheat pennies. What could it be? Her shaking fingers fought with the scissors. She pressed her hands flat on the counter and counted ten slow breaths.

She attacked the box again, freed the brown paper, and removed the lid. A red, white, and blue ribbon attached to a bronze-colored metal touting THIRD PLACE nestled on top of a card written in the same strong strokes as her last note.

You deserve a first-place medal for friendship, but I thought you wanted one to show off your running accomplishments. Good job! Ches

She grabbed her phone. Texted him.

"Are you eating dinner?"

Her phone rang in four seconds. "I'm not eighty-five years old and neither is Jack and Heidi, so no. I'm not eating dinner at 4:30. Why do you always text before you call me?"

Because B.J. always wanted her to text first. "I don't want to bother you."

"You bother me, Josie. But in other ways, not because of a phone call."

She ignored those words and the little flip in the middle of her chest. She had to if she wanted to keep on track. "The medal's great. Thank you."

"Not cheesy?"

"It's perfect. And it's hanging around my neck right now. I'm thinking about texting a picture to my brothers. And I'll plan tomorrow's outfit to match it." She bit it between her teeth like an Olympic athlete. She smiled at herself in the hall mirror.

"You'll wear it to school?"

"Absolutely."

"Share the picture on social media?"

"No. And the medal will be under a sweater. I'm not obnoxious."

He laughed. "Not much. Just enjoying the bling."

"The bling and finally getting my rightful reward. Ben can't take this one away."

"He won't try. He loves you."

She glanced at the daisies. "Yep. I know. How are Jack and Heidi?"

"They're good. She's spoiling me, but as much as I love it here, I need to get back."

"Why?"

"Good question. I don't have a job to go to anymore. I had a few interviews lined up, but now...so—"

"That's not what I mean." Jack and Heidi were good medicine for Ches. Being alone in his empty house might not be a great idea. "They love having you. You love being there. Why not stay?"

"Because I need to pull up my big boy pants and face what's coming down, not keep hiding over here with Jack and Heidi." He took a long breath. "The shock over the arrest is still present, but the sting isn't as sharp now. Jack's reminded me of a few things, taught me a few more. I can handle being back. With you three praying, I'm solid."

"I know how shocked I was. I can't imagine how you...I'm so sorry, Ches. I don't know what to say."

"You don't have to say anything. You think I'm innocent speaks volumes. Believe me."

"So... are you talking with B.J. soon?"

"Another reason to come back. He and Peter are available tomorrow morning, and I don't want to talk here."

"Gotcha."

A noise sounded in the background, then Heidi's voice.

"Heidi just got home." Paper and plastic rattled over the phone. "I'm helping her get the groceries in."

"Okay. We can talk later if you have to go."

"Nope. She just had a couple of bags. She says, 'hi.'"

She grinned at Heidi's greeting, at Ches staying on the phone. "Hey, back."

"So, I'll be in town tomorrow."

"Heidi will be sad to see you leave."

"Yeah, but it's time."

MOVEMENT FLASHED in the corner of Ches's eye. Heidi mouthed to him, "Ask her to dinner."

He shook his head.

She nodded hers. She whispered. "It'll be good for you."

"No." Did he speak the word out loud? He pretended to glare at his aunt.

"I'm sorry. No, what?"

"Nothing. Heidi is trying to carry on a conversation with me while I'm talking with you. Even though she knows what a pet peeve of mine that is."

"I'm ignoring his frown. It doesn't scare me anymore." Heidi raised her voice so Josie could hear.

Ches threw an annoyed glance at his aunt. "As if it ever did."

"When you first lived with us as a teenager, you were such a growling bear. Thank goodness Jack wasn't afraid."

Ches winced remembering that summer. Growling bear described him well.

Heidi chucked him on his shoulder and pulled the phone toward her. "But he's matured into a pretty good guy now. You should get together when he's back in the city."

Too late, Ches snatched the phone back and covered it with his free hand. He glared for real this time at Heidi who grinned and tended the grocery bags, humming to herself. Scenes with Josie and her brothers bickering back and forth flickered in his mind. The good-natured jabbing. The teasing. Love. This is what family felt like.

"Ches? I'm going to let you go now. I hope the interview—"

"Wait. Heidi had a good idea." Maybe. He cleared his throat. "Do you have some time this week to grab a bite to eat?"

"Ahm."

"You're probably swamped with classes. I understand."

"No. It isn't that."

"Right. The reporters, being seen with—"

"For Heaven's sake. You're old news. The NASCAR season is heating up. Big news in Charlotte."

"Oh, I'm old news now, huh? Grateful for NASCAR then. So, just not into it?" Who could blame her if she was having second thoughts about spending time with a suspected criminal?

"No. We don't have to get together because Heidi suggests it."

"I'm done doing things because other people suggest them. I asked you to dinner because I want to. I'd like to see you. If you'd rather wait—"

"No."

Her lightning response raced his heart.

"What did you have in mind?"

What did he have in mind? How about kissing her till she couldn't see straight? How about holding her and breathing in her sweet fragrance that greeted him, along with her smile, every time he came near her?

But no. None of those things could or would happen as long as the charges hung over his head.

He'd take grabbing something to eat with her, sitting on the couch watching TV with her, anything as long as he could be with her.

"I didn't have a place in mind. I don't know where you like

to eat."

"You know I like cheeseburgers. I know a great little place out on the highway."

He chuckled. "Yeah. It is a good place. Maybe I won't wear a tie this time."

"Good idea."

"Tomorrow night?"

"Perfect. And you can tell me all about your interview. If you want to, that is."

"We'll see. You can tell me about your day too."

"Deal."

The phone screen faded to black. Yeah. He needed to get back. Face whatever was waiting for him in Charlotte. An off-the-record interview with B.J. first thing tomorrow morning. Better there than here at Jack's. B.J. in his sanctuary with Jack and Heidi? Not happening.

Sanctuary. At the beginning of that long-ago summer, he'd considered their home a punishment. Then it changed into a secret to hide from his father. Now their home sheltered him, and he didn't want to leave.

He didn't want to, but he had to. He'd go back and fight. That's what Josie wanted him to do. What Jack counseled him to do, but with B.J. as an ally? A new idea to wrap his mind around, for sure.

Jack's house a sanctuary and B.J. an ally all because he was a suspected embezzler. Unbelievable. He squeezed his lids together. Those thoughts were for tomorrow morning. Today, he'd think about Josie.

She loved the medal. He smiled. She hadn't mentioned Valentine's Day, and he'd sidestepped it too. He wanted to send her roses, chocolate, perfume, jewelry...every clichéd gift ever associated with Valentine's, but hearts and flowers would have to wait. He had to concentrate on the fight ahead.

And the interview with B.J.

CHAPTER 31

"So, the interview went well." Josie dragged a french fry through the puddle of ketchup in her cardboard boat tray. She and Ches shared an order of fries, but each had a double cheeseburger to enjoy.

"As well as could be expected, I guess. He asked good questions." He bit the stacked burger, and mustard and slaw dripped onto his tray. He wiped his mouth and chewed.

"Great."

Ches swallowed and took a breath. "Josie, he's a reporter, not a detective. Let's keep a realistic perspective here."

"Don't you watch crime shows?" She wiped chili from her index finger. "Reporters help solve crimes. B.J.'s good at what he does."

"Says his old girlfriend." He watched her over his burger.

"Says someone who sees through his blarney but still appreciates his talent. You enjoy bringing that up, by the way."

He grinned. "Because it pushes your buttons."

"I'll remember that." She slid the boat tray away from her. "I should have remembered not to order a double cheeseburger. I'm stuffed."

"Wrap it up. Take it home for tomorrow." He leaned back in his chair and signaled to the waitress for a to-go box.

She grabbed another napkin from the silver canister to replace the soggy one beside her root beer. "Unless you want it."

"One is more than plenty for me. Thanks." He snagged a fry and popped it into his mouth.

A group of five or six teenagers burst through the swinging doors, phones held at the ready. They rushed the counter and clicked pictures of the menus. They scanned the dining room, spotted Josie and Ches, and two boys pointed their phones.

"Hey." Ches pushed back his chair. "What're you doing?" The bark in his voice tightened her stomach.

One of the females skipped over to their table. She pushed a wad of lime green bubble gum to the side of her mouth. "I'm sorry for these guys, sir. We're supposed to ask permission if we take pictures of people." Tossing her light brown ponytail, she elbowed her friend who apologized with the prompting.

"Yeah. Sorry. We need a picture of two people in love. That's number seven on our scavenger hunt list. For our youth group." The boy's bangs covered one eye. He held out a rumpled piece of paper with twenty-five items. Six were crossed out.

Josie addressed the female with the bubble gum. "I think that couple over there fits your description perfectly." She nodded to a couple sharing a piece of pie, whispering and laughing. A Korean War Vet ball cap hung on the back spindle of the man's chair. "Why don't you ask them?"

And the group scampered off to the octogenarian lovebirds.

Ches relaxed in his seat and focused on a sidewall. "I thought they were—"

"But they weren't. I told you. Old news." She chanced a tiny grin. He met her eyes, nodded, and smiled back.

He transferred his attention to the couple still chatting with the teens and watched for several seconds. "Want some pie?"

"Please don't make me even think about more food."

His eyebrow twitched. "I think they have a cherry. You know, for George Washington."

"Stop." She laughed, covering her ears. "I mean it."

He rested his chin on his palm, attention fully on her. "Another time, then?"

"Yes. Sounds good."

Ches drove the long way home using two-lane roads instead of the interstate. A few minutes into the trip, he asked, "Want some music?"

She shook her head. The silence and the darkness worked in tandem to wrap them in their own world. Other people couldn't reach them. The news couldn't touch them.

He smiled and threaded his fingers through hers. "I like quiet too." He raised their hands and kissed her knuckles. Her breath stalled in her throat.

The fifteen-minute drive from the diner morphed into forty-seven minutes according to the dashboard clock. Her pulse thudded at the looming end to the evening. She inserted the key into the front door lock. "I've got a brand-new carton of chocolate almond ice cream in the freezer. Want to help me crack it open?"

He curved down the corners of his mouth. "Nope. Much as I want to come in, I'm not going to. That's why I took the scenic way back. More time with you." He cupped her cheek, slid his hand to the back of her neck. "It's killing me, but I'm not going to kiss you either. Not until after...I've got to get through this mess. We need to wait, see how all this plays out. You don't need—"

She stepped closer, fisting the edges of his jacket. "You're innocent."

He rubbed his thumb over her lips. "Thank you for saying that. For believing it." He touched his forehead to hers. "Tonight was great. I'll call you, okay?"

Frustration strangled the words from her throat, the zipper

teeth cutting into the soft flesh of her palms. She nodded, gripping the jacket more tightly. He swept the length of her hair with his hand, sifting through the ends, then jogged down the steps for his car.

SITTING in front of the TV held no appeal tonight. Her mind was still full of Ches. History tests would have to wait until she could concentrate on something besides him. Disappointment led Josie upstairs.

She shouldn't feel like an expectant job searcher waiting for an email with an offer for the perfect job. The time with Ches had been fun. They'd laughed. They'd teased each other. They'd held hands.

He just hadn't kissed her.

She blew hair back from her forehead. She should be thankful for the fun evening.

The fun, short evening.

She should be. She was. He'd said it was great. He said he'd call her, but she missed him now. She paced through her brothers' old rooms. Noted the dust. Left it in place. Plodded downstairs and into the living room.

He balanced a lot of stuff, heavy-duty stuff, on his shoulders now. Not pushing anything more between them yet showed wisdom, right? Right. But what about a little peck on the cheek? Could a peck on the cheek have been so bad?

A picture of their last kiss appeared in her mind. She closed her eyes to savor the memory. Heat churned in her stomach. No, a peck on the cheek wouldn't have been a good idea.

She slid onto the piano stool and picked up a book. The *60 Progressive Pieces* book taunted her. Ches. Of course. She had to stop thinking of him if she wanted to have any peace tonight. She dropped the book face down on the floor and positioned her fingers over the keyboard. They hovered there a few seconds before lighting on the black and white keys.

The smooth, coolness of the surface soothed her. All her brothers played better than she did, but she loved playing her favorites when no one was home to hear, to kid her about sour notes. She played a broken C chord and held the sound with the damper pedal. One corner of her mouth lifted. She moved her fingers into the opening measures of an old hymn.

"On Jordan's Stormy Banks" perfectly fit her present attitude, and she knew it by heart. Pounding this hymn always lightened her mood during her teenage years. It soothed her tonight too. By the time she finished all four verses, her fingers throbbed with the force of her play. She flexed her hands then played a few more oldies, adding "Silent Night" and "Joy to the World" for good measure.

By the end of her concert, her heart felt lighter. Her mood, calm.

She picked up her phone as she headed for her bedroom. A text from Ches had come through during her recital. Excitement knocked the calm mood back to the kitchen. She squealed down the empty hall and hugged the phone to her chest.

"Thanks for tonight."

She bounced backward on her bed, holding the phone above her to type the words.

"Thank you. I had fun. I'm still stuffed."

"Me too."

"I may not be hungry for the second half of the burger tomorrow."

"I hear you. It felt good to be out again."

"I'm glad. You need to do something fun more often."

"With you?"

"I hope so."

"You told me something similar last summer."

"Yep. Something that made you happy, I think."

"Yeah. I listened then."

"I remember."

"I'm listening now.

"I'm glad."

"I'll call tomorrow."

She wanted to ask when, wanted to so badly her fingers typed the word. She forced them to delete it. Don't be clingy. Not a good look for a girlfriend, especially when the boyfriend has serious stuff to work on.

"Sounds great."

Forgetting the cheeseburger, she rolled to her stomach, immediately rolled back in starfish fashion, and looked forward to tomorrow.

CHAPTER 32

"One hundred plastic eggs. Stuffed with candy, candy, and more candy. This is great. Thanks so much, Josie." Lucy opened one of the eggs. "Reese's Peanut Butter Cups? You sprang for the good stuff."

"You're welcome. I bought candy I like to eat." Josie scraped the last bit of a spinach casserole into a glass dish and covered it with plastic wrap. One more menu item ready for the refrigerator, waiting for the Easter meal tomorrow.

"It took us almost two hours to finish all those eggs. Each one is pretty well crammed with goodies." She rinsed a dishcloth and wiped the counter.

"Us?" Lucy grinned from her perch atop a kitchen stool. "I hope you're not talking about your brothers."

Josie lifted a shoulder and blinked. "If you must know, Ches helped me fill your eggs. And he was thrilled to do it. I lost count of how many baby Snickers he ate."

"I've lost count of how many dates you've had in the past four, five weeks?"

"Six weeks. It's been six weeks since everything went down. Then about four and a half since he took me back to Harold's."

273

"He took you to Harold's Hamburger House out on the high-way?" Lucy's eyebrows pulled into a frown.

"Yeah, why? You don't approve?"

"I never thought about that place being a destination for a date. I mean, Josh and I've been before because the burgers are out of this world, but the atmosphere—white walls, Formica tables, cardboard boat trays."

"You don't go there for the atmosphere. And it wasn't a date. It was just a get-together."

"A get-together. Did you think about what you wore?"

"Of course."

"Did he pick you up and drive?"

"Yes."

"Did he pay for it?"

"Yes."

"Did you enjoy his good night kiss?"

Josie slid open a drawer with one hand and stirred the contents with the other pretending to look for a utensil. "He didn't kiss me good night." She tasted the disappointment again.

Lucy made a face. "Oh, well. A gentleman. How many get-togethers did you have before he kissed you?"

"We've had a few dinners. Seen a couple of movies." Josie opened a cabinet, stuck her head inside. "But he's not kissing me until this is over."

"What?"

She turned to Lucy with her hands on her hips. "Could we change the subject, please? Are you still going to your in-laws for lunch tomorrow? Because you could come here. The more the merrier, as they say."

"You know my next question, right?"

She nodded. "Yes. Ches is coming, along with his aunt and uncle."

Lucy clapped her hands together. "Wonderful. I wish we could come, but we'll be at Lake Norman."

"Don't sound like it's the last place on Earth you want to be. You love your in-laws. You love the lake. You'll have a blast like always."

"True, but your holidays are so much fun. And I'd love to meet Mr. Windham, finally, not just see him from down the hall." She glanced at the kitchen clock. "Hey, I need to get going. Thanks again for these eggs." She gathered the grocery bags filled with colorful, stuffed eggs. "The Sunday School kids will have a large time at the egg hunt."

Josie circled the island and hugged her. "You're welcome. Enjoy your spring break. See you soon."

"Text me details. Better yet, call me for lunch. I'll need a break about mid-week."

"If Josie'd let us use paper plates, we'd be playing KanJam by now." Sam lifted another china plate from the drying rack and wrapped it in a dishtowel.

"Paper plates on holidays?" Ches rinsed a saucer and placed it into the rack. He smiled to himself. Washing dishes. It felt good.

"Not if I can help it." Josie tore off a sheet of aluminum foil to wrap slices of spiral cut ham. "We've got this lovely china. We have a special day. Washing dishes won't kill you. Ten more minutes and we'll be outside."

"I love it. Men in the kitchen." Heidi dropped whole wheat homemade rolls into a plastic bag. "Strong, broad shoulders huddled over sinks. Big hands drying dishes. Josie and I about to go put our feet up..." She chuckled and zipped the bag closed.

"Honestly, Heidi." Ches shook his head at this new side of his aunt.

"What's the world coming to?" Jack brought in the last dish

from the dining room. "Josie, these Jello eggs are great. Never had them before." He grabbed a wiggly egg and bit it in two.

"They've been staples on our Easter table since we were children. Tradition. We have to have them every year. Or so Josie thinks." Heath tossed his towel onto the corner countertop. "I need a new towel. That one's so soppy it won't dry a fork much less—"

"I have to have them? Have you ever seen me eat one of those slippery things?" Josie opened a drawer to Ches's left and tossed her brother a dry towel. The landline began to ring. "We're not officially finished with Easter, so no phones yet. Ignore it. Do not answer it, Ben."

Walking by the phone with a handful of dirty cloth napkins, Ben glanced at the caller ID screen. His face changed from placid to curious to concerned. "I'm going to take it, Josie. Won't be but a minute."

"It's not an international call, is it? Then anything else can wait." Josie huffed her frustration. "Nobody listens to me."

"Nobody listens to you, huh?" Sam threw a soggy towel at her. "Then what am I doing drying dishes?"

"Hello?" Ben moved into the family room.

"Anything else?" Ches scanned the counter for more dirty dishes.

"Let me spell you. Don't want your fingers to pucker." Jack dunked the Jello egg bowl into the sudsy water, and Ches sidestepped out of his way.

"You don't have to tell me twice. Thank you." Ches caught Josie's eye and smiled. "So, Sam. KanJam?"

"Don't you know it? I'm something of a phenom on the KanJam circuit."

"In his own mind at least."

Heath popped his brother with his towel.

"No joke, man. Last weekend, me and Billy, my partner, were leading the other team by about six or seven points when this girl, couldn't have been more than five feet tall, flipped that Frisbee right through the slot." He shrugged. "You know what that means."

"No. I don't. Until today, I'd never heard of this game." Ches leaned against the counter, hands in his pockets.

"Slam dunk. Game over."

Voices carried from the family room. "Ben, did you turn on the TV?" Josie fixed fierce eyes toward the sounds. Oh, she was cute when she was mad. Who was he kidding? She was cute anytime.

Ben entered the kitchen. "That was B.J. We need to watch the local news. Pull it up on your laptop, too, Josie." He zeroed in on Ches."George Padgett's been arrested. At the airport." He turned back to the family room.

Gasps sounded over the stacks of dried dishes and silverware. Josie bolted to the laptop resting on the kitchen desk. She opened it and drummed her fingers as it powered up.

Alertness cracked and spread throughout Ches's body. People crowded around Josie or joined Ben in the family room to watch the local twenty-four-hour news channel. Ches froze with his back to the sink. Could it be true? George Padgett arrested? Could this nightmare be over?

"There he is, climbing out of the car with a coat draped over his hands." Heath pointed over Josie's shoulder to the screen. "Cuffed his hands in front."

People obscured his view of the screen. Was it real? He couldn't lift his feet. If he moved, would he wake up from this dream?

"Charlotte attorney, George Padgett of Padgett, Gibbons, Tyler, and Rose, arrested at the Charlotte Douglas airport, passport in hand." Jack read from the scrolling at the bottom of the screen. "Unidentified source says embezzling charges are pending." He sought Ches's gaze and smiled.

Roaring in his ears impeded his hearing. What did Jack say?

But he was smiling. That had to be good, right? Everyone was smiling at him. He gripped the counter behind him, held on tight. His pocket vibrated. What was wrong with his pocket?

"Ches. Ches, that's your phone. In your pocket." Jack moved toward him and extracted the phone. "It's Peter. Answer it. Josie won't yell at you." He swiped the screen and held it against Ches's ear.

"Hello." Ches listened for three seconds. "Wait. Here's Jack." He pushed a breath out. Except for the crazy buzzing throughout his body, it seemed to have shut down. "You take it."

Jack moved the phone to his own ear, listened, nodded, then grinned. "All charges dropped."

"They're dropped? Just like that? On Sunday?" Someone asked the question for him.

Jack grabbed Ches behind his neck, smacked his chest with his other hand. "The D.A. assured Peter all charges have been dropped. Sounds like your buddy, B.J., turned in some important interviews that led to crucial evidence. You're good, son."

Heidi's hand shot above her head. "Praise God! Praise God!" She grabbed her nephew as tears flowed down her cheeks. Jack embraced both of them, his head against his wife's. "Thank You, God. Thank You!"

The house quaked with stomping feet. Whooping laughter mimicked the tremors exploding in his body. Ches closed his eyes against the chaos and appreciated the love of his family. He had his life back.

Thank You, God.

He opened his eyes and met Josie's.

She rose from the kitchen chair and glided through the high-fiving brothers, heading straight for him.

JOSIE'S HEART banged against her ribcage. The ridiculous idea knocked on her brain as soon as she saw the image of George Padgett gliding across the screen with a coat covering his wrists. When Jack yelled, "All charges dropped," the idea plopped down in her head and commandeered her body.

She pinned her eyes on Ches. She forgot about her brothers or future teasing comments. She stopped in front of Ches and waited as he straightened and loosened his hold on Jack and Heidi. They parted to allow her access. She stepped closer, planted both hands on either side of his face, and brought his mouth to hers. Tippy toes helped.

Ignoring the stunned silence, she kissed Ches in front of his family and hers. She kissed him like she'd wanted to for months, since she first saw him last summer if she really were being honest.

She kissed him through his stillness, through the silence.

Please kiss me back. It's okay now. You're free. Don't humiliate me in front of Ben, Heath, and Sam, please.

Nothing.

She broke contact and settled onto flat feet. She searched his eyes for something. Anything. Shock? Embarrassment?

What should she do now?

The kitchen clock continued to tick in the funeral-parlor silence. She slid her hands to his chest and dropped her gaze to his lips. Her stomach clenched. Okay. Maybe this wasn't the time. Should she say something?

His lips swooped down over her own. One arm circled her waist. His other hand forked her hair to cradle the back of her head. This time he kissed her with such intensity her mind wobbled like the Jello eggs. She grabbed the collar of his shirt and held on, oblivious to everything except Ches.

His arms crushed her to him. A moan rose from somewhere. A cough barked behind her, then two. Then the whole kitchen sounded like a doctor's office in the middle of a croup epidemic. The whole kitchen. She broke away slapping the back of her hand over her mouth. Her mouth felt like she was allergic to something. Did her lips look swollen to her brothers? To Jack and Heidi? She stepped back, but Ches's arm tightened around her waist and settled her close beside him.

"Pretty good news, huh?" Ches ducked his head and grinned.

The coughing switched to belly laughs, then more high fives and congratulations.

Heidi hugged her from the side and whispered, "This is the best day ever."

"Who's ready for KanJam?" Sam inclined his head toward the front door, a mischievous smirk on his face. All the guests filed outside behind him like children following the Pied Piper.

"That was about the smoothest thing I've ever seen Sam do. I'll have to thank him. Sometime. After a while." Ches turned toward her and lowered his head again.

Sam. Who knew he could be that helpful? She'd thank him too.

As soon as she could think straight.

CHAPTER 33

"*E*xplain this game to me," Ches whispered close to Josie's ear. He didn't need to whisper, but he wanted to get close, smell her floral scent. If he focused on the rules of this new game, maybe he'd forget about her thigh next to his, about that long, slow kiss in front of the whole kitchen.

They sat on the edge of the front porch watching Jack and Ben play Heath and Sam or pretending to watch. Cheerleading, Heidi yelled encouragement to both teams to balance the smack talk. He'd thank Heidi later for being discreet, for letting them enjoy time together but apart from the family.

Winston lay on his other side, waiting for attention. He'd pet him later, but right now he'd rather caress the ends of Josie's hair, pretend an interest in Frisbees, and think about kisses.

Yeah. Kisses.

Josie threaded her fingers through his. Nice. "You want to get the Frisbee into the can. You send it over, and your partner can help you get a point by knocking it into the side of the can or two points by knocking it into the top of the can. If the Frisbee goes through the slot in the front, see it?" She caught a quick breath.

"You're going to have to stop that if you want me to remember all the rules."

He inched away from her. "Where?"

"It's right there in the front above the yellow sticker. You win. No matter the point count. KanJam's kind of like a Frisbee version of corn hole."

He traveled his eyes down her extended index finger, noted the slot in the black plastic can, and followed the line of her arm back up to her profile. "Uh-hum." He kissed her behind her ear. "It sounds fun."

She tightened her grip on his hand. "It's great fun."

The yellow Frisbee landed in her lap. "Hey, you two have the winners of this game. Pay attention." Sam positioned his fingers ready for the return of the Frisbee.

Ches sailed it back to him with a flick of his wrist. "Your brother's a card."

"He should be dealt with. And we were going to thank him for leading the party outside."

"Kissing definitely made us loopy." He grinned and slanted his head toward her. Sunlight glinting off glass shocked his eyes. He glanced at the driveway to see his parents' Lexus sedan coasting to park. His gut seized. He tightened his hold on Josie's hand.

"What?" She followed his gaze. "Company on Easter?"

"Not company. My parents." He flexed his grip and pushed off the porch.

Jack left the game and strolled toward the passenger side of the car. Lloyd Windham opened his door. Jack offered his hand to Alicia. All three walked toward the house. The game suspended, the brothers stood together, watching.

"I suppose I have to say, 'hello.'"

"Of course. It'll be fine." Josie clasped his hand with both of hers and headed for his parents.

Alicia noted the hand-holding with a pursed mouth. "Hello, Ches."

"Mother. Father. Happy Easter."

"Happy Easter? It's more than that. You've been cleared as I knew you would be." Alicia's mouth curved, and she stepped closer to her son.

"Right. Cleared. But you weren't sure if I was innocent, right?"

"Of course, I thought you were innocent, Ches. How could you say that?" Alicia shrank into her Chanel jacket.

"Ches." Jack and Lloyd spoke at the same instant.

Lloyd gestured toward Ches. "We need a few minutes alone with you."

Jack nodded to the brothers.

Ben patted the Frisbee he held. "Come on, guys. Heath, you could use some practice time."

"Speak for yourself." Heath popped the Frisbee out of Ben's hand, caught it, and flicked it toward the can. "Sam and I are putting a hurtin' on you."

Ches caught Jack's eye and dipped his head slightly. Jack and Heidi joined the brothers. "I believe you have one point on us. That's all. Quick work to catch up."

Josie turned toward her brothers, but Ches draped his arm around her shoulders, gathering her closer to his side. Her hand slid on top of his, her touch easing the tension coiling up his neck. "What's up? I explained yesterday I had plans for today."

His father worked his jaw, glancing from Ches to Josie. "We wanted to offer our congratulations. Your mother and I are thrilled with the turn of events. Now we can put this unfortunate incident behind us and move forward. What say we go downtown to the club and discuss your future?"

"We can celebrate Easter and the good news together." His mother lifted her chin.

Ches rubbed his cheek with his free hand. "Well, you see.

I'm not going to be able to leave for several reasons. One, Josie and I have to play the winners of that game." He pointed to the two teams. "Sounds like it's almost time for us." He glanced at Josie and smiled. "Two, there's a piece of bunny cake with my name on it that will be delicious after we beat them." He raised his voice for the brothers to hear.

"You wish. I'm getting ready to lay the hammer down." Jack sailed the Frisbee straight for the can and missed the game-winning slot by inches.

Heath slapped him on his back. "Too bad, buddy. Better luck for me when I show you how it's done."

"And three." Ches paused, making sure he had both parents' attention. I'm not discussing my future with you this afternoon or next week or ever. It's my future. I'll keep you posted, though, when I secure my new position."

His father frowned. "What do you mean 'new position'?"

"I already told you about resigning. George threw me under the bus to give him time to leave the country, according to my attorney. Thank God he got caught before he boarded the plane. I'm not going back to the firm if there's one to go back to."

"You're choosing bunny cake over the almond torte at the club?" His mother's voice held just a touch of whine.

"That's what you're focusing on?" Ches shook his head. "Mother."

"We have a bunny cake. It's a tradition. And German chocolate cake and lemon blueberry pound cake. We decided to have dessert after the game. There's plenty if you'd like to stay."

Ches whipped his head to Josie. She winced and averted her gaze.

Heidi joined the group. "Yes, stay, Alicia. The meal was delicious. I'm sure the desserts will be wonderful too." She smiled at Josie.

Ches ground his molars. What was she thinking?

The last thing he wanted to do was prolong this encounter

with his parents. He wanted to try his hand at KanJam. He wanted to have a piece of bunny cake and maybe have small slices of the other cakes too.

Mainly, he wanted to enjoy the rest of the day with a normal family doing normal holiday things.

He wanted to revel in the knowledge that his future held something more than court dates and a possible prison sentence. He especially wanted to explore the new turn in his friendship, maybe a relationship, with Josie since she kissed him like she was claiming him in front of all her brothers and his aunt and uncle too. His pulse accelerated with simply the memory of her kiss.

She had that sweet look on her face. Open. Innocent. Hopeful. As much as he wanted to, no way could he override the invitation. *Josie, you're opening a Pandora's box by inviting them to stay.*

"We've got reservations." His father slid his sleeve up to reveal his watch.

"Not till six-thirty, Lloyd." His mother turned her head from Jack and Heidi to the brothers, a question hovering on her tight features. *Wondering what was next?*

Indeed, Mother. What now?

"Finish the game, and I'll get the desserts ready." Josie refused to meet Ches's eyes. The tic in his cheek had flashed steadily since his parents arrived. Why did she ask them to stay? Why couldn't she have corralled those words in her mouth? Ches was angry at her. His whole body had stiffened at the invitation. She couldn't blame him for being angry.

Heidi took her sister-in-law's arm. "Come over here, Alicia. There's an iris bed full of six or seven varieties. Truly a beautiful sight."

God bless Heidi.

"Somebody needs to take my place on Ches's team. I'll be inside." Josie turned for the steps.

"Oh, no you don't." He grabbed her hand and pulled her to the porch. "I'll be in the kitchen too."

Her heart banged a crazy rhythm in her chest. Ches was mad. Ches was really mad at her. How to fix this? Take the offense. Confess and beg forgiveness.

She whirled around as he closed the front door. "Please don't be mad, Ches. I'm so sorry."

His arms engulfed her. Sliding his mouth over hers, he walked her backward—one step, two—to the wall beside the coat tree, kissing all thoughts out of her mind. His lips left hers and traveled to the side of her neck.

"I don't know why those words came. They just popped out and—"

He claimed her lips a second time, kissing her until she held onto his arms for support.

She grasped a breath when he raised his head. "No. Listen." What did she want to say to him? "Ches, I didn't—"

He quietened her again. She forgot the importance of talking. She forgot the reason she wanted to talk. She slid her hands around his waist and over the taut muscles of his back and sighed into his long, drugging kisses.

Once more he released her lips, trailing kisses to her temple.

She had to make him understand, something. What? "Ches."

"Don't apologize." He rested his forehead on hers. "You did what any hostess would do when someone drives up in her yard on Easter, uninvited." He gathered her closer and tucked her head under his chin. She felt the frantic pulse in his neck.

"I'm not mad at you. I'm mad at them. And not just for today. For all of it." He blew out a breath. "I can't believe they agreed to stay."

"It'll be fine. I promise." She crossed fingers against the

untruth of her statement. The last time Alicia Windham graced her house she slapped her. A shudder skittered along her spine. Who's to say it wouldn't happen again?

At least this time she'd have witnesses.

Not nice. Not nice. Not a nice thought.

SAM TOOK the seat to Alicia's right at the dining room table. God bless him. Who knew he could be so helpful? Ches stabbed another bite of the bunny cake. Josie hadn't taken a seat yet, so he'd stand too.

Alicia cupped her hands around the teacup. The coffee, full of cream and sugar, appeared almost white. She'd passed on the German chocolate cake because of coconut, considered the lemon blueberry, and refused to look at the bunny cake. Lloyd, meanwhile, had generous slivers of the German chocolate and lemon blueberry on his plate.

Tapping his toe, Ches watched his parents, heat growing in his stomach. "This bunny cake is fantastic, Josie. I love it."

"Yes, sir. I told you." Sam nudged Alicia. "You need to try it. Let me get you a little piece."

Alicia frowned. "No, thank you." Sam had already risen from the table.

Josie laughed. "Thank you, but it's just a yellow cake mix. Nothing special."

"It's the jelly bean smile." Heath popped one in his mouth. "They add a certain I-don't-know-what."

Sam slid a square of cake complete with two jellybeans in front of Alicia. "There you go. Try it. My sister's a great cook, but don't tell her I told you."

Everyone laughed except Alicia and Lloyd. She looked toward her son and startled. Too late, Ches realized he'd been glaring at her. He scraped icing from his plate.

Alicia straightened her back. "Joselyn, how is your library work coming along?"

"Oh," Josie laid her plate on the sideboard. "We're still working on the fundraisers to match the grant money."

"Are you close to succeeding?"

"Every time we raise money, it's a good thing for the library. We still need four thousand dollars or so to make our portion. We'll see what happens later this year."

"You're talking about the firm's grant payout." Lloyd sipped some coffee.

"Well..."

"Seems the firm has much more to deal with than those grants right now."

"Father."

Josie clutched his arm. "Right. Sharon, the director, talked with a secretary a few weeks ago. Everything's tied up, and no one knows what the outcome will be."

"Of course. Ches, the firm would need a steady hand to help navigate through all this."

Was that a compliment from his father? It sounded like it, but he had nothing to compare it to. "I think I'm ready to try the German chocolate now." He returned to the dessert table, dismissing his father's suggestion.

CHAPTER 34

*J*osie fingered the envelope and studied the return address again. A check for five thousand dollars to the library arrived in the mail with no note or explanation. Diamond Properties, LLC cut the check, but the signature remained a mystery. She couldn't make out either the first or last name from the fierce vertical strokes on the signature line.

Coupled with the money from the 5K, the crafts fair, and the book sale, the library would reach its goal of ten thousand dollars and then some. The chocolate tasting night and the antique evening would be more icing on the cake.

A thrill skittered through her heart. Good job, Josie girl. We did our part. Now we wait to see if the firm will be able to make good on the rest of the grant.

But who sent the final donation for matching the grant challenge? And why mail it to her instead of the library? Interesting questions, but not important in the long run because the library reached the goal. She pumped her fist in the air three times.

Yes. Yes. Yes.

She hugged herself and enjoyed the moment of victory.

Thank You, God. Ches would be excited too.

He answered before the end of the first ring.

"Guess what just came in the mail?" She rolled to her tiptoes and back down again. Her body refused to stand still.

"Hello to you too."

"Sorry. I'm super excited. Are you guessing or do you want me to tell you? Five thousand dollars. I just got, I mean, the library just got a check for five thousand dollars." She traced the numbers with her fingers. Five. Zero. Zero. Zero.

"Wow. Great news."

"Yep, it is. This check put us over the goal. I can't wait to tell Sharon. Now we wait to see what happens with the firm."

"Good job, Josie. You worked hard."

"Thank you." She read over the envelope again. "Have you ever heard of a company named Diamond Properties? The return address lists a post office box in Winchester—"

"Virginia."

"You know it? Good. I can't make out the signature, and I want to write a thank-you note."

"Josie, I—"

"Can you believe it? This is wonderful news. I'm so excited. This five thousand dollar puts us to—I'm just ball-parking here—but the total is close to twelve thousand dollars. We made our portion of the challenge. And we still have the antiques night.

"Sharon will be thrilled. I'm sorry. I'm talking too much. So, you know the company. Do you know the person to write the note to?"

"Lloyd Windham III."

"What?" She frowned. "What about your dad?" When did they start talking about his dad?

"Diamond Properties. My parents own that company. They wrote you a check for the library." Ches's voice sounded flat, lifeless.

The thrill singing through her insides for the last fifteen

minutes sank to a cold place in her stomach. Lloyd and Alicia Windham donated money to the library? "But why?"

"My guess is it's their apology."

"For what?"

"Josie, I know what went down between you and my mother last December. She let slip about the slap by trying to defend herself. I saw how she treated you at the reception with my own eyes."

"All that was months ago. It doesn't matter."

"It matters to me. They know how I feel about you, and they're trying to fix things like they always do, by writing a check." He sighed into the phone. "They're trying to make you like them, ingratiate themselves into our situation. First, horning their way into Easter. Now, this."

"Our situation?" How about a relationship? "Sounds like a business deal."

"To them, it's a calculated move. They know you're impor-tant to me, that I want you in my life. They're trying to win you over with this monetary apology."

Josie sobered. "I'll send the check back. They can't buy their way into—"

"No. Don't penalize the library."

"Ches, I'm serious. We have a couple more fundraisers. We can probably raise the amount we need without their check." She'd raise the money now if she had to take another job to meet the goal.

"I'm serious too. Take their money. Let them help the library."

Honestly, she wanted the money. Five thousand dollars, quick and easy. But it wouldn't be easy if it came with strings attached. She wouldn't take it if it hurt Ches. "I'm tearing it up right now."

"Stop! Don't do it!"

The force of his voice made her drop the check. "Ches—"

"Is the check made out to you?"

She retrieved it from the floor. "No." Oh. It wasn't hers to tear up. She laid it on the counter and walked away from it. "This money will not come between us. I won't be swayed by it, but I want you comfortable with the idea of the donation."

Air sounded in her ears. Was the tic back in his cheek? She fisted her hand, familiar anger simmering against people she barely knew.

"They've always believed money talks."

"It can talk all it wants, but I don't have to listen. Your feelings are important to me. You are important to me. I know the way they've treated you in the past. An easily-written check isn't going to change my opinion of your parents."

"That bad, huh?"

"I'm not going to disparage them, but some stories you've shared from your childhood...They've offered pretty much zero support over the past few months. Not my idea for parents of the year." She bit her tongue. "That's all I'm going to say."

"Did I tell you they tried to give money to the firm? To pay back what they thought I—"

"All charges were dropped. It's over."

"Sort of like my reputation."

"Not true. B.J. wrote a nice piece regarding your innocence. Social media has calmed down too." She summoned her teacher's voice. "Let's talk about something else. What are you doing today?"

"I have a date tonight with a spectacular woman who's kind of scaring me with her I-mean-business voice."

She chuckled and softened her words. "What about the rest of the day? Are you busy, or...?"

"If you're suggesting something, I'm ready. Tell me when and where."

"Whoa. I didn't have anything special in mind. I just didn't want to wait all day to see you."

"Mmm. Spending time with you is always special. See you in an hour, maybe less."

She blew messy hair away from her face. Pretended to blow away her animosity toward those difficult people.

Ches had taken some hard hits this spring. The false charges and character slams on social media had engineered part of the damage, but his parents laid the groundwork for his battered self-esteem for years.

Mr. and Mrs. Windham would never be able to buy her affection. It would take a long time and a lot of effort and prayer before she could be more than cordial to them. She'd work on ridding myself of resentment toward them.

She groaned.

I'm sorry for not liking the Windhams. They're horrible people.

She scrunched her face together. Not exactly how to pray.

Sorry. Sorry. Sorry. Forgive me, God, for how I feel about Ches's parents. Help me change my terrible attitude. Maybe see them through Your eyes.

Wow, Josie girl. Pray for a miracle, why don't you?

CHES MASSAGED the fuzzy-covered feet resting in his lap and glanced at Josie at the other end of the couch. He liked her disheveled look he'd created.

"You don't have to fix your ponytail back on my account. In fact, why don't you leave your hair down."

"I will if you promise to stay at your end." She pressed a hand to her mouth.

Did her lips still tingle as his did? His heart did some sort of bouncy move in his chest. What had this girl done to him? He wanted to climb back down to her end…He concentrated on the pink socks in his hands. He'd try to be good.

"Are you feeling better?"

He could feel a lot better if—stop. Play nice.

"Yeah. I'm good."

"Because you weren't exactly when you got here."

Yeah. He didn't know what to expect. His parents had proven to him all his life that money talks, fixes things, buys most everything. Even after all these months with Josie, he wondered how their money would affect her. He should have known she'd be rock solid.

No, she was more than that. She was angry at his parents. Furious in fact. Furious for him. Again, standing with him against them.

They thought they could ruin her feelings for him. Or at least try to warm her feelings for them. Anger boiled in his gut. He wrenched her feet with the force of his anger.

"Hey. Ouch." She scooted back against the arm of the couch. He loosened his grip but held on.

"Sorry. I was just thinking."

"Well, stop thinking about whatever made you crush my toes." She wiggled her feet. "So you're good with the donation going to the summer reading program?"

"Whatever you want."

"I want your input. Sharon will gladly receive the five thousand dollars for the children's program. She was thrilled when I called her. With this money, they can afford a master storyteller from Asheville, a topnotch puppet troupe from Durham, plus all kinds of other good stuff. Ours will be the best summer program in the city.

"She'll write a wonderful thank you note. I'll write one, too, but just a general thank you for supporting public libraries. No mention of the firm, the grant, the ten thousand we had to raise."

"You don't have to write a thank-you note."

"Well, I'm going to. I want them to know, money received. Message received, too, and ignored. End of story. I accept the money for the library, but I'm not being swayed to join the Windham Fan Club. Except for the Ches Windham fan club." She grinned.

He pushed her feet off his lap and grabbed the top of the couch cushions, planting a knee beside her legs. Crawling toward her, he grinned back at her. "I'm coming to your end."

She squealed. "No." She stalled him with one hand on his chest, one on his cheek. "You promised."

"That was before you mentioned my fan club. How many members are we up to?"

"Just me."

"Perfect." He bent down for a quick kiss. He enjoyed turning it into a long one. He broke contact and matched his forehead to hers. "We need to get out of here. Feel up for a cheeseburger?"

"That's a fan club favorite."

CRADLING AN EMPTY BOWL, Josie lounged in her father's recliner, one leg bent under her, the other draped over the arm. Ches relaxed on the couch, licking a spoon.

"So. I was right. Right?"

He smirked. "You were right. Coffee grounds sprinkled over ice cream is pretty tasty."

"Vanilla ice cream works, but chocolate ice cream kicks it over the edge, don't you think?"

"Delicious."

"And ordering singles instead of double burgers at Harold's was a good idea, too, since we can enjoy ice cream now, true?"

He chuckled, scraping the last spoonful from his bowl. "You love being right, don't you?"

"What's wrong with that?" In fact, she did enjoy being right, but she loved making Ches relax and smile and laugh even more. When he'd first walked in the door earlier in the afternoon, he'd been cautious and withdrawn. Had he really thought the money would make a difference to her?

Just you wait, Ches. You'll see. I don't want your parents' money.

I want you.

Gradually, the tic in his cheek subsided as he listened to her plans for the five thousand dollars. His smiles and warm eyes chased any lingering doubt about raising the rest of the funds for the library. She'd reach the goal or die trying.

"Confidence out the wazoo, eh? I like it." He grinned again and glanced at the time shining on the TV receiver. "As much as I hate to, I need to get going." He rose and stretched. "Jack and Heidi invited me to church with them in the morning." He grabbed her bowl and headed for the kitchen. "Wanna come too?"

"You know I do if the invitation included me."

"You know it did. Heidi complained she hadn't seen you in an age. Her exact words." He rinsed the bowls and placed them in the dishwasher.

"Great."

"Lunch is included. Jack wants to talk about some job opportunities." He reached for her and pulled her close.

"Sounds wonderful. You're going to get something soon, Ches. It takes time."

He exhaled. "Time, huh? Last year this time, I was a downtown Charlotte lawyer, and I thought you were a Park 'n Go girl."

"I was a Park 'n Go girl."

"And then I discovered who you really are at the grant party. And now I'm an unemployed—"

"You're not unemployed. You're doing consulting work."

She leaned back in his arms. "Hey, I forgot to tell you. The library is planning a party next month to coincide with the year anniversary of receiving the grant. Just a little punch-and-cookie celebration. Nothing fancy. Would you like to escort me?" She raised her eyebrows, an innocent look shading her eyes. "Or I can always ask Ben."

"Ben won't be needed. His escorting-his-sister days are over. I'll handle those duties from now on. Thank you very much."

CHAPTER 35

$\mathcal{T}$he car engine was quiet except for a few pings after Ches shut it off. Parked a few feet down the street from Josie's house, he watched her front door, waiting for the courier service to hand-deliver the special package. He raked his hand through his hair and gulped in long draughts of air. Still, his heart beat like he'd just finished a set at a CrossFit gym.

Ordering the courier service had sounded like a good idea an hour and a half ago, but now second-guessing added to his distress. Would she think the gesture cheesy? Over the top? Ridiculous? Would she recognize the song?

He wiped his sweaty palms down his thighs.

Hey, God. I need some help here.

Praying had become a new normal. Not just before he went to sleep. Not just to ask for something. It felt good. It felt right to have a running dialog. Jack had taught him. Josie had confirmed it.

Jack.

He checked his watch. He'd paid extra for one-hour delivery. He had a few minutes before the hour would be up. He grabbed his phone. Jack answered with a smile in his voice.

"Hey, buddy. Ford Macomb is excited for you to join his operation. Your lawyer know-how will help a lot of people with legal needs. I know his office is worlds away from the Charlotte firm—"

"Yeah. Thanks for the good word. Ahm. Ah."

"What's up?"

"Ahm. I got something going on. It's kinda important."

"Anything to do with Josie?"

"Everything to do with her."

"And your grandmother's ring?"

"Yep."

"Gotcha."

"I'm kinda having a hard time breathing."

Jack laughed. "Son, it'll be all right."

"At least I have a job now."

"There was never any doubt you'd land on your feet. And for the record, Josie loves you, not—"

"Yeah, well. If you could send up a prayer or three, I'd be grateful."

"Will do."

A beat-up Toyota with Charlotte Delivers on a side placard coasted to a stop in Josie's driveway. Not exactly impressive.

"Thanks. Call you later."

"You better. Heidi will want all the details."

The delivery person, a teenager sporting shoulder-length hair and ripped jeans, sauntered to the front door. Doubly not impressive. But if he got the job done...

Josie appeared in the doorway. Her face registered confusion then pleasure.

Okay. Give her a few minutes or so, then put the second part of the plan into motion.

THE BEAR HUG and kiss Josie'd planned for Ches dissolved into confusion as she opened the door to a lanky delivery person holding a package and a clipboard.

"Special delivery for Joselyn Daniels."

"Yes, I'm Joselyn."

"Then this is for you. Please sign on this line." He offered her a pen with the same logo as his golf shirt.

"Okay and wait right here. I'll get a tip."

"Nope. Already been taken care of. Have a great day." He hopped off the porch two steps at a time and strolled back to his car, his focus centered on the phone in his palm.

Josie examined the package. No return address, but Ches liked to send packages. She liked receiving them. She tore the opening tab and shook the contents onto the kitchen table, a note and a mini tape recorder.

She opened the enclosed note with the familiar strong pen marks. *You told me a few months ago to play music I like. I like this song. I hope you do too. Ches*

A tape waited for her in the recorder. She pressed the play button. Strains of a familiar song played on a piano filled the kitchen. The name of the song flitted along the edges of her brain, teasing her but not identifying itself.

What was the name of it? She'd heard it lots of times before. She loved this song. "What a Wonderful World." That's it. She laughed out loud. Ches played "What a Wonderful World" for her. A special sign?

Three knocks sounded on the front door. She turned to it, but it opened while she stood at the table, the recorder still in her hand.

"Are you laughing because it's the cheesiest thing you've ever heard?" Ches hesitated in the doorway, one hand on the doorknob, one wrapped around the edge of the door.

"I'm laughing because it makes me so happy." She ran to him and jumped into his arms. Still clutching the tape player, she pulled his mouth to within a half-inch of hers. "I love this song. You recorded it? You could have just played it for me."

He shook his head. "It's more romantic and took more effort this way. Plus, I was too nervous. Guess how many takes to get that rendition?"

She closed the gap before answering him. "How many?"

"A lot."

She laughed as he carried her to the family room couch. Tucking one leg under her, she faced Ches and hit the replay button. "This is your favorite song?"

He licked his lips. "Yeah. It's special." He placed his hand on top of her bent knee. "There's this man, Clyde, who eats at the Red Door Tavern every time I'm there. Always alone. Eating at the bar. Talking to the bartender. He likes this song too. One night at dinner, he fed quarter after quarter into the jukebox. He must've played it six or seven times in a row. Somebody finally pulled the plug."

"Meany." She traveled her fingers along his arm and up to run them through the hair behind his ear.

"I think about that night every time I hear this song." He shook his head. "I don't know why I told you."

"It's a sweet story about a man who loves music." She leaned close and kissed the corner of his mouth. "Now you have another good memory with this song."

"I hope so."

HE RUBBED his thumb over her cheek. "I've been trying to come up with a way to do this to equal how I feel about you or to equal your worth as a fantastic human being, but I can't. So, I'm just going to do it right here, right now. And that works because I love being in your house. I love being with you. I. Love. You."

Every breath in her lungs evaporated.

He hit the replay button this time and slid off the couch onto his knee. "We've known each other since last summer. We've run together, volunteered together. You've cooked for me and seen me through rough times." He clasped her hands with both of his. "You told me to play music I like. I want to play music with you. I want to create a wonderful world with you." He stopped and shook his head.

"Oh, man. That sounded better in my mind."

She bit her lip as her heart flipped hard in her chest. "It sounds great. Keep going."

He kissed her left palm and pulled a silver ring out of his pocket. The large, round diamond nestled in a square setting caught the light on the tip of his index finger. Delicate filigree comprised the band. "This ring was my grandmother's. My mother wanted a modern style, so Jack was able to give it to Heidi. She wore it for a long time, but now she wears only her wedding band. She wants you to have it if you want it, but if you'd rather choose—"

"It's beautiful."

"I thought it'd be some special bling to wear to the library party tonight. I mean, the library kind of brought us together, don't you think?"

Josie lifted her gaze from the ring to his eyes. Tears clogged the back of her throat. "She wants me to have it?"

"She loves you. Jack loves you. So do I." He swallowed. "Please marry me."

No mention of his parents. But they had apologized. Sort of. That was a start.

His parents? What about her parents?

"My parents?"

"Know and have given me their blessing along with every one of your brothers. We Skyped a couple of days ago."

She slid to kneeling in front of him and placed both hands

beside his face. "I can't wait to marry you, Lloyd Chester Windham IV. Talented carpenter, faithful texter, sweet friend."

He reached for her left hand and slipped the beautiful ring on her third finger. "Not a hotshot lawyer?"

"How about a hotshot husband?"

"I like the sound of that."

ACKNOWLEDGMENTS

This book may have my name on the cover, but many people contributed to the final product. I'm humbled by their friendship, their help, and their prayers.

Anna, Hattie, Lane, Quinn—Thank you for praying, being interested in, supporting, and sharing about my writing. Your smack talk over the euchre table, during Steelers games, in family texts (and everywhere else) was the inspiration for the Daniels clan. Thanks a million!

Kevin—you're the real deal. I knew it the first night we met at Manzetti's in 1986, and you've proven me correct every year since.

Tiffany Bracco—Thank you for reading an early draft and helping me figure out those pesky hyphenated and compound words. Your characterization comments made the story better.

Timothy Jackson, R.Ph., M.D., FCAP—Thank you for answering questions about bleeding ulcers and explaining difficult medical words. Your lifetime friendship is no small thing.

The Honorable Stafford Bullock (ret.)—Thank you for answering questions about legal matters through your wife and my sweet BSF friend, Velma.

Grant Scott, Esq—Thank you for answering questions about law firms, loving our family, and driving in Italy.

Jim Hart of Hartline Literary—Thank you for continuing to encourage me and championing my writing. I'm thankful to be one of your authors.

Mantle Rock Publishing—Thank you, Kathy Cretsinger, for publishing another story of mine. Thank you, Kathy McKinsey, for editing this book. Thank you to Diane Turpin for another beautiful cover. I'm thrilled to be with this team.

Thank you, readers and friends, for encouraging me with kind words about my stories, for asking questions about my progress, and for praying me through this journey.

Praise God from Whom all blessings come! You gave me the dream and made it come true.

READING GROUP GUIDE:

1. What does the phrase, "Play music you enjoy," mean to you?
2. Who was your favorite character in *Forever Music* and why? What appealed to you most about Josie and Ches? What frustrated you?
3. What did you like about the Daniels family? What did you dislike?
4. Josie is a nurturer. She shows love through food. Do you know someone like this? How do you show love? Discuss the importance of food in the story.
5. Discuss the differences between the Daniels clan and the Windham family. Do you see your family reflected in either one? How?
6. Jack is Ches's spiritual role model. Do you have a spiritual role model in your life? Do you play that role for someone else? Why or why not?
7. Though friends and family warn Josie about spending time with Ches, she develops a friendship with him that blooms into something more. Discuss the idea of emotional affairs using the book as well as our

current social media age. Do you think it's possible for men and women to have platonic friendships? Why or why not?

8. Although Josie Daniels is an outwardly strong professional woman, she realizes a new version of herself, an inwardly weak one who can succumb to an off-limits relationship. Have you ever had to change your opinion of yourself or seen yourself in a new light? Please explain.

9. Ches struggles with what he should do to honor his parents versus what he wants to do. He's torn between two paths. Compare earthly expectations with what Christians term God's calling. Have you ever felt like you were on a wrong path? What did you do to right your course?

10. Discuss the title. Do you understand the meaning behind it? Do you like it or hate it? Why or why not?

ALSO BY HOPE TOLER DOUGHERTY

Irish Encounter

After almost three years of living under a fog of grief, Ellen Shepherd is ready for the next chapter in her life. Perhaps she'll find adventure during a visit to Galway. Her idea of excitement consists of exploring Ireland for yarn to feature in her shop back home, but the adventure awaiting her includes an edgy stranger who disrupts her tea time, challenges her belief system, and stirs up feelings she thought she'd buried with her husband.

After years of ignoring God, nursing anger, and stifling his grief, Payne Anderson isn't ready for the feelings a chance encounter with an enchanting stranger evokes. Though avoiding women and small talk has been his pattern, something about Ellen makes him want to seek her —and God again.

Can Ellen accept a new life different than the one she planned? Can Payne release his guilt and accept the peace he's longed for? Can they surrender their past pain and embrace healing together, or will fear and doubt ruin their second chance at happiness?

Mars … With Venus Rising

A meddling horse, paper bag floors and a flying saucer on the town square. The little town of Mars has it all—including a brand new resident who might spell heartache for one of its own. Twenty-something Penn Davenport yearns for an exciting life in the big city and wants to shed the label of orphan that she's worn for years. To achieve that dream, she must pass the CPA exam then move away from the two aunts who reared her after her parents died in a plane crash. When John Townsend—full of life and the joy of living—moves to town, he rattles Penn's view of herself, her life, and her dreams... which isn't such a bad thing until she falls for him and discovers he's a pilot.

Rescued Hearts

Mary Wade Kimball's soft spot for animals leads to a hostage situation when she spots a briar-entangled kitten in front of an abandoned house. Beaten, bound, and gagged, Mary Wade loses hope for escape.

Discovering the kidnapped woman ratchets the complications for undercover agent Brett Davis. Weighing the difference of ruining his three months' investigation against the woman's safety, Brett forsakes his mission and helps her escape the bent-on-revenge brutes following behind. When Mary Wade's safety is threatened once more, Brett rescues her again. This time, her personal safety isn't the only thing in jeopardy. Her heart is endangered as well.

Four Contemporary Romances
Four Coastal Locations
COASTAL PROMISES

All Yours, Art and Soul by Diane Turpin
For the Love of Dolphins by Kathy Cretsinger
Pawleys Aisle by Regina Merrick
Surf Song by Pam Harris

When Mary Clare Casteel (Mac) discovers her contractor stuffed in the display coffin of Pocket Change, her soon-to-open eclectic business, it puts the skids on secret plans to use her recent *Publisher's Clearing House* winnings to assist at-risk businesses in her small town of Pocket, Arkansas.

Enter her quirky family and tantalizing new neighbor, Mick Walker.

Murder, techie mishaps, and a host of Southern traditions accompany Mary Clare as she juggles her fortune while dodging demanding deadbeats. What ensues is an investigation led by a new millionaire, her fun-loving family, and a handsome bait shop owner.

Pocket Change by Debbie Archer

Stay up-to-date on your favorite books and authors with our free e-newsletters. Sign up today at mantlerockpublishingllc.com. Follow us on Facebook.

CPSIA information can be obtained
at www.ICGtesting.com
Printed in the USA
JSHW030515300420
5383JS00003B/13